A SPY'S LEGACY

A SPY'S LEGACY

SECRETS
BOOK 1

P. A. DUNCAN

Printed in the United States of America.
ISBN: 979-8869369161 (Print Edition Only)
FIRST EDITION: June 2024
Published by Unexpected Paths. www.unexpectedpaths.com
Edited by Sylvan Echo Editing.
Cover art by: www.SelfPubBookCovers.com/Unique_Digital
Created with Vellum.

DEDICATION

For my baby brother, Edward Eastham "Speedy" Duncan II,
Gone far, far too soon and always missed.
And for my mother, Frances Anne Pierce Duncan, who didn't think
I could accomplish anything remotely like this.
They each left me different legacies.

EPIGRAPH

When sorrows come, they come not single spies. But in battalions!

— WILLIAM SHAKESPEARE, HAMLET

CONTENTS

AUTHOR'S NOTE

Secondary characters have jobs to do in a novel: give us a break from the antagonist and maybe the protagonist; give a different perspective or point of view to the story; and aid in advancing the plot to its logical conclusion.

I've always been careful to flesh out my secondary characters but not let them take over the story. My readers had other ideas.

Among the feedback I've received on these secondary characters were suggestions that three specific characters needed their own stories. One of those is a character who has never made an actual appearance except by reference or someone's memory—Katherine Maitland, Mai Fisher's mother. I've established almost from the beginning of writing these stories that Mai lost her parents when she was five years old. One day, however, the thought came to me: What if one of her parents survived?

A Spy's Legacy is not a spy novel, per se. It is, however, a novel from the ***Secrets*** Box Set about the people behind the scenes of a spy's life—notably the one who quite possibly left a legacy of espionage to her child.

PROLOGUE

1963

Taipei Airport
Taiwan, Republic of China

The man at the British Overseas Airways Corporation check-in desk took his time to affix the appropriate labels to their luggage. Finally, he pushed the suitcases through an opening in the wall behind him, and the two oversized bags slipped out of sight.

Another man, likely a Chinese national, down in the bowels of the airport, would load them in a cart he'd push to the belly of a four-engine BOAC Comet.

One hurdle surmounted. One more to go.

Katherine Maitland-Fisher had always been organized, a skill that had distinguished her as first a codebreaker then an intelligence analyst at Bletchley during the war. She'd brought that skill to the United Nations Intelligence Directorate when she'd joined her husband there.

Whenever they left for a mission, she would pack two bags for each of them. One they'd open and use on the mission. The other stayed unopened, to be grabbed for a quick getaway.

Much as they'd done this morning.

The arrest of their long-time translator in a secret police sweep for closet Communists was reason enough to leave Taiwan—in a hurry.

Katherine didn't regret the clothing left behind, no doubt to be picked over and given to a policeman's wife. The dull, shapeless dresses a prim missionary wife would wear. She was no missionary, but she knew the espionage business. If her cover was as a missionary, she had to dress the part.

Her outward calm and composure, like her husband's, she'd honed in dozens of missions over the years with Freddie. She knew the importance of displaying no overt sign of her inner anxiety, that her heart pounded against her ribs, or that she wouldn't feel safe until she was aboard the BOAC aircraft and it was rolling down the runway.

But, damn it, she needed this clerk to hurry up and stamp their bloody passports.

At last, he handed both passports and their boarding passes to Freddie. The clerk pointed to the gate and said, "Best hurry, sir, madam. The flight is boarding now."

"Thank you, old chap," Freddie said, calm as a cucumber. His hand cupped her elbow and squeezed it with affection. For her ears only, he murmured, "Step lively, darling. Almost there."

She matched her pace to his. Not a casual stroll but an intent one. They stopped to queue at the door leading to the ramp. Several people queued behind them.

Good, Katherine thought, camouflage.

The agent at the door gave their boarding passes a cursory glance and waved them onto the tarmac.

Airports were always windy, whether from the whirling propellers, jet engines, or some quirk of weather or location. Katherine put a hand to her well-pinned hat to keep it from flying off her head. She felt Freddie increase their pace, and she did the same without hesitation. She ventured a glance at his profile.

A chiseled, handsome face with a trimmed mustache always kept neat.

How she loved him. Almost twenty years ago now, she'd known he was the man she would marry when she met him, even given the fact he was English. She'd gotten over that.

His dark brown eyes were focused ahead of them as though on a target. Today's target was the air stairs from the tarmac to the open boarding door of the Comet. Katherine focused her attention there as well.

Vague sounds of a commotion behind them reached their ears. Raised voices. Running footsteps.

"Pick it up, shall we, darling?" Freddie said and walked faster, his grip on her elbow tightening.

The stairs were twenty feet away.

Ten.

The footsteps grew closer, the shouts in Mandarin louder.

A few more steps and their feet would be on the bottom tread.

A line of panting, sweating Taiwanese policemen appeared between them and their goal, forming a barrier. One policeman motioned for the other boarders to go around them, and they obeyed, looking over their shoulders at Katherine and Freddie and gossiping about what might be the problem.

"I say, gentlemen," Freddie said, calm with the authority of an earl behind his words, "you're going to make us miss our flight. Stand aside like a good chap."

The ranking policeman was a young man, his face hard and serious, his eyes old beyond his years. In Katherine's experience, this type of policeman was often the most zealous and unfortunately, the least bribable.

"You will come with us," that policeman said.

"I think not," Freddie said, his imperiousness upped a notch. "Move aside and let us board our flight."

For a moment, the slightest portion of a second, Katherine thought the policeman might step aside, but his eyes hardened even more and seemed to grow darker. He barked instructions to the other officers, and they surrounded her and Freddie, hands grasping their arms, shoulders, necks.

Katherine fought down panic when the police separated them. Two large, black vans roared up and screeched to a halt. The policemen hustled their prisoners toward the vehicles.

Staying within your cover also meant no resistance, but Katherine longed to administer a few good kicks and karate chops. She looked over her shoulder, imbuing her face with enough dismay she hoped the passengers or crew would be compelled to intervene.

Instead, the passengers hurried toward the airplane, heads down. Only a lone stewardess watched from the top of the air stairs, her dismay expressed in her widened eyes and the hand at her mouth.

Katherine looked at Freddie, and he at her. Her brave stalwart husband. How proud she was of him. If they got through this, it would be because his strength and will fortified hers.

Katherine squared her shoulders and rendered her face void of emotion. They would live. They had to. They had the most important reason in the world to get back home.

They'd had to wait so long to have her, and five years of her wasn't enough. They needed a lifetime with their child.

Their child.

Oh, my God, Katherine thought. Mattie. Mattie, Mummy and Daddy love you so very much.

❧ ❧

Two months later . . .

WHEN THE DOOR to his cell creaked open on rusty hinges, Frederick Fisher prepared himself for another sound thrashing. The German SS hadn't broken him, so some Taiwanese secret policeman didn't have a chance. Even so, his ribs ached, and bruises covered almost every inch of his torso. Cigarette burns, fresh and healed, marred his arms and legs like an obscene rash.

The man who entered was alone. He wasn't one of Fisher's usual interrogators. This visitor's face twisted in disgust, and he brought a neatly folded handkerchief to his nose.

Fisher had become inured to the smell of his unwashed body, to his own dried blood, the effluvia of his piss and shit. The man's reaction told Fisher the cells in this part of the prison or what went on in them wasn't his milieu.

Someone new, eh, Fisher thought, I do love a fresh challenge.

He pushed himself onto his bare feet, their soles bruised and lacerated from a truncheon, but he rose to his full, rather intimidating height.

"My good man," Fisher said, "I am Rev. Frederick Fisher, a British citizen, and I demand to see someone from my embassy."

The same litany he'd recited on every interrogator at the onset of every interrogation for the past two months.

"Interrogation" made what he'd endured sound almost civilized. When he would make his official report, he'd refer to it with its proper nomenclature.

Torture.

In perfect English, the newcomer said, "Let us not attempt to fool each other, Mr. Fisher. Here, I am Ju Yu, a minor police functionary. My real name is Yazhu Fan, a member of State Security, People's Republic of China. We do not have much time."

"For what?"

"For lengthy discussions. One of Ju Yu's duties is to apply the official government seal on a death warrant. Yours and your wife's came across my desk this morning. You betrayed nothing and neither did she, and that was likely your mistake. The commandant of this prison is a brutal animal, and he sees your defiance as a personal affront to his honor, an insult. So, you must die. I, of course, had to affix the seal, but I delayed that long enough to communicate, requesting instructions. I have been directed to . . . ah, misplace one of the death warrants."

"Why one?"

"I do not question my orders. I merely execute them."

"Pardon me, sir, if I'm skeptical that the Communist Chinese Ministry for State Security ordered you to save one of us. Surely, you don't expect me to believe that?"

"You can trust me because, yes, officially, I work for State Security, but I also take orders from the same man as you."

Ju or Yazhu or whoever he was had spoken English to this point, but his next words were in Latin.

"*In vertiate tua justitia. In justitia veritas.*"

The unofficial motto of the United Nations Intelligence Directorate: "In Truth, Justice. In Justice, Truth."

Fisher had recruited and handled many double agents during the war and since, but a triple agent? And to which entity did this man attach his loyalty?

"I cannot stress more ardently that we must hurry," said Ju. "You must decide quickly."

Fisher understood at once what he meant. He wished he had the strength to thrash the man. With no hesitation, Fisher said, "My wife. For our daughter's sake, save my wife."

Ju smiled, though Fisher sensed annoyance behind it.

"I made this same offer to your wife, and she said to save you for the same reason."

"No. Save her."

"You are certain? I will not have this on my conscience."

Bloody bastard, Fisher thought, but there was only one choice.

"Prove to me my wife is alive, and I'll clear your conscience," Fisher said.

Ju turned to his right and motioned to someone outside the cell. A large, bulky Chinese man entered, carrying a limp Katherine. Her prison shift was blood-stained, torn in places. The sight of the bruising on her arms and legs, her beautiful face almost undid him.

"Come see for yourself she is alive," Ju said. "She is sedated. For the journey."

"Journey? Where will you take her?"

"Off this forsaken island," Ju replied.

Fisher went to his wife, his battered hands giving her filthy hair a gentle, loving stroke. He checked the pulse at her neck. Strong. Steady. She was alive, and he wanted her to stay that way.

He kissed her forehead and murmured, "Tell our Mattie Daddy loves her so very much. And I love you, my dearest, my darling. Forever."

Bitterness came close to overwhelming Fisher. How like his spymaster, Nigel Hume, to hide from him and Katherine that the Directorate had an asset in Communist Chinese State Security.

Why Hume would order the rescue of only one of them, he had no clue.

No, he knew. First, there was that botched SOE mission in World War II where Hume had left behind several Resistance fighters to be shot by the Nazis. Fisher had always thought that had been on purpose, that Hume, whose preferred lifestyle was far beyond his SOE salary, had sold them out to the Nazis. Then, there was Hume's belief that a woman's place in espionage was in the typing pool or to be used as a honey trap. If Katherine died, Hume could use that as an excuse to block other women from being operatives. Worse, he'd use her death as an example, to say women were incapable of being successful operatives.

Bugger you, Nigel, Fisher thought.

Fisher stepped away from his wife with reluctance, taking one last look at her before he glared at Ju.

"You better be telling me the truth," Fisher said, knowing it was an empty threat.

"I assure you, she will live."

"Then, get on with it."

A nod from Ju, and the other man took Katherine away, almost taking Fisher's last nerve with him.

He squared his shoulders and scowled at Ju.

"Grant me the dignity of my own death," Fisher said. "Provided that doesn't go against your orders."

"I had hoped you would make that offer, but I must witness. For my report."

"Of course, we must feed the bureaucratic gods."

Fisher pulled off his soiled undershirt and fashioned it into a makeshift noose. He upended his shit bucket and placed it beneath the narrow, barred window. He stepped up onto the bucket and attached the undershirt to a bar. He pulled the "noose" over his head.

With a final, triumphant glare at Ju Yu or Yazhu Fan, whoever he was, Fisher kicked the bucket aside.

The short drop was insufficient to break his neck, and the strangulation took a while under the watchful gaze of Yazhu Fan's unblinking eyes.

1

BAD NEWS

1963

Directorate Headquarters
Somewhere near Washington, D.C.

Sir Nigel Hume debated whether attempting to fool Sir John Stone was a good idea. Stone had an uncanny ability to ferret out the truth, which had worked well for him as chief of the Directorate's London Station. However, if Stone suspected that what Hume had to tell and show him was a fabrication, Stone wouldn't rest until he found the truth.

The jig, as they said, would be up.

Hume could have sent a facsimile, but Stone would expect him to deliver this news personally. If Hume didn't, that might solidify any suspicion he would have. In his grief—and Stone would grieve because he indulged in emotions—Stone might accept this news and the evidence if it came from Hume's lips.

Good thing, then, Nigel Hume was a practiced liar.

Hume's secretary buzzed him upon Stone's arrival and got the curt reply, "Send him in."

Stone entered smiling. The man always smiled, making Hume think he didn't treat espionage with the solemnity required. Hume had been British Army intelligence in World War I and supervisor of a team of Special Operations Executive agents in World War II. When the United Nations had formed the ultra-secret Directorate and appointed him its director, he'd recruited heavily from the surviving pool of SOE operatives, Freddie Fisher and John Stone among them. Fisher and Stone had grown up on neighboring Sussex estates and had been effective operatives, usually working together as a team. They had, however, never quite given up the improvisation the SOE lived for. Hume believed in protocols, and the Directorate had plenty of them.

"Nige," Stone greeted. He didn't take authority seriously either. "How are you?"

"I'm super, Johnny, and you?"

"I didn't think I would like being behind a desk, but I'm coming into my own, I believe. It was good, however, to get away for a jaunt across the pond.

The two men shook hands, and Hume adopted his most serious expression. "Have a seat, Johnny," he said.

Stone sat, still smiling. "Oh, dear. That tone sounds rather like the headmaster at Eton when I got in trouble, which was far too often for his liking or mine."

"I am afraid it is bad news, Johnny." Hume paused, not rushing ahead to maintain his facade. "We've lost, I'm sorry to say, Freddie and Katherine."

Stone's patrician face scowled. "What do you mean, lost?"

"It seems their long-time translator was picked up in a routine anti-Commie sweep by the Taiwanese secret police. The translator was terrified, I suppose, and told the authorities she suspected

Rev. and Mrs. Fisher were not true missionaries. The translator was quite a devout Christian woman, fire and brimstone and all that, whereas Freddie's cover persona preached love and kindness. Whatever the translator told her interrogators, it was enough for the police to come after Freddie and Katherine. They made it to the airport, almost to the airplane, when they were taken into police custody."

Hume had watched Stone's face as he'd spoken. The perpetual amusement had faltered at last.

"Now, as you know, they quite often stayed out of contact when they were in Taiwan, so we weren't alarmed when we heard nothing from them," Hume said.

"They were operating as Freddie and I would on an SOE job," Stone murmured.

And that's the problem, Hume thought; this isn't the SOE.

"Several weeks after their detention, the Taiwanese government notified the British Embassy of their capture. They also informed the embassy that under interrogation, they confessed to being spies—"

"Not a bloody chance in hell!"

"For the British government," Hume continued, "and they were executed, their bodies incinerated."

Stone's lips pursed, and he shook his head.

"I'm sorry, old boy," Hume said. "I know how close the three of you were. I've already prepared a cover story for the Maitland and Fisher families. By coincidence, a few days after they were taken into custody, a private plane went down in the mountains on a flight from Taipei to Taitung. I had Freddie's and his wife's names added to the manifest. A mission trip, of course."

Stone's hand shook as he brought it to his mouth. Hume forced himself not to react to the tears in Stone's eyes. Stone looked up at Hume, his eyes narrowed.

"No bodies, you say?" Stone asked. "How convenient."

"There is no hope," Hume said.

With the proper amount of reluctance to let Stone believe Hume was sparing him, Hume extracted photographs from the file before him and handed them to Stone.

Stone donned his reading glasses and flipped through the photos: the BOAC tickets with their names, the suitcases that had been loaded onto the plane and had arrived in England without them, their passports, the clothing they'd been wearing.

Stone paled when he came to the final photo.

The bodies.

Hume remained quiet, molding his face into a solicitous expression. He forced himself not to hold his breath as Stone gave that photo extended scrutiny. Hume didn't relax, even when Stone handed back the photos.

"Unbelievable," Stone said. "We had dinner, the three of us, right before they left for this trip. Who investigated in Taiwan?"

"Our station chief there, of course. The CIA and British Intelligence corroborated his findings."

"Hadley Quiston? Yes, I know him. Thorough chap. Very thorough. Might I have a copy of the report, Nigel?"

Hume had known Stone would ask and had had a copy prepared and sealed in an Eyes Only envelope. He handed that to Stone.

"May I contact Quiston or you if I have questions?"

"Of course, old boy. Ask any time. I'm so sorry to have dragged you here for bad news, but in this case, I thought it best delivered in person. I wanted to notify you before I sent the message to all stations to shut down any operations Freddie and Katherine were aware of."

"Have you had anyone or any operation blown?"

"No, but that's not to say that won't happen."

Stone shrugged and nodded absently.

"Would you notify the families, Johnny?" Hume asked, mentally crossing his fingers. He had no desire to deal with that officious shanty Irish bitch who managed Katherine Maitland's business affairs or Frederick Fisher's doddering father.

"What? Oh, of course. Give me a few days after I return to England. Freddie's father is quite infirm. That'll have to be done delicately. The O'Saidhs will handle advising what Maitlands are left, and, of course, I'll explain to Mattie."

"Mattie? Oh, the child. She's what? Four, five?"

"Five, but she's old enough to inquire where they are and to notice they haven't returned."

"Well, the plane crash scenario should be sufficient for her and anyone else who needs to be notified. Except Her Majesty. I'm in no position to travel to make that formal notification. I can arrange for you to be received."

"Of course, Nige. Thank you."

"You appear quite gobsmacked, Johnny. Understandable. Why don't you stay overnight and head back in the morning?"

"Yes, yes, I think I shall do that."

"Again, sorry to be the bearer of awful news. It does rather confirm my ongoing concerns over Katherine Maitland's efficacy as an operative."

"What do you mean?"

"Freddie might well have been able to effect his escape had he not been worried about his wife. A distraction, as I always suspected and warned about."

"Good God, man! They're dead, and you're second-guessing the circumstances and ignoring their thirteen years of success."

"No offense intended, Johnny. I'm sorely disturbed by this. A child has lost a mother and a father, but the mother should have accepted her traditional role and stayed home with her child.

Now, that's neither here nor there. We have suffered a grievous loss."

Stone nodded, his face expressionless, and Hume feared he might have fallen out of character.

"I understand, Nige. Completely. Well, I should be . . . Say, is Nelson on site? I could use a drink and some company tonight. The last time he was in London, I beat him rather soundly at billiards. He owes me a dinner."

"He's not on assignment right now. You'll likely find him in Analysis. There's a new clerical there he has a fondness for."

"I see. Not surprising, considering."

"Yes. I certainly don't mind his proclivities when he's recruiting assets, but there's a quaint American expression. One should not defecate in one's own back yard."

Stone opened his briefcase and dropped the Eyes Only packet inside. He rose, Hume with him.

"I'm sure either or both families will have some sort of memorial service," Stone said. "I'll advise you of the particulars in case you want to send flowers."

"Yes, of course. Splendid."

"I take my leave of you, Sir Nigel," Stone said, rather formal for an informal man.

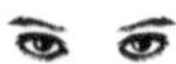

Nelson wasn't in Analysis but in his private office, where Stone went first. The door was open, but Stone heard soft voices from inside, one a woman's. Stone stopped in the hallway, out of sight of the doorway.

"This weekend?" the woman said. "Yes, I'm free."

"Here's my plan. Dinner Friday night at that French place in Alexandria. Back to my place for cocktails. I'll make you breakfast

Saturday morning then a drive in the countryside. The colors on Skyline Drive are at peak. We'll find a cozy hotel along the way and on Sunday make our way back in a leisurely drive. How does that sound to you?"

"Divine, but . . ." The woman's tone shifted to a definite pout. "What if you're called away like last time?"

"My knee has been acting up. I'll beg off. What do you say?"

"Yes. Of course."

"Perfect! I'll pick you up around seven Friday evening. Wear something sexy."

A titter, and Stone heard high heels headed for the door. He backed away and moved forward again as the tall, striking blond exited. She did blush a bit as she passed Stone, but Stone put her aside as he knocked.

"Johnny!" Nelson said. "What a pleasant surprise. What are you doing here?"

Stone pointed to the hallway. "The clerical from Analysis?"

"No. Clerical from Personnel, but don't tell the clerical from Analysis," Nelson said with a wink.

"You live dangerously, old chap."

"Makes it exciting, though. Why are you in the Colonies?"

"Freddie and Katherine are . . . Dead."

"What? When?"

"Nigel hasn't told you?"

"First I've heard."

Stone closed the door, and Nelson opened a desk drawer and flipped some sort of switch.

"White noise generator," he said. "Are you certain about Freddie and Kate?"

"Nigel is. Look, I can't be here long. Nigel thinks I'm only stopping by to arrange a dinner with you. He gave me a copy of the investigative report, pictures. I want you to look those over and see if you find what I did. Seven tonight at my favorite spot in Chinatown."

"I'll be there. Johnny, I can't believe this. Where's the baby?"

"With her governess and staff in Sussex, and she's five now."

"Damn. Old enough to remember them."

"Yes, that's what's facing me when I return. I better be off. Knowing Nigel, he'll check to see when I signed out."

Nelson opened the drawer again and flipped the switch.

"Thanks for stopping by, Johnny. Looking forward to dinner," Nelson said.

"Cheerio," Stone replied and left.

After clearing Security, Stone exited onto the relatively quiet streets of an Arlington neighborhood called Rosslyn. He spotted a cab and hailed it.

He had the driver take him several miles away to Fairfax, Virginia, where he made a call at a public box. The driver was then happy to take him into D.C. and drop him near the Smithsonian Castle on the National Mall.

Once the cab was out of sight, Stone walked to 7th Street, turned left, and walked a few blocks to Chinatown. When he knocked on the door of a modest row house, the Chinese woman who answered seemed happy to see him.

2

UNCERTAINTY

Dragon King Restaurant
Chinatown
Washington, D.C.

The neon sign indicating the restaurant was open flickered and reminded Nelson of Morse Code. He jogged up the steps from the street, past the gilded, plastic dragons, and opened the door. The dining room on the first level was all Chinese kitsch, what tourists expected to see: lanterns, jade dragons that were really plastic, paintings of pagodas, a well-worn photograph of the Great Wall, a collection of Buddhas, and photographs of President Chiang Kai-shek and Madame Chiang.

The hostess could have been anywhere from thirty to sixty, her svelte figure set off in a gold, embroidered Cheong-sam dress decorated with red dragons. She'd pulled her jet-black hair back in a taut French twist, held in place by lacquered hair sticks from which tiny, gold dragons dangled.

Her eye shadow was light blue with a white highlight, her eyeliner black and applied to make her eyes seem round, and her false eyelashes were thick with mascara. Her lipstick was a medium pink, and her long nails were painted to match the color of the dragons on her dress.

The waitresses were similarly attired and coiffed, except their Cheong-sams were blood red and embroidered with gold dragons.

The odors from the kitchen were tantalizing; the waitresses gave the orders to the cook in Mandarin. The patrons were a few local residents, white men and women attired in suits and dresses. Others were tourists in casual dress, all also white.

The hostess bowed to Nelson and said, "A pleasure to see you, Mr. Nelson. Please, follow me."

She led him through the restaurant, down a corridor, past the restrooms, and to a narrow stairway. She went first, allowing him to appreciate the sway of her hips in the form-fitting dress.

John Stone was alone in the upper dining room, but that wasn't unusual. This room wasn't for the public but for special guests of the owner, who happened to be the hostess and a long-time asset for several intelligence organizations.

Stone puffed on his pipe and rose when Nelson entered. They shook hands. In the center of the table was a bottle of what had to be Baijiu, a potent white liquor made from sorghum. Stone already had a glass in front of him, and the hostess, Soong-Ju, poured some for Nelson. She pointed to a buffet laden with various dishes Nelson knew wouldn't be served to the downstairs clientele. He and Stone warranted authentic Taiwanese cuisine.

The buffet was so the two men could converse without interruptions from servers. The hostess bowed to both men and left the room, closing the double doors behind her.

"Let's plate up while it's warm, eh?" said Stone, rising and heading for the buffet.

The two men returned to the table with bowls of beef noodle soup and plates laden with rice and a variety of dishes: gua bao, zong zi, scallion pancakes, stinky tofu. They started with the soup but used chopsticks to eat the soup's noodles and to sample the food from their plates.

They dined in silence for a while, and Nelson remembered why he liked this place as much as Stone did. Every bite he took exploded with flavor, far more satisfying than the bland offerings downstairs intended for tourists.

Stone dabbed at his mouth with a napkin and passed an Eyes-Only envelope to Nelson, who noted the seal had been broken. Nelson took out a report he considered too sparse for an investigation into the deaths of two long-time operatives. He continued to eat as he looked over the contents.

Stilted bureaucratic language.

Euphemisms for torture.

"Did the embassy get the bodies?" Nelson asked.

"No. Incinerated after execution."

"How long were they in custody?"

"The station chief isn't certain. They were headquarters operatives and generally operated independently of the Taipei Station. The chief had no idea they were missing until the embassy was notified of their deaths."

"Ah! The airline tickets. June 27. Nearly three months ago."

"Yes," Stone said in a low voice. "A week past their eighteenth wedding anniversary."

When Nelson got to the pictures, he studied them closely. He pushed his plate away; his appetite had fled.

The naked bodies of a man and a woman, their severed heads placed on their stomachs. Nelson would know Freddie Fisher anywhere: the aristocratic looks, the Clark Gable mustache though now obscured by a months-old beard, thick mop of hair he usually wore slicked back with some typically British styling concoction.

Now, his eyes were bulging, his tongue protruding, but almost no blood came from the severed head. He had to have been beheaded post-mortem.

Katherine's red hair had been moved back off her face to show her identity. Her mouth drooped open. The eyes were half-closed, but Nelson saw they were the right color of dark blue.

"The beauty mark on her upper lip," Nelson said.

"Yes, that's what I noticed."

"There is a great deal of bruising on her face. That could be hiding it. It's not a good-quality picture. Blowing it up wouldn't help with clarity."

He set the picture aside, face down.

"I have no doubt that's . . ." Stone began then stopped. "That's Freddie. I'm not certain at all that's Kate."

"I don't know, Johnny. You're putting a lot into a missing blemish. Again, the bruising on her face . . . What did Soong-Ju downstairs say?"

"Her sources say it happened, but I don't believe that is Katherine."

"And if you decide to challenge that?" Nelson asked.

"The goal would be to find her, then." He thumped the table with a fist. "And bring her home. I'll wager a double was involved. Someone in Taiwanese intelligence who's a double for the Commies took her. The Taiwanese didn't want the embarrassment and staged her death."

"If that's the case, if it's the Chinese Communists, they've had time to turn her and—"

"Never! She would never—"

"Johnny, your heart's too much into this. You're seeing what you want to see because you and I both know you've always loved your best friend's wife."

Stone blinked, his eyes hardening, and Nelson saw murder in them. That passed as quickly as it had occurred, and Stone stared at an indefinite point across the room.

"Johnny, your responsibility now is Freddie's and Kate's little girl," Nelson said with uncharacteristic concern. "They'd want you to make sure she has the best possible life, the one they would have given her. They wouldn't want you to chase their ghosts."

Stone's chin crimped, trembled, but a steadying breath later, his face relaxed.

"For a traitorous colonist, you're right, Lord N.," Stone said.

Nelson smiled at the nickname. Nelson's father had named him Horatio, the reason why Nelson never used his first name. Stone had always called him "Lord N."

Stone gathered the report and the photos and slid them into the envelope. That, he tucked away in his briefcase. He turned to Nelson, his expression jaunty. His eyes, however, were haunted.

"I'm ready for seconds," Stone said and returned to the buffet.

3

TAKE A BREAK

Later that evening . . .

Directorate Headquarters

Alonso Zamora was always unnerved when the operative named Nelson emerged from the shadows into Zamora's dim domain, the Directorate's Archives.

First, the man was absolutely silent, and second, the way he accessed the Archives was supposed to be known only by Zamora and Nigel Hume.

Zamora had fled Italy when an anti-fascist mob hanged Mussolini upside down. He'd landed in England, where Hume had recruited him for the Directorate. Only after his recruitment did Hume discover Zamora liked killing. He wasn't an assassin but a serial killer of women, but by the time Hume discovered that, Zamora had also shown his penchant for archival duties. When Hume made the evidence of one of Zamora's murders disappear, Zamora was Hume's. For life.

The ingress Nelson used to enter the Archive was the way Zamora himself came and went, which Hume allowed for Zamora to sate his desires. Zamora had discovered that autoeroticism gave him enough satisfaction that he didn't have to kill. Hume made a deal with him: Come and go as you please, use only willing sexual partners, but don't kill anyone.

Ever one for the details, Nelson had noticed Zamora's comings and goings and had followed him, witnessing the fact that Zamora had gone too far and accidentally murdered a call girl. Nelson had offered to keep that secret from Hume for access to the Archives and access to Zamora's secret ingress and egress. Zamora found himself held in thrall by two men and could do nothing about either of them.

When Zamora had asked Nelson how he'd known about his forays, Nelson had smiled in that smooth, charming way he had and said, "Between missions, I often have a lot of time on my hands, and I'm learning everything—*everything*—about this organization. Who knows? I might be in charge one day."

Zamora wouldn't be surprised if that became reality.

Nelson told Zamora what he wanted and waited while Zamora retrieved two files, whose seals were not yet applied. For some files, sealing could be put off for six months to a year, in case further information became available.

Nelson's dark eyes studied the two files Zamora placed on his desk.

"It's a lovely evening, Mr. Zamora. I've had a pleasant walk back from Chinatown after a wonderful meal. Have you been out of the Bunker lately?"

"You know I only go out on Saturdays, Mr. Nelson."

"Yes, that's true. It's supposed to rain Saturday." He looked up a Zamora. "Take a break, Mr. Zamora. Five minutes."

Without a word, Zamora went to a door that led to his quarters and disappeared.

NELSON FIRST PICKED up the file that was a match for the copy John Stone had shown him. The originals of the photographs were clearer, of better quality than the facsimiles Stone had.

As he studied the photos, Nelson frowned. Stone might be right, something was off about the "body" of Katherine Maitland.

However, there was no leverage in that knowledge unless Nelson could prove someone had made a switch.

Besides, even if Chinese State Security had taken Kate alive, she was surely dead by now, months later. Stone was also right that Kate wouldn't have broken and told her interrogators anything. They would have killed her for that.

The second file, marked "Private - N. Hume," provided the leverage Nelson wanted. A report from an asset inside Chinese State Security, interesting in and of itself because Nelson wasn't aware there was one. As headquarters' top operative, Nelson was a designated advisor to Hume. So, Hume had compartmentalized this from him.

The report was a single sheet of paper, handwritten, the English good. Nelson read it quickly and went directly to Zamora's xerographic machine to make a copy of both sides, which he folded and slipped into his inside jacket pocket.

By the time Zamora emerged from his quarters, both files were on the desk precisely where Zamora had placed them.

Nelson was nowhere to be seen.

NELSON KNEW BETTER than to re-read the document he'd copied while he was in headquarters. He waited until he was in his apartment, alone for a change, with a glass of Scotch.

One thing the report proved: Nigel Hume could be fooled. He wasn't the infallible spymaster everyone in the organization thought he was.

The other thing was, at least at the time of the writing of the report, Katherine Maitland was still alive. John Stone would want to know that, but . . .

Telling him would send him or operatives working for him on a mission that would likely never succeed. Kate was either dead or turned. Either way, missions in the area would be paused or halted altogether. Other operatives in the Far East would be recalled for their safety. Codes and cyphers would be abandoned and new ones distributed to all far eastern stations.

Then, the waiting game would begin, the wait to see if anyone or any operation had been compromised.

The knowledge Nelson had would ease John Stone's pain, and Nelson admired him enough he almost wanted to do that.

But if he passed this along to Stone, Stone would confront Hume, and Nelson would lose his leverage.

In the end, the decision was easy. Nelson locked the copy of the report in the safe behind a false wall in his linen closet.

As he tossed and turned for most of the night, he wished he wasn't alone. A comely companion would have chased away the images banging around in his head of Katherine Maitland-Fisher being tortured.

4

UPSETTING THE SCHEDULE

1990

Directorate Headquarters

Alexei Bukharin parked his car in his designated spot in the underground garage, the space with the sign that read, "Reserved for A. N. Burke, Burke Financials."

The mid-rise building above the World War II bunker that housed the Directorate housed legitimate businesses, and mingled among them were cover businesses for various operatives. Burke Financials was Alexei's cover.

For a man raised under Communism, he had a talent for investing. Of course, he had few real clients; the investments he pursued were for himself and colleagues in the Directorate. The business was a front, a way for him to manage his human assets as well as his personal financial ones. Even Mai, who was the titular head of a global business conglomerate, pronounced his investment efforts exemplary.

He shut off his car but paused for a moment, running the bizarre conversation he'd had with Edwin Terrell through his memory again.

"She used a Chinese name when she introduced herself, but the family resemblance is more than obvious."

"Up close, I couldn't mistake this woman for Mai. She was close to seventy. Wasn't Mai born when her mother was almost forty?"

"Yes, but—"

"Damn it, Alexei, I was closer to the bitch than I am to you when she cut my fucking arm off."

Alexei pushed the memory away, exited his car, and locked it. He checked, as usual, for any unauthorized people on this level and only headed for the Directorate's ingress when he saw no one.

He went straight to Nelson's office, relieved as always he didn't have to deal with Nigel Hume's no-nonsense, old school secretary, as she preferred to be called. Penelope had been Nigel's secretary from his SOE days. When Hume had died two years before, she'd begged to stay, to assure "Sir Nigel's legacy."

Nelson, as acting director, had forced her to retire right away, but with a generous pension so she wouldn't be embittered enough to spill any secrets.

Nelson had been the permanent head of the Directorate for only six months after having been "acting director" since Hume's death. A transition between Secretaries General and confusion from the new Sec-Gen over the Directorate's role and jurisdiction had delayed the formal appointment.

Nelson hadn't wasted time, though. He'd begun to make his mark right away, while he was acting. The old bunker had become crowded as personnel and departments increased. First, Nelson had reduced the size of what had been Hume's office and living quarters, which the old man had styled like an expansive country house. Nelson's office and quarters were a fourth of what Hume's had been.

Next, Nelson had opened more stations worldwide and moved operatives and analysts specializing in that part of the world to those stations. He'd started to shift the Directorate into the information age and freed as much space as he could for the Information Technology and Analysis Departments to expand and work in less confined quarters.

Alexei knew Nelson had other plans; some he'd shared, some he hadn't. Nelson had waited a long time for his opportunity to make the Directorate into a modern COINTEL organization, one on a par with the CIA or NSA or British Intelligence, and he was succeeding handsomely.

"Good morning, Ms. Greene," he greeted. Nelson had opted for an older woman for his secretary, so he wouldn't be tempted to fuck her, he'd said. She wasn't quite a Penelope but close.

"You are not on his schedule today," she said.

"You know I'm someone who can go into his office at any time and without an appointment."

She sighed and moued her displeasure. "I am aware, Mr. Bukharin, but when you do that, it upsets the day's schedule."

"I do have something urgent to speak to him about."

A finely plucked and precisely penciled eyebrow rose toward her hairline. "Is this 'urgent' matter of a personal nature or an operational one?"

"It is a matter between him and me."

Ms. Greene looked at him with the expectation of a further explanation. He said nothing. The stare-off lasted nearly a minute, and Alexei became aware of everyone in the operations center watching them with anticipation.

Another sigh, a long-suffering one, and Ms. Greene put her glasses back on and returned to her typing.

"Very well. Have it your way," she said.

Alexei passed her desk, knowing she'd be pissed when he didn't thank her, and knocked on Nelson's door. Without waiting for an answer, he opened it.

👁 👁

THANKFUL for the interruption to his phone call, Nelson grinned at his oldest friend and held up an index finger. Give me a minute, he was saying. Alexei didn't sit. He paced.

It took longer than Alexei wanted, but Nelson ended the phone call, with an abruptness the person on the other no doubt found rude, not to mention vexing.

"London station chief offering me his sage advice. Again," Nelson said.

Alexei grunted a response and kept pacing.

"What's up, Ice?" Nelson asked.

Alexei stopped in front of Nelson's desk. "I had an interesting conversation with Terrell this morning at Bethesda and . . ." He stopped, looked at his watch, and asked, "May I use your interoffice phone for a second?"

Nelson frowned but said, "Sure." Nelson watched as Alexei lifted the receiver and punched in two digits.

"Hi. I'm back from Bethesda. I'm in Nelson's office right now. Lunch in about a half-hour? All right. Yes. See you soon."

After Alexei hung up, Nelson grinned again. "Look at you, checking in with the little woman."

That drew a grimace of a smile from Alexei. "It's her test. A couple of times a week, she randomly suggests lunch."

"Test? Oh, I see. To check and make sure you aren't on a nooner, which you gave up years ago. You did, didn't you?"

"Yes, of course, but she's still unsure of that, despite evidence to the contrary."

"Okay. I won't make you late. How's Snake doing?"

"The doctors had to remove more of his arm because of infection. The CIA has cut him off, told him they couldn't be sure he wasn't compromised."

Nelson rolled his eyes. "That should be obvious to them if no case officers have been rolled up, but our CIA siblings are a totally different animal. What was so interesting about your conversation with him that had you pacing the floor?"

"Is Mai's mother alive and working for Chinese State Security?" Alexei blurted.

"Well, shit," Nelson said. In times of stress, his slight southern accent thickened. "Shit" had come out as "shee-it."

"What the hell?" Alexei said, blood draining from his face.

"Yeah, you better sit down."

Alexei dropped into one of the chairs before Nelson's desk.

"Tell me exactly what Snake said," Nelson ordered.

Alexei recounted the conversation about the special interrogator from Chinese State Security who had questioned Terrell in a North Korean prison, a Caucasian woman who looked like an older version of Mai. He reminded Nelson of how Terrell had reacted to Mai when she and Alexei had broken him out of that prison.

"I thought he was out of his head," Alexei said. "Is it true?"

Nelson snatched his cane from where he'd hung it on the edge of his desk. He went to the safe in his office. Blocking the keypad with his body, he unlocked it and extracted a thin file folder. Returning to his desk, he sat again, his hand atop the file he'd taken from his safe.

"What do you know about Mai's parents?"

"Only what she's told me, and she knew only what John Stone told her. They were betrayed by a local employee of theirs. They made it to the airport and almost to the plane before being arrested by the Taiwanese secret police. A few months after they were taken, the Taiwanese government notified the British embassy they died in custody."

Nelson nodded and said, "More or less matches, except that the Taiwanese told the embassy they'd been executed as spies. Supplied pictures of the bodies, but Nigel Hume knew long before anyone else because he was running a man who turned out to be a triple agent. He informed Nigel of their capture, and Hume ordered his asset to save one—only one—of them. He even gave his preference. Freddie, but Freddie overruled that and told the asset to save Katherine."

Nelson paused, rubbed his face, and sighed.

"I'll wager Freddie thought the asset was going to repatriate Katherine to Great Britain and ultimately to us, but instead, he took her to China."

"Why only one?"

"You're well aware Hume was a chauvinist's chauvinist. He hated every woman operative he encountered because they threatened the sanctity of his misogynist world view. Up until the old bastard died, every woman operative almost didn't get certified, but the U.N. had goals for hiring women and minorities. He couldn't ignore that."

"Yes, I remember how he treated Mai."

"In Hume's eyes, Freddie was worth saving. Kate was not. He even told Stone Kate's death would dissuade other women from seeking operational status and that if she'd stayed home with her child where she belonged, she would still be alive."

"He knew she was alive but told Stone she was dead?"

"So it seems. However, there was some question whether she was alive or not. We still don't know. We don't have any assets in China who would know. Our attempts to recruit assets there over the years have been unsuccessful."

"Doesn't the Hong Kong station chief have an in-road there?"

"A possibility, and one I will explore." Nelson slid the file toward Alexei but kept his hand on it. "Hume archived two reports about Freddie and Kate. The official one, the one for the record which indicates that they were executed as spies, doesn't contain what's in this file. Hume filed this in his personal archive, but I managed to get a copy of it from the Archivist."

"From Zamora? How is that possible?"

"Don't ask." He lifted his hand and leaned back in his chair.

Alexei frowned at him but picked up the file and removed the single sheet of paper.

5

CONSIDER YOURSELF SUBDUED

Ministry of State Security
People's Republic of China

October 14, 1963

Dear Nigel,

Here is my report on the disposition of the two Directorate operatives in Taiwanese custody, Frederick Fisher and Katherine Maitland-Fisher.

I must confess, I have varied from your specific instructions because I did not wish to kill the woman. You see, the interrogators quite often allow us "minor officers" to observe their torture sessions. This has a twofold purpose: to recruit from among us and to show us what will happen if we stray from the path.

I admired Katherine's strength and determination.

She endured for weeks that which has broken many a man within hours. On that alone, I decided I wanted her for myself.

I did offer a choice to both, though separately: One of them could live, but one of them would have to choose which one that was. As I expected, Katherine insisted her husband live. Frederick insisted his wife live. They both had the same reason: their child.

So I could have Katherine, I deferred to Frederick's request. However, as a reward I ended his torture and allowed him to kill himself.

Now, I am safely ensconced back in Beijing where I am my best self and can serve the great Mao Zedong.

Not you. It was never you.

As for Katherine, I will subject her to a new reeducation process our behavioral scientists have experimented with, a remapping of sorts of the mind and memory. It is, however, a dangerous process involving chemicals and certain forms of stimulation, reward, and punishment. Most have not survived this experimental process, but after witnessing Katherine's demeanor under torture, I am convinced if anyone can survive it and be successfully reeducated, it is she.

I promise you, I will not send her back into the dark world you and I inhabit. I have a daughter close in age to Katherine's daughter. My daughter's mother did not survive reeducation, and when Katherine finishes her reeducation, I will channel her maternal proclivities into my child, who is in desperate need of a loving mother.

I suppose you, with your western civilization-centric attitudes, would call Katherine my concubine. So be it, but she will be cared for and protected and will live out her life in a glorious socialist paradise.

I am rather proud I managed to fool you, that you genuinely believed I worked for you. I am not sorry to tell you that my country has learned well from our Soviet allies. Most of what I gave you was disinformation. I laugh at how much time you will spend trying to figure out what was useful and what was shit.

I do regret that Katherine's family has to believe she is dead. If the process is a success, she will have a good life as the companion of a rising member of the Communist Party, and she will have a child to nurture and to raise to be a good Communist. Of course, since it would be a significant embarrassment for you, you are unable to admit any of this to anyone.

By the time you receive this report, her transformation will have begun, and I look forward to my future with her as part of it. Sadly, she will forget her own child. I think you will agree, that will be for the best. Remembering that child would be a torture she might not survive.

You may, therefore, correctly conclude this is my final report to you, indeed, my final communication to you. I am sure your people and mine will encounter *each other on the field of battle that is espionage. You were an excellent player in that game, but now you are old, backward. Time to cede the battlefield to those of us who have the stamina to endure.*

As the master Sun Tzu has said, "The supreme art of war is to subdue the enemy without fighting."

Consider yourself subdued.

Yours truly,
Yazhu Fan

Alexei looked up at his former partner.

"Yazhu Fan, as in the former head of the Ministry of State Security?"

"Yes. Quite the survivor, one of the few in Mao's inner circle to be allowed to retire in actuality and not as a prelude to execution. Also, a crafty man, who has my admiration for pulling one over on Hume," Nelson replied.

"Did Hume know you had this?"

"Of course. Why else do you think he allowed me to make the changes I did?"

"You're lucky he didn't try to have you killed."

"Oh, he did," Nelson said and held up his cane. "He only crippled me, but I forced him to put me where I am now. I fully expected him to task you with killing me."

"But you knew that would never happen."

Nelson smiled at his friend. "I was reasonably certain."

Alexei returned the letter to its file. "We don't know if this reeducation process he spoke of was a success or not?"

"No. Stone tried to find out if it was possible from our own behavioral scientists. All he got was, 'It's a theory, no known indication of its practical application.' However, if what Terrell told you is true, it worked."

"And, it also appears Fan lied about not putting her back into espionage work," Alexei said.

"Or he used her to advance his career but kept her in the background. What we do know of Yazhu Fan was his rise after 1963 was meteoric. He was indeed a widower who never remarried, who was never associated with any other woman."

Alexei slumped in the chair. "It's possible the process worked, and Katherine Maitland has been his willing tool all these years."

Nelson sighed and said, "Yes, it's possible."

"*Boizhe moi*," Alexei muttered. He looked at Nelson. "Mai can never know this. Never."

"I agree."

Nelson returned the file to his safe and sat again.

"We somehow need to get ahead of this," Alexei said.

"I'll put a feeler out to Hong Kong."

"A carefully worded feeler."

"Granted. If the Chinese push back, it's likely true. Silence will mean she's in a mass grave at some reeducation camp or cremated and her ashes scattered. Is Snake likely to confess to Mai?"

"No. He agreed with me that she shouldn't know."

"It's risky. All she'd need is a tiny hint, and she will dig until she hits gold. And if she finds out you and I knew . . ." Nelson broke off with a shrug.

"I'll take that risk and do whatever I need to do to keep that secret, but I don't think she could be more upset with me than she has been lately."

"What's up? Not taking to playing mommy?"

"No, she's marvelous with Natalia, I think because they have the shared experience of losing a mother at a young age. She's upset with me because you're throwing missions my way instead of hers. Roisin O'Saidh has offered one or another younger O'Saidh as a nanny, but Mai doesn't want that. And we can't exactly approach a service and ask for a nanny with a clearance and personal security experience."

"A tall order indeed. All right, I'll put that feeler out as soon as possible, and I'll brief you if I get anything back." Nelson smiled again. "And you've got a lunch date with your wife. Don't be late."

6

AN UNKNOWN ROOM

2002

Dublin, Ireland

Six months.

Roisin O'Saidh, the one person left whom Mai Fisher had known her entire life, who had been the only constant in that life, had been dead and buried six months.

That should have been enough time to mourn properly, to keen and lament, to light candles and say Rosaries, to accept and move on.

A casualty of the collapse of the South Tower of the World Trade Center on September 11, Roisin's death had surprised Mai, shocked her, gobsmacked her. Worse, she'd had to wait to bury her until international air travel was safe again.

And when the time had come to bring Roisin home, when her bronze casket had rested in the cabin of a EuroEnterprises jet, Mai had taken the left seat to fly to Dublin.

That was more than the responsibility of an aristocrat for a retainer. It was duty and love.

Mai was certain the O'Saidhs, the family inextricably entwined with hers for centuries, had mourned in a traditional Irish Catholic way, but Mai hadn't participated in that. She'd been preoccupied, tracking a rogue Alexei across Afghanistan during his hunt for Osama bin Laden. Now, with both of them home and safe, Mai could see to the things associated with the death of an extended family member.

For instance, closing out Roisin's residence in Dublin.

The Maitland family, Mai's mother's family, owned several houses in various upscale neighborhoods in Dublin, one of which was always given over to the highest ranking O'Saidh, the one who was the business manager and main advisor to the Maitland heirs. Mai was currently the only Maitland heir left. There were, however, plenty of O'Saidhs.

The woman married to one of Roisin's many cousins, God knew how many times removed, had inherited Roisin's role, per Roisin's will. Somewhat unprecedented since Moira Pearse wasn't an O'Saidh by blood but marriage. Once Mai had given her endorsement, the O'Saidhs had no option but to accept it.

Moira had already removed Roisin's clothing and personal effects from the house, but her personal papers remained, both analog and digital. Moira had also seen to Roisin's business papers, those relating to EuroEnterprises, but tradition was that the Maitland heir would see to the personal papers because they might contain secrets only a Maitland should see.

Mai Fisher had always chafed under the O'Saidhs' arcane traditions, but she'd established a decent relationship with Moira. This tradition Mai would indulge.

To Mai's surprise, Alexei had offered to help her. "What on earth for?" Mai asked him. "You loathed the woman."

"I didn't loathe her. I was, almost as often as you were, annoyed with her. First, I'll help so you don't have to do it all yourself, and second, perhaps I'll find something to exonerate me fully."

"Exonerate you from what?"

"Ah, remember when Roisin hired a woman to seduce me?"

"Quite well, and I did believe your side of the story then."

"I was never sure of that."

Mai had raised an eyebrow. "Well, I'm still here, aren't I?"

"For which I am beyond grateful. Maybe a better word might be vindication."

"Ah, yes, that sounds more like the Alexei Bukharin I know."

"And love?" he prompted.

"Don't push it, Bukharin."

"I know the woman is dead, and I should have respect for the dead, but . . . "

"But," Mai said, "this is Roisin O'Saidh, who could be a pain in the arse."

THE ATTIC of Roisin's Dublin house had a footprint as large as the house itself. It had been put to the usual use for an attic in a large house. Old or out-of-style furniture filled a large section of it. The presence of dust covers over most everything tempted Mai to peek beneath them, and she decided the furniture, in particular, was best hidden from view.

A smaller section of the attic was devoted to the boxes of Roisin's papers. Her usual sense of organization was ever-present in their arrangement. Each archival quality box had been labeled by year. Inside each were dividers labeled by month. Some months had a great deal of content, others scant.

The historian in Mai longed to pick through page by page. After all, these would be Roisin's non-business notes, her impressions of people she'd encountered in her personal life and somewhat in her business life.

Why, who knew what Mai might learn of her mother and father since Roisin had become COO of EuroEnterprises when Mai's mother was still alive.

Maitland family history might be among Roisin's personal papers, perhaps even an explanation of how the two families had become so critical to each other.

Moira must have considered that, too, because she sent someone from EuroEnterprises to . . . assist.

Brendan O'Saidh Jr. had met them with a laptop, a scanner, and a shredder. He wasn't much interested in entering management, preferring instead to scout talent for the Entertainment Division, something Moira said he was exceptionally good at. He'd volunteered to help Mai out, remembering her from two decades ago when his father had been murdered while working with Mai.

Alexei would select a box, in order, of course, Mai would review a document, Brendan would scan it, then feed the paper document to the shredder.

What a team we are, Mai thought, as that process had proved quick and efficient.

In the evenings, Mai saw to the burning of the shredded documents herself, making for a cozy time spent with a "drap of whiskey," a flickering fire, and Alexei.

Within a few days, their work had significantly reduced the number of boxes and revealed a small, sturdy door to an unknown room. To Mai's surprise, it took Alexei most of the morning to pick the door's old and elaborate lock.

"I can call a locksmith or get a pry bar," Brendan had offered.

"Don't bother," Mai said. "He likes a challenge."

Once unlocked, the door opened onto stygian darkness, and Alexei's pocket penlight revealed more boxes, wooden ones this time, each with its own padlock. Alexei's movement into the room stirred up a cloud of dust that set everyone to sneezing, and the dust on each box was thick enough to obscure the dates stenciled on it.

To Mai, he called, "Who is Ethny O'Saidh?"

"I have no idea. Why?"

"Come have a look."

She entered the hidden room—it was an old house in Dublin; of course it had a hidden room—and read what his penlight illuminated: Eithne O'Saidh.

"Not Ethny," Mai said. "Enya."

"Like the singer?"

"If she spelled it properly. Eithne O'Saidh Brennan was Roisin's and Aifric's mother."

"Aifric?"

From the doorway, Brendan piped up, "Roisin's older sister."

"I think you're right, Brendan," Mai said. "I recall someone telling me Aifric was my mother's companion or whatever you O'Saidhs call it."

"We call ourselves retainers," Brendan said.

"How medieval," Mai replied with an arched eyebrow. "Aifric was my mother's companion and due to take over management of EuroEnterprises at some point. I think she died the year before I was born. Right, Brendan?"

"Correct, ma'am, but Eithne lived until 1960 I believe . . . No, wait. It was 1964, but she and Roisin shared the duty until Roisin took over."

"This is odd," Mai said.

"How so?" Alexei asked.

"Well, what we're doing right now for Roisin's personal

papers, Roisin and my mother would have done for Eithne. Of course . . ." Mai paused long enough for Alexei to frown. "My mother died in 1963, before Eithne, and I was too young to assist Roisin with Eithne's papers."

Alexei had cleaned the top of each box, not stacked like the archival boxes but in a chronological row: 1931-1940, 1941-1950, 1951-1960, and 1961-1964.

"Three and a partial," Alexei said. "Eithne, it seems, was far less inclined to capture minutia than Roisin." He leaned down to study the locks.

"These are likely personal papers," Brendan said. "Her business papers would have been at HQ."

"Let's pop the first one open and read all the gossip from the thirties, shall we?" Mai said.

Alexei straightened and sneezed again. "How about we clean them off and move them someplace a bit less dusty?" he said.

"Will you pick those locks, too?" Brendan asked.

"I think you should procure some bolt cutters," Alexei replied.

7

EITHNE O'SAIDH

After Brendan wielded a hand vac with a dexterity men seldom displayed for cleaning, the three of them dragged each box into the attic's main area. Alexei closed the door to the hidden room because the dust seemed to have waited forty years to escape.

Alexei used the bolt cutters on the padlocks, and they stood for a moment, staring at the boxes.

Mai opened the 1930s box, which yielded personal diaries, the first one beginning on the day Eithne had taken over her father's duties at what was then Maitland Enterprises after his death. The hand-bound, leather-covered diaries were the size of an A4 sheet of paper and an inch thick. The pages were undated, except for a hand-written notation at the beginning of each entry.

Some day's entries were but a paragraph or two; others went on for a few pages. The dates were sequential. Eithne wrote something every day, even if it were only a commentary on the weather and, occasionally, world events.

Again, the historian in Mai came to the surface when she

caught glimpses of phrases like, "My decision to cease all business with Germany will prove to be an appropriate one." That entry was dated "30 Jan 1933," the day Hitler was appointed Chancellor of Germany.

Eithne's handwriting was fluid but precise and easy to read. The ink in her pen was excellent quality; the fading was minimal. Indeed, the writing looked as though she'd penned it only a few days before. The diaries' pages were thick but still flexible. No ink had bled.

Mai returned to the first diary's initial entry, dated 4 Mar 1930 and read aloud, "'Da passed today, peaceful, in his sleep. Though we had expected it, to see that boisterous giant of a man look so small and shrunken in his bed was still quite the shock.'"

Mai closed the diary, an index finger marking the page, her eyes on something indistinct.

Alexei frowned and asked, "What is it?"

"Nothing. I thought the same about Roisin when I saw her on a gurney and covered with a sheet," Mai said.

Brendan blinked rapidly and stared at the floor.

Mai opened the diary and read more, "'My mother wailed for a good hour until I ordered the bloody doctor to sedate her so we'd have some peace and quiet.' Jesus Wept, I like Eithne already. Brendan, do you know if there are any pictures of her? Did Roisin look like her?"

"I don't recall seeing a picture of her, and Moira would have already removed any family portraits Roisin had here," Brendan said. He brought out his Nokia and typed on it. After re-pocketing it, he said, "I sent Moira a message and asked."

Mai nodded and flipped a few pages ahead in the diary. "Oh, this is all too familiar," she said. "Listen, 'The bleeding board of directors object to my taking Da's position, even though it was his directive, and for the most insane of reasons: my children. Who will raise my children, they asked. I wager none of the stuffy old buggers asked my father who would raise his twelve children when he rose to the position. I had to bloody agree to have Ciaran . . .'" Mai looked at Brendan. "Her husband?"

"Yes. He was an O'Saidh, too, a third cousin twice removed, I believe, and through his mother. Brennen was his surname, but I can check for certain."

"Not necessary, but thanks." Mai resumed reading, "'I had to bloody agree to have Ciaran *advise* me on business matters. Jesus Wept, I love the man in my own way, but he can barely manage his own pocket money. I'll not be letting him anywhere near a multi-million-dollar company. I can, however, trot him out at board meetings and tell him what to say. He'll be amenable to that because it won't take too much time away from breeding and racing his horses.'"

Alexei smiled at Mai. "I see now where your irreverent mouth came from."

WITH BRENDAN GONE HOME for the day and a light dinner and a bottle of wine in front of them, Mai and Alexei watched Roisin's shredded papers burn in the fireplace. The four wooden boxes they'd lugged downstairs and stacked in a corner. Several of the 1930s diaries lay on the sofa table.

"I don't think the O'Saidhs knew about Eithne's boxes," Mai said. "Brendan seemed shocked to see them, so I told him not to say a word."

"Do you think he'll keep quiet?" Alexei asked.

"He's an O'Saidh. They always, well, most of the time, do what they're told."

"Would Roisin have locked those boxes away in that room?"

"What are you getting at?"

"Her boxes were stacked in such a way to hide that door, almost as if she didn't want anyone to know what was inside."

"But she would have known that eventually someone would go through her personal papers and in doing so, discover that hidden room."

"Someone or only you?" Alexei asked, and Mai frowned at him. "Mai, she knew it would be you. Maybe she wanted you to find Eithne's boxes."

Mai pondered that but joked, "Though the fact you're here and discovered them should have brought her ghost roaring from the walls. Why do you think she wanted me to be the one to find Eithne's diaries?"

"I'm still thinking about that," he said.

"One thing is obvious from them," Mai said. "Eithne had a fondness for that green-dyed leather. Every single one of them was the same except . . ."

She and Alexei looked at each other.

"Those smaller diaries in the 1940s and 1950s boxes. Ones that could have come from any stationery store," Alexei said.

"Why would she have switched?" Mai said, frowning. "We didn't really look at those."

Alexei rose and unstacked the boxes, removing the lids on the two, more "recent" boxes.

Mai picked up one of the smaller diaries and opened it. "Oh, my God, this is beyond unusual. These belong to Aifric. She never took over the concession because she died before her mother, and that meant it went to Roisin."

"Eithne must have put these in with her diaries for some reason," Alexei said, flipping through the pages of another of the smaller diaries.

"It had to have been her. Jesus Wept, Alexei, Aifric went with my mother to Bletchley. She was there when my mother and father met. She went to live with them in Sussex after they were married." She looked at Alexei, some emotion in her eyes, something he hadn't seen in a long time.

"Alexei, these . . . These diaries will have details about my mother. Roisin made sure . . ." Mai's voice trailed off.

"Roisin made sure you would find them," Alexei said, but his thoughts spun at a particular possibility.

Aifric had died before Mai was born. Her diaries would not be a problem, but Eithne's diaries went up to 1964. How much had John Stone told Eithne about Katherine Maitland's "death?" Would he have shared his suspicions with her? If he had, Eithne surely would have written about it, and Roisin's diaries from a decade ago could be a problem, too.

"We have to be back in the U.S. by Monday," Alexei said. "We should take these four boxes with us. You can go through them as you have time."

He wasn't sure she had listened.

"This is odd," she repeated. "Why didn't Roisin simply tell me she had these?"

"I've often thought she'd have made a good spy, as secretive and devious as she was. She wanted you to find them, and she knew you'd be thorough."

"Yes, if Moira had known about Eithne's diaries, she would have disposed of them before we got here. The O'Saidhs have always known everything about the Maitlands. It was rarely the other way 'round. Which is why they so often have to be reminded who works for whom."

"If we were to ask Brendan to ship the remainder of Roisin's boxes and Eithne's boxes to our house, would he do it without letting Moira know?"

"With the proper incentive; however, I'm not entirely certain he's not fiercely loyal to Moira. If we work our asses off and finish Roisin's boxes before Monday, we won't have them to worry about. It'll all be digitized anyway, and I'll have access. We'll have to sneak Eithne's boxes home somehow."

Alexei said, "I'll work on a way to sneak Eithne's boxes onto your airplane. We'll take those home, and you and I can review them at our leisure."

Mai smiled at him. "You're rather secretive and devious yourself. I find that stimulating."

"Do you?"

"I do, but first . . ."

She resumed her seat on the sofa and picked up one of the leather-bound diaries and turned to a specific page. Alexei noted the date on the page: 15 Feb 1958.

Mai said, "Let's read what she wrote about my birth."

8

OUR DAUGHTER

February 15, 1958

Uxfield Manor
Sussex, England

Frederick Fisher, Fifteenth Earl of Uxfield, couldn't see much difference between English nurses he'd encountered and the Irish midwives his wife had insisted upon. The midwives wore the same type of uniform, though gray instead of blue, the same white caps, the same style aprons. The only difference was the accent.

British nurses were encouraged to use the "BBC accent," that distinctly English but more or less neutral accent, as a courtesy to patients who might be uncomfortable with a Cockney or Scot. To the biased mind, both implied a lack of education.

The Irish midwives were as uncompromising as his wife could be, and Fisher suspected that was on purpose because they were among *sasanaigh*. His own wife could sound like a Tinker when she wanted to make a point to the aristocracy she'd married into, but he had to concentrate to understand what the midwives were saying. His understandable excitement and fear made it difficult for him to do that. He had the impression that as the soon-to-be-father, he was a mere appendage who got in the way and who had no need to know what was going on.

His wife's business manager, Eithne O'Saidh, had wanted this child born in Ireland, but Fisher had insisted on his family estate. His heir would be born in his family home, but he'd compromised on the Irish midwives, including the one who'd lived here with them for seven months. Eithne made it clear she wanted no English doctor anywhere near his dear Katherine, and Katie had tried to bridge the cultural divide between her husband and the woman who'd been like a mother to her.

But really. Surely, Eithne understood it wasn't as if Lord Fisher needed to use the National Health Service, perfectly adequate as it was. He could afford the best private obstetrician from, well, anywhere in the world. Midwifery, Eithne explained, was a Maitland family tradition. He'd long since learned trying to sidestep one of that family's obscure traditions was ill-advised.

Frankly, if he'd done so, he'd have been a hypocrite. His own family's traditions were rooted in history but were often absurd to the point of eccentricity. His father, for example, had insisted the birth take place in a particular room of the sprawling manner, one "where all Fisher heirs have entered this world."

Now, a half-dozen midwives scuttled about the large bedroom. They'd opened the tall brocade drapes, and so far the room had moved through twilight, nighttime, dawn, morning, and into afternoon sunlight as his wife's labor had progressed. The head midwife, the one who'd come out of retirement for this birth, who'd lived in a room next door to Katherine's, and who'd attempted to ban him from his and Katherine's bed, had the take-charge demeanor of a British Army sergeant major, though Fisher doubted she'd appreciate the comparison. She marshaled and directed the midwives with short, clipped commands, and they obeyed without question.

Hovering in the background, where she always seemed to be, was Eithne, dressed in black, thin as a rail, and sallow-complexioned, her small, dare he say, beady eyes reminding Fisher of a gigantic crow.

Bad simile, old boy, he told himself. For the Irish, the crow was a symbol of the Morrigan, who foretold doom in battle. And wasn't childbirth exactly that, a battle between the mother, who wanted dominion over her own body again, and the child, who preferred lazing about in the warm, comfortable womb.

Fisher had decided upon his introduction to the formidable head midwife that when she commanded him to leave, he'd retreat with haste. So, when she settled her gray-eyed gaze on him and jerked her head toward the door, he jumped to.

"Freddie?" said his wife, Katherine Maitland-Fisher. "Where is it you think you're going?"

"Well, darling, Sister Moyna has indicated it's time for me to depart," he replied, trying to smile.

He recognized Katherine's expression of displeasure, the crease in her forehead, her flinty eyes, an arched eyebrow.

"Oh, no, me boyo, you're staying right here," she said, labor having leached her affected British accent, leaving the Irish behind.

Before either he or Sister Moyna could respond, Katherine stopped pacing, one hand latching onto a bedpost on a bed at least three centuries old. Each of the four posts had been a tree from the estate, carved with elaborate scenes of what could only be, well, fertility rituals.

Katherine's other hand pressed against the side of her

distended belly. She bent slightly at the waist. The sound she made began as a vibrato "mmmmmm" but built to a near-scream that raised Fisher's hackles. At Sister Moyna's direction, Katherine panted through the pain, and it passed in less than a minute. It had seemed like forever to Fisher. He released the breath he'd held.

Sister Moyna and two other midwives guided Katherine to the bed and helped her onto the rubber sheet that had been covered with crisp, clean white towels.

"Lass," said Sister Moyna, "it is time to start the pushing. Himself needs to leave."

"He is not leaving," Katherine said. She looked at Fisher. "You did this to me, and you're watching every second of it."

Her mass of thick, red hair was bound in a bun atop her head, but wisps had escaped and curled into ringlets from the sweat of her labor. A cliche, he knew, but Fisher thought she was never more beautiful.

"Lass," Sister Moyna said, her tone more firm, "the father always waits outside."

Yet, outside this room was his father and his harridan of a step-mother, the former eager for a Fisher heir, the latter hoping her son, the step-brother, would get a share of the estate even if he couldn't have the title. Waiting with his father and hearing yet again a recitation of the Fisher family history and its connection to the Crown while dealing with his stepmother's sour looks was not something Fisher wanted to do.

Neither was watching someone expel another human being.

"Fuck that," Katherine said, setting the younger midwives to blushing. "I'm countess here. My baby, my rules. He stays."

"I have found, Lass, most fathers don't have the fortitude to witness what's to come. It tends to make them queasy and prone to fainting."

"Then, one of youse hand him a bucket or hold him up if his knees buckle, but he stays."

Sister Moyna folded her hands over her girth and said, "Well, then, if he stays, I go."

"Fine," Katherine replied. "There's five more of youse, and if youse all go, Himself and I will do this on our own."

Dear God, Fisher thought, one of you stay.

Her next labor pain began, and a younger midwife took over the coaching to pant while Eithne took Sister Moyna aside, murmuring to her in Irish.

"Very well," Moyna said, her scowl broadcasting her displeasure, "he can stay but out of my way."

"Yes, of course, absolutely. Out of the way," Fisher babbled. He'd find a nice corner of the room and stare out a window until this was over.

That wasn't Katherine's plan, however.

Fisher ended up on the bed, behind her, holding her upright when she didn't have the strength to do so herself, murmuring encouragement even after she told him "to shut the feck up."

The whole of it was a blur, minutes or hours, he didn't know. Katherine panting when the pain came, screaming as she pushed, bewailing the child would never be born, and telling him it was all his fault because he needed an heir.

Well, you do, too, he'd wanted to say but stayed silent.

However, his heart also raced with excitement and anticipation. After all the years of false hopes ending with no pregnancy and false starts ending in miscarriage or stillbirth, he and the woman he loved were about to become parents.

Over Katherine's labored breathing, Fisher heard Sister Moyna say, "All right, Lass, one more big push, and we'll have the wee-un here. Push!"

Katherine's final cry of labor was prolonged and grated down

Fisher's spine, but she stopped abruptly and lay back against his chest, panting from exertion.

Fisher held his breath again. They'd been here before—with a baby who'd never drawn breath.

A lusty, full-bodied, annoyed crying filled the room, and Fisher wanted to laugh and cry, too.

"Let me see. Give it here," Katherine commanded.

Sister Moyna said, "One moment for cutting the cord." Then, she straightened, holding a squirming jumble of towels. There was blood on them. Not much but blood all the same. Sister Moyna smiled and said, "Let us get her cleaned up and presentable."

Katherine gasped and turned to Fisher, her eyes bright with tears, her smile unbelievably gorgeous.

"A girl, Freddie. Our daughter. You're not disappointed she's a girl, are you?"

"Of course not," he said and kissed her.

An heir was an heir. His estate and title went to any child of his, born or adopted, no matter the gender. That aside, he and the woman he loved more than life itself had a child. Their child.

While two of the other midwives still did something he didn't want to think about behind the sheet covering Katherine's bent knees, the other midwives and Eithne gathered around the baby, who continued to scream indignantly.

Some emotion passed over Eithne's usually stoic face. Brief, but Fisher saw. The sudden stiffening of Katherine's body against him told him she'd seen it, too.

There could be no god if he dashed all their hopes now.

"What?" Katherine demanded, sitting up. "What is wrong?"

The baby's loud crying had to mean nothing was wrong. Such cries hadn't been heard in this house since his own birth, and he'd despaired they'd never be heard here again. No, a baby crying that strongly had to be healthy.

"What is it?" Katherine demanded again.

"'Tis nothing," Eithne said.

"'Tis good luck, is what it is," said Sister Moyna. More cooing from her, and the baby quieted from screaming to whimpering. Moyna began wrapping the baby in blankets, and Fisher caught a glimpse of a tiny arm freeing itself from the swaddling, a minuscule clenched fist.

A fighter, she was. Good girl.

"What do you mean, good luck?" Fisher asked.

Eithne said, "Only half the face was covered. She won't have the Sight, this one."

"What on earth are you talking about?" Fisher said. "What was on her face?"

Over her shoulder, Moyna replied, "Sometimes a baby brings part of the birth sac with it as it's born. It's called a caul. It's said a baby wearing a caul will have the Sight, that she'll see the future. This wee-un only had half a caul. She won't have the Sight, but she'll have good instincts. Intuition, they call it."

"Fine and good with all the fairy tales," Katherine said. "Give me my daughter."

Sister Moyna handed the swaddled baby to Eithne. Another Maitland tradition: an O'Saidh gave a new Maitland mother her first child. Eithne took a small bottle of water from a pocket of her dress, unscrewed its cap, and sprinkled some water on the fingers of her right hand. She made the sign of the cross on the child's head, murmuring, "I baptize thee in the name of the Father, the Son, and the Holy Spirit. Amen."

A blessing from a Catholic to tide the baby over until a priest could baptize the child.

The Irish midwives all blessed themselves.

Katherine reached for her daughter, and Fisher was glad his father wasn't in the room to see that last bit.

THE MIDWIVES HAD ERECTED a folding privacy screen between Fisher and the bed, and all he could do was wait, his hands aching to touch his child. The midwives finished whatever mysterious things they needed to do. Sister Moyna made an entry in her book of births then filled out and signed both the British and the Irish birth certificates.

The screen came down, the midwives filed from the room, and there was Katherine, holding their daughter, Eithne hovering, crow-like as usual.

"Freddie," Katherine said, smiling at him. "Come see her. She is so beautiful."

He climbed onto the bed and got as close to Katherine as he could. A rare thing for him to have no words, but he was without speech when he looked into the face of a cherub with a head of dark hair tinged with red and alert, dark eyes that seemed ancient. An arm again pushed free of the blankets, the tiny hand coming to rest on Katherine's cheek. Fisher leaned forward and kissed that little hand.

"She is absolutely beautiful, darling," he managed to say.

"Freddie, I thought this would never happen, but we have her. We have her."

"That we do, my darling."

The emotion welling in him was a surprise. He was a cold, calculating covert operative about to weep at the sight of his long-awaited first, and likely only, child.

"And the name?" Eithne asked.

Katherine looked at her husband. "We didn't discuss a name for a girl. Typical."

"I have an idea," Fisher said, "that might satisfy everyone." He looked at Eithne.

"What?" Katherine asked.

"My daughter's name is Maitland Katherine Fisher. Lady Maitland Katherine Fisher, of course, later to be Countess Uxfield." He looked at his wife, and she was smiling.

"But," Katherine said, "we'll call her Mattie."

9

REVENGE FROM THE GRAVE?

2002

Dublin, Ireland

"Well," Alexei said, "Eithne was quite the diarist. I felt as if I was there."

"Yes, that was rather descriptive," Mai said. "I knew they'd been married more than a decade before they had me, and I do understand how they felt about the lack of success."

Knowing she wouldn't want to discuss that any further, Alexei brushed her cheek with his fingers.

"Let's get to work scanning the rest of Roisin's papers and get Eithne's ready to sneak home."

"Of course," Alexei murmured, eyes on the box that held Eithne's final diaries. From their brief examination of the boxes' contents, Alexei saw Eithne had filled three to four of them per year. He wanted to extract the ones for 1963 and 1964 and examine them before Mai had a chance to read them—in case John Stone had voiced his suspicions to Eithne.

And the fiction he'd told Roisin a decade ago, had she put that in a diary of her own? Knowing Mai would eventually see Roisin's diaries, he hoped not. Or would Roisin have exacted some revenge against him from the grave?

Damn, Alexei thought, I'd hoped this was over and done with.

"You know," Mai said, "I'd like to read Aifric's diaries before reading Eithne's."

Careful not to show his relief, Alexei said, "Why?"

"Because Aifric was with my mother at Trinity, at Bletchley, at Uxfield. Her diaries could be the closest I'll ever come to knowing anything about my mother."

"Mai, you knew your mother."

"For five years, and those memories have faded. Aifric's diaries will introduce me to her as a young woman. Maybe I'll learn how and when she met my father, about their life together as a couple. I read their operative files. I know them as that, but now I could see them as . . . Well, people."

Mai rose and went to the crate that held the first of Aifric's diaries. She looked at the dates on several and selected one.

"Nineteen forty," she said. "The year my mother was recruited for Bletchley. Oh, I should get Eithne's for the same period. We could read them separately and compare versions of the story."

She smiled in a way that often rendered him unable to deny her.

"I thought you wanted to hurry up the scanning," he said.

"True. All right, only the Bletchley recruiting, then scanning."

"I was, however, thinking a seduction scene might be preferable," Alexei said. "We have the wine, we have the cozy fire. I'm here. You're here. No one else is here, well, except for perhaps Roisin's ghost."

"I'm still in the process of forgiving you for dashing off to Afghanistan on a fool's errand. You'll have to work pretty hard to get that seduction, me boyo."

"All the more reason to get started, don't you think?"

Mai shook her head. "Which O'Saidh do you want? Eithne or Aifric?"

"Neither. I want you."

"You'll have me. After this indulgence and finishing with the scanning."

"You, madam, are a tease."

"You've never complained before. You know, the sooner we get started . . .?" She raised an eyebrow.

Alexei chose Eithne's diary.

👁 👁

1940

Trinity College, Dublin

WALKING among the stately buildings of Trinity College brought pleasant memories for Eithne O'Saidh.

For the most part.

The most pleasant, of course, was being one of the first women admitted in 1904 when she was only sixteen. After that, the memories lessened in pleasure; the ridicule of professors and fellow students, the threats of interfering with her unless she left, a few attempts to do so.

Thirty-six years later, she was more confident, less fearful, but still grateful for the former Garda walking with her.

Certainly, more women attended Trinity now, though that was likely because men had left to join *an tArm*, not to fight the

Brits' war but to protect Ireland in case the Brits' war threatened to spill over here.

She smiled when she recalled that none of her tormentors could quibble with her success: top in all her classes; honors in all her subjects; concomitant degrees from Oxford and Cambridge. She'd spent thirteen years here, through her undergraduate, graduate, and doctoral degrees plus the law.

A dean told her, "No one will hire you in any law office in Ireland or anywhere else."

No matter. She had no intent to practice law, but, like her father, she needed to know the law to fulfill her destiny as manager of Maitland Enterprises, as O'Saidhs had done for centuries.

Despite the good memories and the pushed-aside ones, Eithne wasn't sure why the Dean of Mathematics had requested a meeting with her to discuss the only pupil here Eithne cared about. Caitrin Chláir Maitland, only child and heir of Maigret and Upton Maitland, may they rest in peace, and the person to whom all of Maitland Enterprises would belong when she turned twenty-five.

Eithne knew of no issue with Caitrin's academic performance. She, too, was top of her classes and had honors in all her subjects, but Eithne's curiosity had the best of her. She was here, albeit with reluctance, for the requested appointment.

The Dean's secretary, an efficient but effete young man, received Eithne and her bodyguard politely but asked only Eithne if she wanted tea.

"No, thank you," Eithne said. "This is not a social occasion."

The young man blushed and led the way to the Dean's inner office. Dean Keegan Burns and another man in a British Naval uniform stood before Burns' massive desk. Eithne took in the entire office in a glance, its overbearing masculinity, the martial paintings, leather chairs, dark paint, and polished wainscoting. A massive, dark wood humidor sat on one corner of Burns' desk, and he puffed a cigar, smoke swirling about his head like mist over a bog.

How fecking rude.

Eithne removed a hanky from her purse and pressed the cloth over her nose and mouth. Burns should have known better than to smoke that offending thing in a woman's presence, but he was Scots, after all.

Indeed, it took him a few moments to comprehend the intent of her gesture. He turned to a stone ashtray in the shape of a man's cupped hand and knocked the ember from the cigar, which he placed in the ashtray.

Fine and good, but the disgusting stench lingered.

To Burns left, the naval commander stood to the full extent of his six feet. His fading yellow hair had receded a bit, baring a forehead that would have been high anyway. He'd combed back his hair, and his eyes were a piercing, no-nonsense blue, his face lean and angular, but bags of exhaustion and worry marred an otherwise pleasing face.

The naval officer's scrutiny passed over Eithne and stayed on her tall and burly companion.

"And you are?" the officer asked, his accent Scots, from the west. It almost had an Ulster inflection.

"O Cochlian," Eithne replied. "My personal detective."

The thin, light naval officer and the thick, dark O Cochlian began a stare-down. Eithne knew O Cochlian would win; that was why she'd hired him. Indeed, the navy man averted his gaze at once.

To Eithne, he said, "I'm sorry. The matter we will be discussing is not for all ears."

"You're wanting him to leave?"

"Yes."

Eithne looked at O Cochlian, who shook his head and said, "*Ar lá fuar in ifreann, b'fhéidir.*" Maybe on a cold day in hell.

"Excuse me?" said the navy man.

"Merely O Cochlian stating that the likelihood of being separated from me is small."

The navy man smirked at Burns. "Why does one need a bodyguard here at Trinity?"

"There were, uh, several unfortunate incidents when Mrs. O'Saidh matriculated here," Burns said. "Incidents of inappropriate, unwanted, uh, attention."

Eithne sighed. Technically, she was Mrs. Brennan not Mrs. O'Saidh, but she never allowed anyone to address her as Mrs. Brennan.

Eithne said, "Mr. O Cochlian can wait outside with your secretary after he ascertains there are no dangers here."

At her nod, O Cochlian examined every nook and cranny of the Dean's office, under Burns' disinterested gaze and the navy man's amused smirk. O Cochlian gave Burns a pat-down then stood before the navy man, who blinked in confusion.

"Am I to understand he means to search me?" the navy man asked.

"Yes," Eithne replied. "For weapons. Explosives and so forth.

"Bloody hell!"

"Watch that language before madam, sir," O Cochlian said.

Eithne pinched back her smile. O Cochlian had heard Eithne say far worse.

The navy man held his arms out from his sides, and O Cochlian's search was thorough, more so than usual because he'd taken offense at being dismissed by a *sasanach*. The navy man's lips squeezed to a thin, grim line, and that massive forehead crimped in displeasure.

With a nod in Eithne's direction, O Cochlian left.

"Shall we sit?" Burns said when it was the three of them.

Her back ramrod straight, Eithne said, "Not until I know with whom I shall be sitting."

After a sigh, Burns replied, "Commander Alastair Denniston, Mrs. Eithne O'Saidh."

Denniston didn't offer a hand to shake, and she wouldn't have accepted such anyway. With a bob of his head, he said, "Madam."

Eithne had noted the arrangement of the three chairs before the Dean's fireplace, which popped and crackled with a distinct warmth as the wood burned. Eithne went to the largest of the three chairs and stood before it until the two men, after more confusion, stood at the other chairs. Eithne kept them waiting a moment longer then sat, poised at the front half of the cushion, purse tucked behind her back, hands folded and resting on her lap.

"Now, what may I do for you, gentlemen?" she asked.

10

NOT AN IRISH WAR

Burns cleared his throat and leaned toward Eithne.

"Alastair is a chum of mine from the University of Bonn," he said. "What I'm about to tell you from this point is at the highest level of secrecy and cannot be shared. I'm certain you understand what that means without further explanation. Since immediately after the Great War, Alastair has been the head of the Government Code and Cypher School."

"That's—" Denniston began.

"I'm aware of GC&CS," Eithne said. "What I am not aware of is what that has to do with me or Caitrin Maitland."

"Caitrin?"

"Katherine," Burns said. "I was getting to that, Mrs. O'Saidh. Alastair and I have a long-standing agreement where I identify students of exceptional proficiency in mathematics as potential candidates for GC&CS. Miss Maitland is one such candidate, not only for her mathematical acumen but for her superior ability to solve unique and challenging problems in both higher mathematics and logic."

Eithne's snort was unladylike and startled the two men.

"You want Caitrin Maitland, heiress to the largest fortune in Ireland, to be a codebreaker? For the *Sasanaigh*?"

"The what?" Denniston asked.

"Foreigners. It's what they call the English."

Denniston narrowed his eyes at Eithne. "We are at war, Madam," he said.

"Your war. Not an Irish war," Eithne snapped back.

"Against an enemy the whole world must fear and defeat."

"That's a pat answer, Commander. Your war is not my concern nor that of my ward. GC&CS is a military organization. A *British* military organization. Caitrin Maitland will never be part of any aspect of the British military, whom all Irish perceive as conquerors, murderers, and colonizers."

Denniston's lip curled in a sneer. "That attitude is wholly expected from a people who are allowing Hitler to court them."

"And if you'd done sufficient research, Commander, you would know the loudest voices against any sort of relationship with Nazi Germany are those of the Maitland family."

"I am aware of that, but since the Maitland family consists of a few cousins several times removed and the only Maitland heir studies here, that voice comes actually from the Maitlands' retainers, who are the O'Saidhs."

The sneer became a smirk, that haughty expression the English used when discussing anything Irish.

"Of course," Denniston continued, the sneer deepening, "you may carry more Maitland blood in your veins than some of the Maitlands, but you can never lay claim to the fortune or the name, which was a Norman one."

"Alastair," Burns said, "that was unallowably crude."

His eyes were flat and listless when Denniston looked at Eithne and said, "My apologies, Madam."

"Accepted. Now that we have that settled, I shall be on my way, gentlemen."

"Nothing is settled," Denniston said. "I am authorized to make you an offer."

"For what?"

"To make Miss Maitland a civilian employee of GC&CS. We are, of course, prepared to pay a fair price for her services."

"She has no need of British money nor will she be an employee of the British."

"Very well. How does 'expert consultant' sound?"

"Marginally better. As an expert consultant, would she have to live in England?"

"Her work would not be something that could be conducted over the telephone or the wireless, Mrs. O'Saidh. We have a facility at an estate named Bletchley Park. That is classified, by the way. She would have quite adequate accommodation there."

"And her consulting fee?" Eithne asked.

"Thirty thousand pounds a year."

"You consider that a serious offer?"

"It is as much as we're paying our top scientist, Alan Turing."

"I see. Mind you, I have not agreed to this, and if I were to agree, which I doubt I will, Miss Maitland would have to be accompanied by my daughter, Aifric Brennan. This would not be negotiable. Aifric's presence is necessary as a chaperone and to assure there would be no undue, negative influence exerted on Miss Maitland."

"Negative influence exerted by whom?"

"The British, of course."

"Mrs. O'Saidh, Miss Maitland is twenty years old, I believe. Old enough, surely, to make up her mind about who influences her and who doesn't."

"Per the tradition of her family, she is not recognized as an adult until she is twenty-five years old. Until that time, I or my elder daughter make decisions for her. This is how it's been done in the Maitland family for centuries. I do not expect the likes of you to understand, nor do I seek your understanding. Fifty thousand pounds. Thirty thousand for Miss Maitland and twenty thousand as a stipend for Miss Brennan."

When Denniston smiled, Eithne had a glimmer of dread that she'd been had, that she could have gotten far more from the snotty English bastard.

"Done," Denniston said. "We shall expect Miss Maitland and her chaperone at the end of term."

"Oh, I've not given consent yet," Eithne said. "Do not be making any plans."

Denniston's smile broadened. "Why don't we hear from the lady herself as to her desires in this matter?"

"I have explained—"

"Yes, you have, but I would like for you to hear from Miss Maitland on this matter."

Eithne lurched to her feet and took a step toward Burns, who pressed back in his chair.

"Am I to assume you have allowed this, this foreigner to speak with my ward without my being present?"

"Miss Aifric Brennan was present," Burns said. "Miss Maitland was entirely comfortable with the situation."

"Impossible. My daughter would have apprised me of this."

Burns rose, moving sideways to avoid Eithne, and went to a door leading to a private annex off his office. When he opened the door, Katherine Maitland entered, Aifric Brennan close behind her.

ALASTAIR DENNISTON GOT to his feet when the young women entered, but Eithne didn't acknowledge his manners.

Caitrin's hair had been styled well, parted on one side, trimmed to shoulder length, and rolled under. Her outfit was a charcoal-colored wool, pleated skirt, stopping an inch below her knee. The matching peplum jacket-blouse had three large, white buttons. The slight vee neckline showed no décolletage, and the sleeves were three-quarter length, the shoulders slightly padded. Black pumps with a modest heel, some eye shadow and mascara, and an apple red lipstick completed the look of a wealthy, well-heeled young woman.

Satisfactory, though Eithne objected to the length of the skirt. Someone else's war shouldn't mean higher hemlines.

Aifric wore a grey one-piece dress with pockets on the skirt portion. Her hair was styled similarly to Caitrin's, and she wouldn't meet her mother's eyes.

"Eithne," Caitrin said, "this is something I want to do."

"You've had your head filled with nonsense."

"No, Eithne, I am quite capable of figuring these things out on my own, and I won't have you blaming Aifric. She conceded to my logic and followed my instructions not to discuss this with you. I want to go to Bletchley and help however I can."

"Help the British?"

"Help the people in Europe under Nazi oppression and stop them before they decide capturing Ireland might be the way to defeat England." Caitrin looked at Commander Denniston. "How much can I tell her?"

"I'll let you know when you're overstepping," he replied.

"Eithne, they think I can help Alan Turing decipher a Nazi code machine. Turing is probably the most brilliant mathematician in the world. I could learn more from him in a year than I did in my time here. No offense, Dean Burns."

"None taken, Miss Maitland."

"Eithne, it is the opportunity of a lifetime," Caitrin added.

"And the German bombing can end your life in a second."

"Bletchley is well north and west of London, Eithne. The danger is minimal."

Eithne looked at Denniston. "How many other women work at this Bletchley?"

"Well, Bletchley has quite a few women in clerical positions. Mr. Turing has one other woman who works in the lab with him. The rest of his team are men, most of them married," Denniston said. "However, Miss Brennan would not be allowed in Miss Maitland's work area."

"Then, no deal."

"Eithne, I can take care of myself. When I'm not with Aifric, I'll be with the other woman on Mr. Turing's team. She's older, I believe, Commander Denniston, isn't she?"

"Yes."

"Commander Denniston has addressed all my and Aifric's concerns in this matter."

Eithne addressed her daughter. "So you at least asked some questions." Her words were a rebuke Aifric felt, given her blush.

"As Miss Caitrin has said, her arguments were beyond reproach. Had I had doubts, I would have advised you," Aifric told her mother.

"How long have these discussions been going on?" Eithne demanded of Aifric.

Caitrin was the one to answer. "Dean Burns initially discussed the opportunity with me a few weeks ago. I completed a little test Mr. Turing uses on all applicants."

"She had one of the highest scores," Denniston said.

"Commander Denniston and I met earlier this week to explain what the work would be."

"Were you present for that?" Eithne asked, again of Aifric.

"No, the details were top secret, and I am not cleared, I believe is the word."

"You left her alone with this *Sasanaigh* military officer?"

"Eithne," Caitrin said, "that is quite enough."

"Excuse me," Eithne said, "exactly to whom do you think you're speaking?"

"Why, to my employee."

Eithne's hand went to her throat as if to stop her heart from rising into it. That was how it felt, as if her heart were about to lurch from her chest.

To be spoken to like this in front of men, in front of a foreigner; it was beyond humiliation.

"Commander Denniston," Caitrin was saying, since Eithne had yet to find her voice, "I have spoken with Dean Burns, and my obligations for this term can be completed within a week. We have no need to wait for the end of the term. I can be at Bletchley within no more than a fortnight."

"Excellent news, Miss Maitland," Denniston said.

"And thirty thousand pounds is quite sufficient for Aifric and me to live on since you're providing accommodations and one meal a day. Should I require something out of the ordinary, Mrs. O'Saidh will certainly supply it at no cost to the British government. However, I would like a contract to be drawn up as soon as possible reflecting these terms and several other conditions, which I have prepared in writing."

Katherine turned to Aifric, who produced a folded letter from skirt pocket.

Blinking, Denniston took it from her, unfolded it, and read what was there. He looked at Eithne and smiled.

"Not to worry, old girl," he said. "You trained her quite well." To Caitrin, he said, "The contract with these terms will be prepared, and I will deliver it personally in two days. The clearance for Miss Brennan would take considerably longer unless you will accept a restricted one."

"That will be fine, as long as she's not shut up like a prisoner in our quarters all day."

"I am quite good at clerical work," Aifric said.

Caitrin looked at her. "That's all right with you?"

Aifric smiled and said, "I'll adapt."

To Eithne, Caitrin said, "That should alleviate your concerns."

"I'll still want to read that contract before you sign it, and I will want to witness it," Eithne replied.

"That's fine," said Caitrin.

Denniston tucked the letter inside his tunic, retrieved his cover from Burns' desk, and stopped at Caitrin's side.

"In two days, then, Miss Maitland. Good day."

"I'll see you out, Alastair," Burns said, and the two men vacated the office.

11

REASSURANCE

2002

Dublin

Alexei closed the green diary. "Again, I think I see where your infamous stubborn streak comes from," he said to Mai.

"Stubborn? I think of it more as tenacity," Mai replied.

"You would, of course, but it makes you that much more stimulating to me."

He moved in for a kiss, but she backed away.

"Easy, me boyo. Scanning documents first, then a shower, and you can *attempt* your seduction."

"Our priorities are off-kilter. However, showering together could pass for seduction. How did Aifric's version match up?"

"Compared to Eithne's detail, it was more like, "Mam came to Trinity and heard Commander D's proposal. She eventually and reluctantly agreed.'"

Mai took both diaries, rose, and returned them to their crate. Alexei followed her and embraced her from behind.

"I might need some reassurance that my seduction attempt has a chance of succeeding," he murmured against her neck.

"A couple of hours of work first. I think you'll find the shower in the main bath is narrower than what we're accustomed to, but we'll manage. Reassuring enough?"

"It is, indeed."

He released her and jogged up the stairs to the attic.

WITH MAI SLEEPING the sleep of the sexually sated, helped along by a Benadryl he'd encouraged her to take after a bout of sneezing from the attic dust, Alexei pulled on a pair of sweatpants and tiptoed up to the attic.

He went right to the box holding Roisin's personal papers from November of 1991, selecting the folder for a specific week. No mention of a meeting with him. He scanned the folders for at least a month afterward. Again, no mention of meeting with him.

After a check that Mai still slept soundly, he went to the living room. In Eithne's 1960s box, he skimmed through four diaries and saw nothing about any sort of meeting with John Stone regarding the possibility that Katherine Maitland had survived her capture and torture.

The only relevant thing he found was a single entry:

> I was informed today that Caitrin and her
> husband were killed in an airplane crash in Taiwan.
> On an approach over the water, the plane lost control
> and plunged into the sea. The wreckage cannot be

recovered, but the plane's manifest clearly shows their names. All my attempts to contact them have gone unanswered, and I am forced to accept the reality of it. My heart is broken into so many pieces.

I tried my very best to protect her, but she knew what she wanted, which was her own life lived her way and with <u>him</u>. I can only thank God they never took Mattie with them on these ridiculous Prot mission trips. She is the only reason I didn't slit my own wrists at the news. I will do better with Mattie. I will protect the last surviving Maitland at all costs.

I am also grateful my Aifric was not alive to receive this news. She would not have survived it. Now, I must do the difficult thing and inform the board of directors. And Roisin. I only pray that Caitrin's will indicates the O'Saidhs will be Mattie's guardian, but I will dispatch Roisin right away to Sussex. I won't last until Mattie is 25, but I know she will be protected under Roisin's care.

Goodbye, my darling Caitrin. May flights of angels sing thee to thy rest.

Again, he skimmed through subsequent years up to her death, but the only time John Stone was mentioned was with resentment that he'd been named Mattie's guardian.

He replaced the diaries exactly as he'd found them, took a one-use phone from a pocket of the sweat pants, and texted a single word to Nelson.

Nothing.

In a few seconds, Alexei received the reply.

Acknowledged. Whew.

Alexei re-pocketed the phone he'd dispose of later.

The knot that had coiled in his gut since Mai had told him about this excursion to go through Roisin's papers eased. Only two people in the world knew this secret. Considering one was him and the other Nelson, it would remain a secret.

He tiptoed up the stairs to the bedroom and shed his sweatpants. He eased into bed beside the person who would never in his lifetime learn that secret.

12

SURPRISE

1991

Thomas Beach, Bali

Hong Kong was a growing and bustling city, and its noise was constant. When Haru "Harry" Tompkins took his allotted leave, he wanted sun, sand, turquoise water, and a willing woman or several. Bali's Thomas Beach was precisely what he craved.

Off the beaten path and down a gravel lane and accessed by a steep, rickety set of wooden stairs, it fulfilled all his needs.

Harry had learned early on in school in the south in the 1960s not to use his given name, Haru. His mother had picked that name because he was born in the spring. His father was an American pilot who'd fallen in love with a Japanese woman during the post-war occupation.

They'd had to leap through several paperwork hoops to marry, even more to get permission for her to come with him to the States. Harry had thought they were happy. Well, his father probably was, but his mother was shunned on every Air Force base where his father was stationed. The other wives ignored her. Their children would taunt Harry with chants of "slant eye" and "chink." If they let him in on their World War II games, Harry was always the "dirty Jap" everyone else got to kill.

When Harry was ten, his father crashed a plane on a test flight, and his mother took the survivor benefits and moved to California, where she had friends who had also married American servicemen and who had also been widowed or divorced. There, he'd freely learned his mother's culture and language, and as he'd grown to look more like his father, his "slant eyes" had rounded out. Many times, people didn't know his Japanese origins until he spoke perfect Japanese.

His affinity for Asian languages had made the Far East, specifically Hong Kong, the perfect posting for him after becoming a Directorate operative. Harry was twice divorced, because of all the willing women he sought, and he was glad to be on his own at last. At least no children had complicated his life as an operative for the U.N.'s intelligence service and later as station chief in Hong Kong. He figured another ten years as station chief then retirement. Maybe right here in Bali, because of sun, sand, and that unending supply of willing women.

HARRY TOOK a long swim in clear, inviting water of a perfect temperature. He'd always worked on his physique, and many of the woman lounging on the beach—and a few men—looked him over when he emerged from the water. He headed for his chaise longue and umbrella.

About six feet away from his spot was another chaise longue that hadn't been there before he started his swim. A woman in a silken cover-up, a wide straw hat, and large, round sunglasses stretched out on her chaise under her own umbrella. Her black hair was loose about her shoulders.

Ignoring her, he went to his chaise, dried himself off with a towel, and stretched out, his eyes closed.

"Surprised to see me?" the woman asked, her English good and with only a slight hint of Mandarin.

"I am," Harry replied. "Did you follow me?"

"Harry, please. No need to. You come here every time you take leave. So predictable."

Well, damn, he hadn't varied his pattern because he loved this place. Now he'd have to find a different paradise.

"I'm on vacation," he said. "If you have something for me, Zhen, wait until I'm back in Hong Kong."

"This is way too much fun, and, you know, too many eyes and ears in Hong Kong. You did a good job of pretending not to know me, though. You can keep that up later. You know, a little fucking a stranger fantasy?"

"All right, Zhen, what do you want?"

"Why don't we fuck first, and then I'll tell you?"

Since this place had lost its allure now, he said, "Why not?"

ZHEN WOULD HAVE MADE sure her hotel room hadn't been bugged. They spent an afternoon being a little wild and more than inventive. Their encounters were rare but always memorable.

More than sated, Harry lay back on the pillows, eyes on the ceiling, hands behind his head. Zhen smoked, a stereotype, he knew, almost as much a stereotype as two spies from opposing organizations fucking each other. Harry had kicked the covers aside, but Zhen kept the sheet over her. Chinese women were overly modest about nudity, though Harry had had a good look at all of her when he'd gone down on her.

"So, Harry," she said, expelling smoke, "remember the query you posed last year?"

He had to think about that. Almost a year had passed during their last encounter, but what had he asked . . . Oh, right. The request from Nelson.

"Yes?" he said.

"I have some information for you in that regard."

"It took this long for you to get back to me?"

"No, silly boy, it took me this long to decide to tell you."

"Okay. Why did you decide to tell me?"

"My father died, and I no longer owe him my obedience."

"I didn't know that, Zhen. I'm sorry."

"Not likely you would know when an obscure retired Communist intelligence officer died. Nor would you know that the sympathy is not needed."

Of course, he did know because Yazhu Fan was not obscure, as he knew that Zhen downplayed her father's status for some reason known only to her.

"All right," he said. "What can you tell me?"

"The woman is alive and has been for nearly thirty years as Li Daiyu, companion to Yazhu Fan, former head of Chinese State Security. I have no idea what her real name is. Fan would never allow it to be spoken."

Oh, shit, Harry thought.

"Seriously?" he asked her.

"Yes. She was re-conditioned, re-programmed to forget her former life, and Yazhu put her to work interrogating betrayers of

Communism. This is something she excelled at, received medals for, but she had to remain behind the scenes because Yazhu wouldn't risk someone recognizing her. He was besotted with her or some such. I never quite understood why he protected her so diligently, but he did. The Party had no issue with her performance until a few years ago. Yazhu loaned her to the North Koreans, and she botched an interrogation there. After that incident, she wasn't the same. She and Yazhu argued about her past. I think perhaps she'd begun to remember, that something about that botched interrogation triggered her memory. Then, Yazhu died. I figured the Party would dispose of her, but someone along the line didn't want that, so she's been under house arrest for close to two years. And she's ill. Gravely ill."

Zhen lit another cigarette and smoked in silence.

That was a lot for Harry to take in, and he wondered if this was one of Zhen's usual games.

"You seem to know a lot of details about this, far more than your current position in state security would allow," Harry said.

Zhen laughed and turned toward her night table. From a drawer, she took a stack of a half-dozen 3.5" computer diskettes held together with a rubber band.

"These contain all the details you need. Photos. Very convincing," she said.

Harry took the diskettes. "These don't explain how you know so much about her," he said.

Zhen laughed again. "Harry, darling, sometimes your naïveté is endearing. Most of the time, I find it annoying. Li Zhen isn't my real name."

"Oh, big surprise."

She laughed at his sarcasm. "My name is Yazhu Zhen. Yazhu Fan was my father."

Tell me something I don't know, Harry thought.

Zhen continued, "And the English woman you asked about was the woman he brought home nearly thirty years ago? She was essentially my mother."

13

FROM A RELIABLE SOURCE

1991

Directorate Headquarters

The only way to get someone into Directorate Headquarters, someone you didn't want seen, was via Zamora's secret entrance and exit. When Zamora Sr. had died from a heart attack in the throes of one of his auto-erotic escapades, Nelson had considered sealing the secret passage. It was a huge, potential security risk, after all.

When Zamora's wife and son, Enzo, took over the Archives, they continued to live in quarters in the Directorate. Enzo didn't have his father's proclivities, or, if he did, he didn't have to leave the bunker to indulge them. Nelson decided he might have occasions when he needed to go off-site or when he needed to see someone he didn't want the rest of the Directorate to know about.

He'd left the passage intact but made sure no one except him had the passcode.

Young Enzo's efforts at digitizing boxes and boxes of paper files had freed space for Nelson to have a special room installed. Shielded against electronic eavesdropping, soundproofed, and bullet- and bomb-proof, he used it to have some of his most sensitive conversations. He also made it his safe room within the Bunker, stocked with rations, water, and weapons, plus a cot.

When Harry Thompkins' encrypted message arrived, indicating Harry had "highly sensitive" information he needed to deliver personally, Nelson opted for the clandestine ingress and the ultra-secure room. Harry had been a bit nonplussed by the blindfold, but he adjusted rather quickly. He'd always been good at that.

👀

HARRY OPENED his briefcase and placed a stack of diskettes on the small conference table in the room.

"So, I have it from a reliable source that someone fitting the description you gave me is alive," Harry said.

"Fuck," Nelson muttered. "How reliable a source?"

"My asset from the Hong Kong station for Chinese State Security, but there's . . . I guess you'd say, a complication."

Harry related his and Zhen's pillow talk.

"Shit. Shit," Nelson said. "What's on the diskettes?"

"Corroborating information." Nelson and Harry stared at each other. "According to my source. I haven't examined them," Harry said. "I didn't want to on our network."

"Good move. I'll review them on an off-network computer. Why is she giving up the woman who was her mother?"

"I'm not clear on that. Zhen is enigmatic to say the least. She knows who I am—we attempted to recruit each other—who I work for, and she's never outed me. I'm not her only bed partner, and even when we're together, it's rarely more than once or twice a year. She has, on occasion, passed on information she feels I might find useful. I suspect she does that for her other romeos."

"I've read your reports. Sleeping with her, even only once or twice a year, is enough to compromise you."

"And vice versa. If you'd found it a problem, you would have addressed it, I'm sure. I call her my asset, but it's not a formal arrangement. She's never taken a dime of our money."

"Are you some kind of wizard in bed, then?"

Harry smiled, blushing. "She told me she likes western men. We're not boring in bed. Who knows? I may turn her yet or burn her if it becomes necessary."

Nelson nodded, thoughtful. "Did Zhen indicate what her next steps would be regarding this woman?"

"She's open to negotiation about the woman's return."

"And what does Zhen want for that?"

"What do most of them want? Money she can bank somewhere untraceable. She did say if we're not interested, she'll approach British Intelligence."

"I want to keep British Intelligence out of this."

"An internal matter?"

"Don't ask those questions, Harry. How does she want the negotiations to proceed?"

"She'll negotiate with someone with authority. Not me, obviously. One-on-one. Someone who wouldn't have to consult with the powers that be for approval of a deal."

"Ah, she knows a station chief wouldn't have that authority. When does she want an answer?"

"Whenever we're ready, she said. However, she seems to think her government is growing tired of keeping the woman under house arrest and might execute her."

"That would solve a lot of problems," Nelson murmured.

"You didn't hear that, by the way. All right, I have someone in mind, but I'll have to work a few things out. Can the negotiations take place outside of Hong Kong?"

"She's amenable to that."

"I want Zhen to bring the woman to the negotiations for an immediate exchange. No way I'm paying her without the goods in sight. Anything else I should know?"

"Zhen said the woman was gravely ill."

"All right. I'll get things ready as soon as possible. Oh, and I don't want the negotiator I'll send inside a state security locale. A neutral spot. I'll work it out and let you know. I don't want you involved or to know the identity of the negotiator." Nelson paused and added, "For your safety. Clear?"

"Yes, sir."

"Did Zhen offer a figure she's interested in?"

"She has expensive tastes. Fits with her cover as a fashion designer. She didn't offer a figure, but I'd say she wouldn't take anything less than five million. Dollars."

"Damn. I loved my mother, but five million is asking a bit much. However, it's doable. I shouldn't have to say, but I will, that this is absolutely on the down-low. I already feel as if too many people know about this. Does her government know she's involved in this?"

"She was more secretive than usual and insisted it was between her and me. I doubt she'd want the Party to know she's negotiating for cash."

"And I don't want this to come back and kick me in the nuts. Zhen will have to concoct something good to get her out of China to Hong Kong."

"Perhaps a medical consultation for whatever illness she has and it wouldn't be a surprise if the woman were to 'die' there."

"Pitch that to Zhen, though I suspect she's come up with that on her own. I also have a hunch the Chinese government might want the woman out of their hair."

Nelson reached for the diskettes and slipped them into his jacket pocket. He and Harry stared at each other again.

"You are absolutely certain you didn't look at what is on those diskettes? Because my guy here can determine that."

"I did not review anything on the diskettes."

"Did you copy them? Because I can find that out, too."

"I did not."

Nelson's eyes narrowed at him for a moment. "All right, Harry. I appreciate the discretion," Nelson said.

"Of course."

"And if you're not discrete, I'll know that, too."

Harry smiled and said, "I'd expect nothing less."

Nelson tossed him the blindfold. "You'd better get back to Hong Kong, then."

14

TWEEDS AND LEATHER

January 1942

Bletchley Park

Commander Alastair Denniston had always liked the spotlight. After all, he was in charge of the single most important program to win the war. Turing might be the one to crack Enigma, but Denniston would make the critical decisions.

Still, this was all top secret, probably not known to the public in what was left of Denniston's lifetime, certainly not until after the war was over. What Turing and his team were doing here might bring that end sooner, but Denniston would be the public face of that, not Turing. Good God, please, not Turing.

Denniston rose from his neat desk and went to the windows overlooking Bletchley's grounds. At one of the picnic tables on the lawn sat Katherine Maitland and Aifric Brennan, bundled in their coats because they'd wanted "fresh air."

The two women didn't seem like employer and employee. Not sisters, either. Sisters were often in conflict with each other. Over parents' affections. Over men. Not for the first time, Denniston considered they might be lovers. Indeed, women could often get away with that more than men could, as he'd quite often had to explain to Turing.

Katherine and Aifric sat on opposite sides of the table, eating lunch and talking animatedly. He'd given the Brennan girl a modified clearance because she might hear something by chance. He'd had her sign an official secrets oath, and he'd had her watched, had her room searched, had her phone calls and mail monitored. Nothing amiss.

Indeed, he felt as if the girl was happy to be here, likely glad to be out from under the thumb of the harpy of a mother.

The Brennan girl smoked, but, then, most girls did now, an aspect of the modern era Denniston could be without. Katherine didn't, and good for her. The more Denniston saw of Katherine, the more he was impressed with her.

She'd fit well with Turing, who could put off anyone with fifteen seconds of meeting him. She and Turing spoke the same language, mathematics, but Turing had also identified Katherine as suited for analysis and mission planning. The SOE often consulted with Bletchley and would continue to do so. In response, Denniston had brought in photographic specialists, people who could interpret what they saw on aerial photographs, and analysts who could predict human behavior under stress.

Katherine had an affinity for analyzing photographs and for solving puzzles. Turing often created puzzles and logic problems that would stump everyone . . . Except Katherine, who could solve them, often in seconds. At Turing's recommendation, Denniston had tried Katherine out in planning an SOE sabotage mission to derail a German ammunition and supply train headed to the eastern front.

She'd studied maps, rail lines, the model of the train's engine and cargo cars, and even the dossiers on the train's engineer and crew. She studied weather charts for the past year and determined the moon's phase for the time of the proposed operation. She examined the photographs of a bridge over a small river and determined its weakest point. From that and knowledge of its construction materials, she calculated how many pounds of explosives it would take to take down the entire bridge, what time of day would be best, the gear the agents would need, and even some things the SOE hadn't considered.

And she'd done it quickly.

She'd presented Denniston with a thorough mission plan, answered all his questions—in truth he'd had few—and when he'd briefed it to SOE, they'd been in awe.

Denniston had received word the mission was a success. Tons of ammunition, rations, and winter coats for the Nazis fighting in Russia. The agents had been safely picked up and returned to England. Katherine had recommended a process for that.

The SOE now wanted Katherine full-time, but Denniston wouldn't have it. She'd shown she could do her work with Turing and do mission planning, and that had to content SOE. He'd told her himself that the operation she'd planned with such diligence had gone precisely to her plan.

What he hadn't told her was that he'd identified her to the SOE only as K.C.M. SOE, despite its record of using women agents, had assumed she was a man. After each successful mission she consulted on, kudos and commendations accumulated in Katherine's personnel file.

Denniston was hoping he could keep her around after the war. Surely, even after Enigma, other codes would need breaking and peacetime missions for British Intelligence she could plan. Anything so he could start the day seeing her.

A black Rolls Royce Phantom III came up the drive. Its occupants must be allowed since the guards at the gate had let it pass, but Denniston was expecting no appointments today. Like most days recently, his calendar was clear.

The car stopped at the front of the mansion, and a man in chauffeur's livery exited and hustled to open the rear passenger door. A tall man emerged. Expensive suit. Haughty expression. Dark, slicked-back hair. A Clark Gable mustache.

Frederick Fisher, the Earl of Uxfield.

The second man was as tall but less effete looking. Tweeds and leather. Every bit the country squire.

Sir John Stone.

Boyhood friends. Eton together. Oxford together. SOE together. A good team, so Denniston had heard. He knew of them. Before the war, they'd frequented the same clubs as Denniston had, gone to Ascot, been at court.

Why were they here?

As they walked from the car to the mansion's main entrance, both men looked toward the picnic table where Katherine and Aifric sat. Stone said something to Fisher, who nodded and smiled, tipping his hat to the two girls. The two men jogged up the front stairs, disappearing from Denniston's sight.

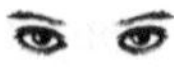

KATHERINE MAITLAND WATCHED the car's progress from the guard house to the mansion. She murmured to Aifric, "Rolls Royce Phantom III. I'd say a 1938. Gorgeous car."

"It's a car," Aifric said. "Your family are partial to Benz."

"Yes, but they're out of favor right now."

Still watching the car, Katherine opened her thermos of tea and poured more into her cup.

A chauffeur got out and opened a door for two men, who emerged into the winter sunshine.

"Look at that first one," Katherine said. "The mustache, the hair. Positively a rake."

"But rather handsome," Aifric said.

"Absolutely."

When the man tipped his hat their way, neither of them acknowledged it.

"Who on earth could they be that they can cruise so casually into a secret facility without an escort? I wonder what they're here for," Katherine said.

"Probably here to see Commander Denniston. They look like they'd belong to the same 'gentlemen's club.'"

Katherine smiled. "Eithne will be delighted to know you haven't lost your contempt for the English class system."

"She won't be happy to hear how often you sound like one of them."

"It's called blending in, Aifric," Katherine said and dropped back into her Dublin accent. "Sure and I can remember how to sound as Irish as you."

Aifric laughed and lit another cigarette.

"You smoke too much, Affie."

"It relaxes me when I'm among all the *sasanaigh*."

"They're not foreigners here. It's their country."

"And despite all the fighting and all the uprisings, they still squat on part of ours."

"Hush," Katherine said. "I've warned you about that kind of talk, Affie. It took a hell of a lot of persuasion to get you that clearance so you can trail me everywhere like some sycophantic puppy. Don't screw it up."

"Yes, ma'am, oh, lady of the manor."

Katherine laughed and shook her head. Aifric had been like a sister to her, older by five years. Aifric's real sister, Roisin, was like Katherine's baby sister, too. With them in her life, she'd never felt lonely as an only child and orphan.

"Have you had a letter from Roisin?" Katherine asked. "She hasn't answered my last one."

"I have not. I asked Mam if she was sick or something, and Mam said Roisin is 'focusing on her studies,' which means following tradition and going to Trinity next year."

"I'm sure your mother has that all planned out and is already preparing Roisin's office for whatever it is she'll be doing," Katherine said. "You didn't want to be a lawyer like your mother, so I suspect she'll push Roisin that way."

Aifric shrugged and exhaled smoke. "Hard to say what Mam has in mind. She complains that Roisin has a mind of her own, and that, of course, won't do."

"A rebellious O'Saidh. Hard to imagine."

"Mam will break her. Mam breaks everyone eventually."

Katherine's smile over her cup of tea was sly. "I don't know. I thought I handled her pretty well about coming here."

"That you did, but watch out. We Irish can hold grudges for a long while."

Katherine laughed again, sipped tea, and looked around.

"I didn't think I would, but I like it here," she said. "I mean, the Brits are hard to take at times, but I'm contributing to eventual peace. What I'm learning from Turing . . . Like I said, I could never learned as much anywhere else, even Trinity."

"You better hope Mam doesn't discover Alan's queer. She'll rip you out of here so fast . . . "

"Well, then, we'd best be quiet about that, hadn't we? I don't understand the issue. It's not like it's catching."

Katherine looked over the grounds some more, her eyes straying to the Phantom III again.

"You know, Commander Denniston has been hinting I might have a position doing the work I'm doing for SOE after the war," Katherine said.

"What? Surely there won't be a need for secret agents and sabotage after the war."

"The Commander says the next war will be with the Soviets. He thinks we should finish them off after we beat the Nazis."

"Typical British. Turn on your allies. Caitrin, if you haven't figured this out yet, I'll be blunt. Denniston wants in your pants."

"Don't be ridiculous, Affie. He's older than dirt and married. With children close to my age. Besides, I'll be no man's mistress. Assure your mother of that. However, it may come to nothing, the job that is. Denniston may be on the way out. Despite Churchill's support for this program and for Turing, Denniston is still obstructive. Commander Travis has been meeting with Churchill's advisers an awful lot."

"You think Travis will push Denniston aside?"

"I do."

Aifric extinguished her cigarette on the underside of the table and tossed the filter end away. "Caitrin, you listen at doors too much. That'll bite you in the arse one day."

"Affie, I'm a woman. I'm invisible. Let's go inside. I'm freezing that arse off."

15

NAME YOUR POISON

The forthcoming shake-up at Bletchley was somewhat common knowledge to everyone except perhaps Denniston. Fisher and Stone supported the change. Turing's project was too critical to the war effort for Denniston to over-manage.

"Denniston was always parsimonious," Fisher had said on the drive to Bletchley. "He's treated the project's budget as if it were his money to save."

"That's true," agreed Stone, "but I think it's more he can't accept that the leader of this project is Turing. To Denniston, Turing is nothing except a deviant, not a brilliant man with an amazing mind."

"Frankly, I don't care if the man fucks chickens or sheep, as long as he breaks Enigma," Fisher had replied.

That was why they'd arranged their trip here with Commander Travis, currently Denniston's second but likely soon to be in charge.

Like Denniston and to fool anyone watching the mansion,

Travis dressed in civilian clothing. Unlike Denniston, Travis seemed comfortable dressed that way. Travis stood up from behind his desk when his two guests were ushered in and smiled, all affability.

"My Lord, Sir John," he greeted them.

"Travis, for God's sake," said Fisher. "I'm Freddie. No 'my lord' here, please."

Travis grinned wider. "Of course, of course. Would you like tea or something a bit stronger?"

"It's afternoon somewhere in the world. Something stronger, of course," Fisher said.

Travis went to an armoire in his office and unlocked it with a key from his trouser pocket. Behind the doors was an impressive collection of spirits, mostly Scotch.

"As the Americans say," Travis said, "name your poison."

Both Fisher and Stone selected a Macallan, and after Travis poured three glasses, the men settled in some plush chairs before an unused fireplace.

"Great to see you two," Travis said. "Good work on the train job. Quite the stunt, and you pulled it off."

"That's rather why we're here," Fisher said. "The mission plan and support were superb. Better than anything I've seen so far. I was amazed by the analyst's depth of knowledge, not to mention the ability to anticipate what we'd need to do should certain things happen. More than comprehensive."

"There were a great deal of contingencies, as I recall."

"Always best to be prepared for those contingencies. This analyst, KCM, is a gem."

"One of Denniston's favorites."

"I don't care. Johnny and I would like to shake this KCM's hand in person. I mean, I understand it's critical to keep such personnel's identity secret, but I assure you that young man's identity won't go beyond us."

Travis stared, frowning, into his Scotch. "KCM isn't a man, young or otherwise," he said. "She's a woman."

"Are you serious?" Stone asked.

"Completely. She's one of only two women hand-selected by Turing to work on Enigma. Denniston learned of her from an old school chum and brought her here in 1940." Travis looked up at the two men. "From Trinity."

"Ah," Stone said.

"So, she's . . . ?" Freddie said.

"Irish, yes. I objected, of course, because she was young, barely twenty, and because though the Republic are remaining neutral, the IRA are courting a relationship with Hitler."

"Or Hitler is courting them."

Travis shrugged in dismissal. "Anyway, Denniston had his way, and here she came. When, ah, Denniston takes his leave, I've a mind to cancel her contract."

"Don't you dare," Fisher said. "We can't afford to lose such skills. All of SOE was impressed with that mission plan."

"Freddie, she's a woman."

"Do you understand how many SOE agents are women?" Stone said. "We've worked with our fair share of them, and they are, in some cases, fiercer and braver than some of our male agents."

"She's bloody Irish."

"And so was my grandmother," said Fisher. "Has she given you any inkling she's a security risk?"

Travis shook his head with reluctance. "We have the woman here under constant surveillance, and she's raised no concerns. It's just that . . . Damn it, man, that accent, even though she tries to sound English. And she has to have this chaperone with her. Now, *her* accent is so thick you can't cut it with a *katana*. Sometimes, they speak together in this guttural language, and I have to constantly remind them only English."

"Irish? They actually speak Irish?"

"I suppose that's what it is."

"How rare, right, Johnny?"

Stone replied, "Close to being a dead language. So, Travis, she stood out in mathematics at Trinity, then?"

"Yes, and logic and rhetoric. Turing was dubious at first. I mean, we already had one woman on that team. We figured there'd be some sort of cat fight."

"Was there?" Fisher asked.

"No. Surprisingly, they get along well."

"Why did Turing accept her?"

"Those little tests that he gives everyone? She solved his puzzle in no time. Now, he's her biggest advocate. He didn't want Denniston to loan her to SOE, but she did her Enigma work and the planning for your mission without a hitch. Besides, we all know the point here is to keep Turing happy."

"Don't knock it, old chap," Stone said. "Turing's complaints are what's going to get you Denniston's job."

Travis sighed and said, "Oh, he's a brilliant man, all right. I've resolved never to be alone with him, and I keep my back to the wall when we're in the same room." Travis chortled at his joke.

Fisher and Stone exchanged a look, and it was Fisher who smiled brightly at Travis.

"Well, may we meet Miss KCM?" Fisher asked. "And, I assume, her chaperone as well."

"And, seriously, a chaperone in this day and age?" Stone said.

"Her family's retainers run her estate for her until she's twenty-five, and a constant companion is a requirement."

"Estate?" Fisher said.

"I daresay she's richer than you, Freddie," Travis replied.

"Sounds like just the type Pater wants me to marry."

"Well, uh, she's, you know, a Papist," Travis whispered, as if he'd blasphemed in the presence of an Anglican priest's hearing.

Stone laughed and said, "Oh, now, he's certain to court her. Freddie loves upsetting his old man."

"How does she manage Mass here in Protestant England?" Fisher asked, smiling.

"Oh, we've had quite the population of Papists here in the area for nearly thirty years. Belgian refugees from the Great War. They took over a large manse on, appropriately enough, Church Street. They call it Saint Thomas Aquinas or some such."

"I see. I still want to thank Miss KCM personally, and, Eddie, do not cancel her contract. I've already told Churchill about KCM's contribution, and he won't care she's a woman. He does love it when the ladies step up to do their part for the war effort."

Travis pursed his lips but said nothing. He understood he had his marching orders.

He set his glass of Scotch aside and rose. "Let's see where she is," he muttered.

He opened the door to his office and called for his adjutant. "Hanlon, would you . . .? Oh, never mind. Miss Maitland, Miss Brennan, would you step inside for a moment, please?"

16

THAT ARISTOCRATIC LOOK

Fisher and Stone were already on their feet when the two young women entered Travis' office. The one with thick, red hair and cool, blue eyes entered first, her appraising gaze taking in both men. She didn't look away from them as most women might.

The two women wore identical dark green wool coats with a thick fur collar and fur cuffs, matching kid leather gloves, which they both pulled off, finger by finger. The shape of their faces bespoke some sort of blood relation. Both women shrugged off their coats and slung them over an arm.

The red-haired one's hair was styled nicely, worn long but with the front and sides rolled into a shape that reminded Fisher of a crown. He realized they were the two young women at the picnic table he'd seen when he and Johnny arrived.

The other woman, a bit older, had close-cropped, jet-black hair and blue eyes almost the same shade as the other. Black Irish that was called, Fisher remembered.

The younger woman approached Fisher and Stone while the

other lingered near the door. Ah, Fisher thought, the one at the door was the companion Travis mentioned, the servant, or whatever she was.

"You're the owner of that fabulous car," the younger woman said. Her voice had an Irish lilt, but not enough to justify Travis' prejudicial remark about it.

"The Phantom?" Fisher replied, smiling. "She's an old girl, but she gets me where I need to go," he said.

"Old girl? She's, what? A '38 model at most."

"You know your cars."

"I adore cars."

"Yes, she is a 1938 model, but the war means I haven't been able to replace her."

"Freddie," said Stone, "not everyone buys a new car every year like you did before the war."

"Frederick Fisher, ma'am," he said to the younger woman. "At your service, old car and all."

She extended her hand. "Katherine Maitland. A pleasure to meet you, Mr. Fisher."

They shook hands, and Fisher resisted letting his touch linger.

"So," Katherine said, her appraisal continuing with a hint of a smile on her lips, "what are you? A marquis? A viscount? You have that aristocratic look about you."

"Ah, well, not that it's important, but Earl of Uxfield."

"Oh, my. Am I supposed to curtsy?"

"Heavens, no, Miss Fisher. Commander Travis says you're Irish. Wouldn't curtsying to a Brit be blasphemous or some such?"

Katherine laughed in a delightful manner and certainly not in the way any "proper" Englishwoman would but with a full-throated, boisterous guffaw. It wasn't coarse or crass but almost musical to his ears.

"Something like that," she said. She turned toward the other woman, whose eyes narrowed. "Allow me to present my companion, Aifric Brennan."

"Ma'am," Fisher said to her. The eyes narrowed even more. Fisher gestured to John Stone. "My friend since we were practically in nappies, Sir John Stone."

"Miss Maitland, Miss Brennan," Stone said, his smile warm as he nodded to both women separately.

Fisher noted Miss Brennan's eyes didn't narrow at Stone but softened in a way Fisher had seen before. Pretty girls inevitably went for Fisher. His worldly looks and obvious wealth were definite lures. The not so pretty girls tended toward Johnny's classic English squire looks. He was attractive but not spectacular, much like this Miss Brennan herself.

"Miss Maitland," Fisher said, "would you be related to the Dublin Maitlands who have a horse breeding business in County Kildare?"

"Yes, that's us. How did you know that?"

"My younger brother bought a racer from you. Well, your family. In 1938. He bought a horse." Fisher smiled at Katherine. "I bought a car."

"And how did the horse do for your brother?"

Almost two years had passed since the Luftwaffe had shot down Tommie's plane over the Channel. Freddie was surprised he hesitated to answer her question.

"Ah, yes. You see, Tommie didn't have a chance to race him. The horse was still being trained when, ah, when my brother's airplane was shot down in the Battle of Britain. My father sold the horse. I don't remember to whom. Sorry."

"No apology necessary," Katherine said, her expression serious, her eyes moist. "I'm terribly sorry for your loss. He was a pilot, then, your brother?"

"Yes. An inexperienced one, I'm afraid, but at the beginning, they all were, weren't they? Except the Germans it seems. Still, my father was distraught. Still is. He's somewhat of a recluse now. Transferred his titles and properties to me, and . . . Sorry again. All that is boring, I'm sure."

Fisher wasn't sure why he'd unburdened himself, except that those eyes were kind.

"Not at all, Mr. . . . . I'm afraid I'm not up on things royal. How do I address you?"

"Oh, not royalty. Please, call me Freddie."

"All right, then. Let's have a huzzah for the not-so-stuffy nobility. I'm Katherine, if you like." She pronounced her name in three syllables. "Or Caitrin, *as Gaeilge*." Two syllables.

"*As Gaeilge?*"

"In Irish."

"Oh, I see."

"Please call me Aifric," the other woman said, her gaze still on John Stone.

"John or Johnny," was Stone's reply, accompanied byFi his own rather rakish smile.

Fisher turned to Commander Travis. "I say, Travis, is there a commissary here where I can buy these ladies a cup of tea?"

Travis checked his watch. "Yes, it's still open. You, ah, you should have it to yourselves this time of the afternoon."

Fisher looked at Katherine Maitland, and she met his gaze again, like an equal, he realized. He liked that.

"Katherine . . . Caitrin, may I interest you and Miss Brennan in a cup of tea?"

"I'd love a cuppa, as you Brits say, Freddie. Come along, I'll show you the way."

17

AN SASANAIGH

Because her afternoon break had extended to more than an hour's conversation in the commissary with Lord Whoever and his friend, Katherine Maitland had worked past the usual time to assure Turing would have the latest calculations first thing tomorrow.

She and Aifric were thankful to retreat to their quarters in the mansion and do nothing for a while. Except that as Katherine tossed her coat aside and kicked off her shoes before flopping on the sofa, Aifric went to the basket their correspondence was delivered to. Without looking, Katherine knew the envelopes would have been opened and the letters read. That was the way of things on a top-secret base.

"Anything in the post, Affie?" Katherine asked.

"The usual. A letter from my mother to me, a letter from my mother to you," Aifric replied.

Katherine smiled; she wagered whoever read their mail got a good kick out of Eithne O'Saidh's stodgy prose. Katherine rose from the sofa and went into her bedroom, where she unzipped her dress and let it fall to the floor. She looked at it there. If she left it, Affie would come in and act like a lady's maid, something Katherine was trying to break her of.

Katherine picked up the dress and hung it in an armoire. She changed into lounging trousers and a thick, Aran sweater—jumper as the Brits called it. Her and Aifric's quarters in Bletchley might be in a mansion, but that mansion had the notorious lack of adequate heating the British were famous for.

Katherine returned to the living area and put some coal in the stove so they wouldn't freeze tonight and could have some water for tea later.

Aifric said, "I don't think you should have given *an sasanaigh* the phone number here."

"I suppose you're going to tell your mother I did that, even after you pointed out to *an sasanaigh eile* that your number was the same as mine?"

"Trust me, I've known for a long time what to tell Mam and what to keep to myself. I don't think you should have given your number so soon is all."

"Why? Want him yourself?"

"No, I saw the way he looked at you. I thought he'd drool in his *tae*. Caitrin, he's a man of the world, a spy, a noble. You're another conquest to him."

"Well, I hope not."

"Why?"

"Because I'm going to marry him." She raised an eyebrow. "Going to tell Mam that?"

"God, no. She'd swim the Irish Sea to get here if I did. Cait, I don't think he's the marrying kind, and certainly not with that title will he think about marrying Irish, especially Catholic Irish."

"We'll see."

The suite's phone jangled, and Aifric started for it.

"I'll take it," Katherine said. "Katherine Maitland," she answered. She motioned Aifric closer and held the phone so they both could hear the conversation.

"Ah, exactly the person I hoped would answer," said Frederick Fisher in a jaunty tone.

"Hello, Freddie. I was hoping you'd call."

"Were you? Well, I am flattered. I say, how about a pub dinner tomorrow evening? You and I, and your companion, of course. Johnny specifically wanted me to ask if she'd come."

"She'd have to come anyway. Family rules. I'd adore a pub dinner. Where shall we meet you?"

"Johnny and I shall pick you up in the old girl. That is, unless there are family rules against it."

"Oh, no. I will have to sign out from here and indicate with whom I'll be. Commander Travis knows you, so that will be no problem. What time?"

"Do you have a curfew?"

Katherine looked at Aifric and rolled her eyes.

"If Aifric's with me, no."

"Then, Johnny and I will come 'round for you at seven."

"Seven it is, Freddie. I'm looking forward to it."

"As am I, Caitrin. Tell me, what plans do you have tonight?"

Aifric's turn to roll her eyes, and Katherine elbowed her.

"Nothing special. Some reading to do. A bite of dinner. Aifric and I play chess most evenings."

"Chess? We must have a game, you and I, sometime. What do you say?"

"I'd love to, but be prepared to lose."

He laughed softly, almost in an intimate way that Katherine found exciting.

"Then, we should make it interesting," Freddie said. "A wager, shall we?"

"That sounds super, but we aren't allowed to have anyone up to our rooms."

"I see. Do you have weekends off?"

"Two weekends a month unless an emergency pops up. My next free weekend is the one after this one upcoming."

"My house in Knightsbridge is still somewhat of a mess after the Blitz, but I have a country house in Sussex. Huge, rambling place, so plenty of room for you and your companion. No hint of impropriety. Johnny lives on the adjacent estate, and I could bunk there. All absolutely above board. The live-in housekeeper, Mrs. Chumley, keeps an eye on everything and runs the place quite like a garrison commander."

"I'll have to check with Mr. Turing and Commander Denniston or Travis, but I don't think it will be a problem."

"Superb! Dinner tomorrow and a weekend in Sussex the weekend following this one. Wonderful!"

"This country house, then, is it your manor or castle?"

"Yes, uh, it is. I shall love showing you around the old place. Have a delightful evening, Caitrin. My regards and Johnny's to Miss Brennan. Sleep well."

"I will, and you, too. 'Bye, yer lordship."

That garnered his laugh again, and he joked in return. "'Bye, you Fenian wench."

Still laughing, Katherine hung up. She sobered rather abruptly when she saw the sour expression on Aifric's face.

"I must say, Affie, you showed remarkable control during that conversation. I expected you to snatch the phone away."

"Dinner at a pub is one thing, Cait, but a weekend in the country? Sussex is hours away. How will we be getting there?"

"In his Phantom III, I should imagine. Or maybe he has a private rail car. Oh, that would be awfully romantic. We can ask him at dinner tomorrow."

"At a country house, with only me and a housekeeper who works for him to chaperone. Mam will have a conniption."

"I think perhaps this is one of those things your mam doesn't need to know about. Come on, Affie, he's an earl. He probably has a large staff that'll be in our business the whole time. I don't see a problem, Affie."

"Cait, you wouldn't because it's something you want. You're putting me in a difficult situation. You know very well, even over the phone, Mam knows when I'm lying."

"Well, you'd better practice then because I am going to dinner with him tomorrow night, and I am having a weekend in Sussex. Now, we have to start planning what to pack. Do you think dinner at a Sussex earl's manor will be formal?"

"God, Cait, I have no idea what these *sasanaigh* do."

"No worries. We have plenty of time to figure it out."

👀

"I say, thanks for including me in arranging your assignation," John Stone said when Frederick Fisher hung up.

"I'm doing you a favor, Johnny. I saw how that girl, Aifric, looked at you."

"You might want to re-think the Sussex trip, Freddie. Your father will be there, and he won't take kindly to Catholics under his roof."

"But it isn't his roof anymore, is it? It's mine because he surrendered the title to me. He, my step-mummy, and her beastly progeny are my guests. Besides, how will he know they're Catholic?"

"Katherine must hide hers, but Aifric—Good God, what kind of name is that anyway?"

"An Irish one, I should think."

"Aifric wears her crucifix for all to see. Your father's eyesight might be failing, but his wife's isn't. She'll definitely point it out."

"Pater had better get accustomed to Katherine Maitland because I'm going to marry her."

"Good God, man, you've had tea with her, chatted for an hour, and now one brief phone call. How could you possibly know you're going to marry her?"

"I know, Johnny. You see, I looked at her and saw my future in her eyes."

"Christ, Freddie, what makes her any different from any other ingenue you've had?"

"That's precisely it, Johnny. She's different from any woman I've ever known. She doesn't put on airs, and you heard Travis. She probably has more money than I do, so my fortune isn't her motivation."

"She's, what? Twenty-two? You're thirty."

"What does that have to do with anything? If I didn't know better, I'd say you're coming up with all these excuses because you want her yourself." Fisher studied his friend. He knew every subtle nuance of John Stone's expressions. "That's it, isn't it? Well, Johnny, we've never argued over a woman, and we won't start now. May the best man win." Fisher grinned at Stone. "And we both know I'm the best man."

18

A BINGO CARD

2002

Mount Vernon, Virginia

When the security system alerted Alexei Bukharin that Mai's car was on its way up the driveway, he put aside Aifric Brennan's 1942 diary. Frederick Fisher's and Katherine Maitland's first meeting was nothing at all like his and Mai's, but Alexei found familiarity in the depiction of Katherine Maitland.

Most of how it played out in his head came from the diaries, the rest from his knowledge of how things had worked at Bletchley, and he suspected Eithne's detail about that first meeting of Katherine and Frederick had come later from Aifric.

The door from the garage to the house opened, and Natalia burst in, chattering a mile a minute about flowers and caterers. Mai's responses were quieter and calmer, mostly agreeing with whatever Natalia had said. Alexei left the office, closing the door behind him.

"Popi!" Natalia exclaimed, tossing her jacket toward the family room sofa, only to have it miss and slide to the floor. "We looked at so many amazing dresses. I have, like, twenty favorites. Next time, you need to come with us. Please, please?"

She was acting like a child, and that annoyed him. "We'll see," he said. "Natalia, are we peasants who toss our coats on the floor?"

Natalia looked at Mai, who said nothing. Natalia picked up her coat and muttered, "What am I? Twelve?" She headed up the stairs to her room.

"You should have come," Mai said, hanging her jacket in the closet by the door to the garage. "That was all she would talk about—neither you nor her father was with her."

"I saw no need to come and pretend to be happy about buying a wedding dress for her," Alexei said.

"Well, you need to put that attitude aside because the wedding is happening whether you want it to or not. Her father isn't here, and she wants to share details with you because you were her father when she needed one."

"I am not interested in the mundane details. All I want is for her to come to her senses and not marry him."

"Again, wishing for it not to happen won't make it so. I'm doing the dress shopping because I'm the only thing she has who resembles a mother. Really, all you need to do is listen to her and try to show her you're happy—for her."

"As the 'father' of the bride, I'm expected to find and pay for a venue, for catering, etc., all while I can't support this."

"Once again, no need for you to do anything. The O'Saidhs are dealing with the 'mundane details' at my direction," Mai said. "And I'm paying for it because she acquired her expensive tastes from me." She smiled at him. "You can write me a check later, or, you know, we can work some sort of trade out."

Any other time, the innuendo would amuse, even arouse him, but not today.

"You know, she should learn that not everyone can afford to have other people take care of every little detail of their lives," Alexei said.

"Why is this an argument?"

He crossed the family room to her and lowered his voice. "Because I'm not happy about any of this. She's too young. He's a soldier who'll be constantly deployed because of his specialty. He's a Terrell. That's why this is an argument, but I'll nip it in the bud. I'll resume my reading."

He let himself back into the office, picked up the diary, and sat on the sofa again.

Mai had followed him.

"In case you haven't done the maths, let me point out she's older than I was when you insisted we get married," Mai said.

"I should have a bingo card to mark off all the things I know you're going to say."

"Since you've done a poor job of nipping the argument in the bud, I'll give it a try. What are you reading?"

She settled on the sofa with him but kept her distance.

"Another of Eithne Brennan's diaries. 1942. Your mother and father meeting for the first time. She even went back years later and commented about a conversation your father had with John Stone. It seems both your parents decided on first sight that they would marry each other."

"Tell me about their meeting."

"They talked about cars and horses. It was rather stuffy, and Aifric, it seems, had a thing for Stone."

"John? Well, he was quite handsome."

Under his breath, he said, "You would know."

"Jesus Wept, Alexei, what is your problem today?"

"I'm not in a good mood over this wedding, then you remind me how handsome a former lover was."

"He and I were lovers before I was ever with you, and by the time you and I were lovers, he was dead. If you want to go there, I might have a list of former lovers, but it's certainly not as extensive as yours would be. At least I stopped adding to mine."

"As I did."

"So you say." She looked away from him. "Natalia said she wanted Chinese for dinner. I'm going into the CIA for a few hours to perpetuate my undercover story that I work there."

She was up and out of the room before he could say anything, and when the door to the garage slammed, he knew it was too late anyway. He tossed the diary aside and went back to the family room as Natalia trotted down the stairs.

"Where did Mums go?" she asked.

"Work."

"Wow, Popi, you're in a bad mood today."

"I'm not in a bad mood."

"Yeah, you are. You know, today should have been fun for me, for the three of us."

"Mai said you wanted Chinese. Order in or pick up?"

"I want House of China, and I want to eat there. That way, you and I will have to have a civil conversation about my wedding because we'll be in public."

This apple had not fallen far from Mai Fisher's tree indeed, he thought. "House of China it is. Get your coat."

19

A BAD MOOD

At half past ten, the security system again alerted Alexei Mai's car had returned. He didn't leave the office to greet her, but after all these years together, he could "see" what she'd do: Hang up her coat, perhaps find a snack in the fridge, or come into the office for a whiskey from the dry bar there, then quietly climb the stairs, almost as if she were sneaking in.

She didn't come into the office, likely because the lights indicated it was occupied. The only possible occupant was him, so she was avoiding him.

He continued to drink brandy until he was sure she'd be in bed, then drained his glass and returned the bottle to the bar. He was unsteady on his feet. All those abstemious weeks in Afghanistan, drinking strong chai, and it hadn't taken that much brandy to get shit-faced drunk.

He headed upstairs, detouring first to Natalia's room.

She was still awake, propped up on her pillows with several of her old stuffed animals. That tightened his throat. In his eyes, she was still his little girl. Her phone was in hand, and she was texting someone. She looked up, saw him, and set the phone aside.

"Mums is home?" she said.

"Yes."

"Popi, are you, like, drunk?"

"Quite possibly. I had an argument with my wife. My grand-daughter is trying to ruin her life. Excuse enough." She rolled her eyes. "All I want," he said, "is for you to be happy."

"I know you don't want to hear this, but with Alex, I'm happy. Good night, Popi. I hope you have a big, fucking headache tomorrow morning."

She picked up her phone.

MAI HAD TURNED onto her side so her back would be to Alexei when he got in bed. She'd heard his unsteady footsteps on the stairs. He'd stopped by Natalia's room, something he'd always done before coming to bed, even if she were already asleep. The depths of Alexei's feeling for his granddaughter couldn't be denied, but those feelings created an overreaction to Natalia's impending marriage.

Mai wondered how her father would have reacted to Alexei.

"Oh, I say, Pater, this is the Soviet defector I'm going to marry, and you can't stop us because I'm already preggers."

That made her smile. She didn't remember enough about her father to predict his reaction, but from what she'd skimmed in Aifric's diary, she could hazard a guess that, initially, it would not have been positive.

Mai feigned sleep when Alexei entered their bedroom. He went through the dressing room and into the bathroom, turning on lights and not bothering to close doors. She heard him urinating, for a long time it seemed. She'd caught the sour smell of too much to drink when he'd passed by the bed. If she'd been so inclined for romance, the prolonged peeing and reeking of liquor had suppressed it.

He brushed his teeth. No shower.

That had been a clue when he'd been with another woman. Alexei took morning showers. If he'd had a nooner with one of his harem, he'd shower before coming to bed with Mai.

But that hadn't happened in a long time.

The light in the dressing room switched off, and he climbed into bed. He lay there a while before he turned toward her, his hand coming to rest on her hip but atop the covers.

"I was in a bad mood today," he said. "I'm sorry."

"For being in a bad mood or for being shitty to me because I want Natalia to see both of us support her marriage?"

"Yes."

Mai turned over, so they faced each other. "Are you apologizing only because you want sex?"

"No, I drank too much. In the morning, though . . ."

In the dark, they looked at each other for a long time, each waiting for the other to speak.

"I'll be there when it counts, as you well know," he said.

"I know. Natalia is the one who needs to know that."

"I'll take care of it."

"So, what else did you learn about my mother and father?"

He condensed what he'd read into a few sentences, and she liked what she heard. She would have to read that diary for herself. Alexei might not want the mundane details of Natalia's wedding, but Mai wanted every word written about her parents.

"I didn't read any more of the diary after you left," Alexei said. "Natalia and I went out for Chinese, where we managed not to say a single word to each other for the whole meal. We came home, and I decided brandy would be good company."

The quiet came again, and Mai broke it this time. "Can you find a way forward from this?"

"You mean, can I bring myself to pay tens of thousands of dollars for a wedding I don't want to happen?"

"Jesus Wept, can't you answer a yes or no question with yes or no?"

"I want her to be happy, even if I question whether she can be with him. I don't want to be inundated with trivia about how many bridesmaids and what colors they're wearing or what kind of flowers or the theme or whatever else is involved. I understand and I do appreciate what you're doing for her, because this is something a mother and a daughter should do. I only care about whether she can be happy with a man she won't see half the time of their marriage and whose work he'll have to keep secret from her. Is that a satisfactory answer, despite the fact I didn't use the words yes or no?"

"Quite satisfactory. Look, I get that you don't like Alex Terrell, but he loves her. That's all that matters because, Bukharin, this is about her and not you."

"Did it feel good to throw my frequent words for you back at me?"

"Immensely. Now, good night."

She rolled onto her other side, giving him her back again, but he spooned with her, arm around her waist.

20

NOT INTERESTED

1991

Chambers
U.N. Commission on Human Rights
Geneva, Switzerland

An old Ukrainian saying was "Look at the mother-in-law, see the wife." When the older woman entered the CHR chambers with the younger, Asian woman, Alexei kept his face neutral.

Terrell had not had a delusion.

Alexei had seen portraits of Katherine Maitland, including a nearly life-sized one at a family house in Belfast. He'd mistaken that one for Mai until he'd looked closer at the eyes. Katherine Maitland's were blue, like the older woman here, but there was also the shape and angles of that flattened face, typically Celtic.

The younger woman was chic, long black hair loose around her shoulders; long bangs that overlay her eyebrows. She wore a knee-length, cap-sleeved black sheath with a mandarin collar, trimmed at the neckline in bright red. A line of red piping and three red buttons slashed diagonally from right to left. Embroidered poppies ran beneath the row of buttons, lower, across the breasts. She wore red pumps with high, stiletto heels. Without them, Alexei doubted she could be more than five feet tall. Her makeup was flashy, her lips and fingernails the same color as the red on her dress and shoes.

The older woman, a caucasian, seemed to have stepped from a propaganda poster for the Cultural Revolution. Her long, white hair was in a single braid down her back. Straight-cut bangs covered her forehead but ended above the brows. The uniform-like clothing consisted of baggy trousers and an oversized tunic, both in blue-gray. The tunic was cinched at the waist with a wide leather belt and buttoned to the throat. Her shoes were flat, black slippers. Alexei almost expected her to flash a little red book of Mao's sayings.

The older woman's face was devoid of makeup, was thin and pinched as if in pain, the skin pale, crows feet at the eyes and deep brackets at the mouth. But Alexei saw Mai in her. Mai had aimed that same dour expression at him more than once. This woman moved slowly, as if weak and afraid she would fall.

Alexei remained standing by the chair at the main conference table. The younger woman went to the seat directly across from him. She examined him in a blatantly sexual manner, and his expression remained disinterested. She smiled at him as if to say, "Good try, but I see lust in your eyes."

Not quite. She *was* beautiful; he appreciated that beauty, but he wasn't interested.

"You must be Sergei," the Asian woman said. "I am Li Zhen. This meeting has been facilitated by Haru Thompkins. This is Li

Daiyu, the reason we are here." Zhen's smile was full of invitation. "Harry never mentioned you were so handsome."

He again gave her no reaction, but her smile didn't change. She sat, Daiyu beside her.

"I understand you picked this locality as a meeting place for its neutrality, but really," Zhen said. "The U.N. Commission on Human Rights? A not so-subtle dig at my government's record in that area. Russians aren't known for their subtlety."

Unbuttoning his suit jacket, Alexei took his seat. "I'm not Russian. I'm Ukrainian, now an American."

"Yes, the decadent life and temptations of the West does appeal to intellectual inferiors."

"Says the woman in at least a five-thousand-dollar designer dress who's about to be paid a decent sum of Western money," he replied.

Zhen's laugh was pleasant. "Didn't you know that's our plan? Extend credit to the so-called world superpowers and have them beholden to us."

"It's not my money. I won't be beholden."

"You believe that, don't you? Now, about that money."

"Check your offshore account. It should have been deposited five minutes ago."

From a hidden pocket in the tight dress, Zhen produced a mobile satellite phone, dialed a number, and spoke in Spanish. She waited, spoke again, and ended the call.

"And so it has," Zhen said.

Alexei sensed some discomfort in her slight frown, and she turned to the woman beside her, taking her hands. Zhen spoke in Mandarin, tears dampening her cheeks. Daiyu remained stoic but nodded when Zhen finished her speech. Zhen kissed both of the woman's hands and released them before she stood.

Alexei did, as well, but Li Daiyu remained seated.

"Sergei, I remand to your custody this spy captured by the People's Republic of China in 1963 and reeducated there. Per the wish of my beloved father, she is released from her obligations to the People's Republic, to his memory, and to me. The People's Republic has no further claim on her. If, however, it becomes known that she has revealed any sensitive or secret information to you or any other intelligence organization, punishment will be swift. She is old and infirm, and my only wish for her now is to live out what remains of her life in peace and comfort. Good day."

Li Zhen left the way she came, the spike heels sending sharp echoes around the mostly empty chambers. At the exit, she turned back to Alexei with her come-hither smile and winked.

WHEN LI ZHEN didn't close the door, Alexei crossed the chambers and did it for her. He returned to the table but remained standing.

"For the record," he began, "state your full name."

"I hope you didn't buy all that 'beloved father' and wishes for my peaceful life," the older woman said. "Yazhu Zhen, her real name by the way, is a superb actress."

Alexei perceived a hint of Irish in the stilted speech, spoken as though she hadn't used English in a long time.

"I don't care what her real name is. State yours."

"My name is Caitrin Claire Maitland-Fisher. Katherine Clare, if you prefer the English version. My God, how odd it sounds to say that again. I have questions."

"No, you don't. I ask the questions," Alexei said. "All I require from you are the answers."

The smirk of a smile she gave him was all too familiar.

"I remember how this works," she said, "but before I answer any of your questions, I want to know some things."

Alexei said nothing.

"Does my daughter know I'm alive?" Katherine asked.

"Yes," Alexei said. "The woman who just left the room was well aware you are alive."

"She was never my daughter. I raised her, yes, from the time she was three, but she was never, never my daughter. As I said, don't be fooled by the clasping of hands and shedding of tears. Since her father's death, she considers me her burden. No one, except perhaps the Paramount Leader, wants me gone from the People's Republic more than she does. Zhen is a climber. She wants power, and my presence in her life held her back from what she believes she deserves, which is to eventually succeed her father as head of State Security."

"Her father was Yazhu Fan," Alexei said. "Your husband."

"No! No. We never married."

"You were his most trusted interrogator is my understanding. For him, you uncovered many enemies of the state, did you not? Either you did that because you were a true believer or for love."

A wince crimped her face, but he couldn't tell if it was pain or a guilty conscience. She collected herself and looked at him again.

"Does my daughter know I'm alive?" she repeated.

"No."

"Is someone going to tell her?"

"That will not happen."

"Why?"

"Because it is not in her best interests."

"As determined by whom?"

"Her husband."

Katherine allowed a small smile. "Husband? I see. Not the O'Saidhs? Oh, but Mattie is thirty-three now, and I'm sure quite capable of making her own decisions. I am surprised the O'Saidhs aren't weighing in. It would be . . . Eithne would be dead by now, I suspect. Aifric, bless her, is gone, too. Roisin? It must be Roisin."

"The O'Saidhs won't know either."

"Well, how are you going to explain me, then?"

"I won't be explaining you to anyone. You are dead to everyone who matters, including your daughter. I will take you to a medical facility for a physical assessment, and—"

"I can tell you myself. Pancreatic cancer. Advanced. The Chinese doctors, despite their herbs and acupuncture, give me at most six months."

"I will take you to a medical facility for a physical assessment, and you will remain there while I conduct your questioning. You will be made comfortable, and despite Ms. Yazhu's warning, you will be well protected. You will be free to answer my questions."

"You told Zhen you were Ukrainian, now American, but you can't be CIA. They wouldn't have it, would they? A defector working operationally. British intelligence wouldn't be interested, so you must be Directorate. Of course, you would be. Fan knew who I worked for. He was a triple, you know. He put one over on old Nigel Hume, who, I hope, is rotting somewhere. Because of Hume, I spent twenty-eight years in hell, but it stands to reason Fan Zhen would turn me over to the Directorate."

"Say no more. We are not entirely secure here. We will have plenty of time . . ." Alexei gave a tight smile and said, "Well, only six months or so for you."

He stood and motioned to a security camera. The door opened again, and two UNSECFOR guards entered with an ambulance gurney. Katherine looked at them and back at Alexei, who'd come around the table.

"What is this for?" Katherine asked.

"To get you out of here incognito. You'll need to lie still and play dead, but you've had some practice at that."

"What do you mean?"

"If you don't cooperate, we'll sedate you."

"Zhen brought me here without all this . . . Nonsense."

"Get on the gurney. Now."

"Do not give me orders, young man."

Alexei stepped close to her chair, and she stood, shakily. She was taller than Mai, at least five-ten, and he and Caitrin were almost eye-to-eye.

"Madam Interrogator, as you said, you know how this works. Your life is mine now. You best remember that. If you don't cooperate here and now, your intel be damned. I will snuff you out without a thought, and I will take pleasure in it. Understand?"

"Yes, you were quite clear." She smiled at him, yellowed teeth but still perfect otherwise. "I look forward to our sessions. I won't go easy on you, either, me boyo."

She stepped toward the gurney, and the two guards lowered it for her to lie down. They raised in again and used zip ties to fasten one thin wrist and a bony ankle on the opposite side to the gurney's rails. They covered her with a blanket, pulling it higher to cover her face.

"A rehearsal of my future," she murmured and went silent.

21

TIGER BEAT

1991

Arlington Condominiums
Arlington, Virginia

With Alexei somewhere in the world taking custody of a defector, Mai hadn't slept well and had barely awakened in time to get Natalia ready for school. Now, Mai checked her watch and swallowed the last of her morning coffee. When she turned to Natalia to hurry her along, she frowned when she saw the magazine the eleven-year-old was reading as she munched her bagel.

"Is that . . . Is that *Tiger Beat*?" Mai asked.

Natalia looked at her. "Yes. You know *Tiger Beat*?"

"Of course," Mai said. She'd clipped all the articles about Ian Flynn and the Ballymurphys from its pages.

"Seriously? You used to read teen magazines?"

"You make it sound like I'm ancient. It wasn't that long ago."

"Mums, you're, like, thirty-plus. That *is* ancient."

"How sharper than a serpent's tooth," Mai muttered. "Well, put it down and bring your bagel and OJ along. We can't be late today. It's the field trip to the middle school."

"You're going to let me eat in your car?" Natalia said, wrapping her bagel in a napkin. She finished her orange juice instead of bringing it.

"Yes, if it means getting you to school on time and avoiding that disapproving glare from your principal."

"I don't even know why I have to go," Natalia grumbled. "We'll be in the new house soon, and I won't even be going to that stupid old school."

"Believe me, I tried to explain that, but your principal is quite the stickler for protocol. All the fifth graders go on the orientation field trip regardless. Come on, coat, book bag. Let's go."

The drive to Oakridge Elementary was not long as the crow flew, but Arlington had an irregular layout of streets plus the infamous rush hour traffic to contend with.

"Do you know when Popi will be back?" Natalia asked.

"Not for certain. He said he'd be gone a day or two," Mai told her, as she had the countless times the girl had asked since Alexei had left.

"I don't see why he had to leave when we're packing to move into the new house."

You and me both, Mai thought, but she replied, "A special project for Uncle Nelson. He explained that."

"Yeah, but you didn't go with him like you used to do. You haven't gone with him on work trips since I came to live with you guys."

Observant, Mai thought. "Well, we can't leave you alone," Mai said. "You'd throw wild parties and invite boys over."

Natalia laughed and said, "Boys are gross."

"Popi will be glad to hear you say that."

"Maybe in middle school, I'll change my mind."

"I suspect you will."

Inwardly, Mai fumed at a slow driver whose dilly-dallying caught Mai at a red light. She checked her watch again.

"You're not upset you're not working with Popi, are you?" Natalia asked.

Of course, Mai was upset but not with Natalia. At Nelson and Alexei for their paternalistic, patriarchal assumption that Mai had to be the one to stay home and mind the baby.

Except she'd hinted to Alexei that maybe, perhaps, possibly, she might want a baby of her own. Roisin O'Saidh would never come out and demand an heir, but Mai was sure it was on Roisin's business-focused mind.

Jesus Wept, if I do have a baby, we *will* have to find a nanny.

"Of course I'm not upset," Mai lied. "I enjoy our girls' time together. You know. Eating pizza. Picking out outfits. Shopping. Reading *Tiger Beat*."

Natalia laughed. "I do like shopping."

"I have trained you well, young padawan."

That made Natalia giggle, and Mai was glad. She'd sensed Natalia slipping into a dark mood, like Alexei sometimes did. Two years had passed since the car accident that had killed Natalia's mother, but the grief sometimes crashed in on the child at unexpected times.

Mai had been much younger than Natalia when her parents had been killed. She was certain grief overwhelmed her at the time, but now she couldn't remember. She'd been so long without her parents, she rarely thought of them.

Lately though, she'd thought a lot about her mother. The only reason she could imagine was Natalia. Dealing with a child, raising that child—Mai had no experience with that. Her time with her mother had been brief and supplemented by a nanny, but surely her mother would have had advice to offer.

Mai pulled into the school, following a teacher's directions to the line of drop-off traffic. She was the last to pull in, but they had two minutes to go. Mai smiled and waved at the principal, whose scowl remained disapproving.

Mai leaned to one side and kissed Natalia's cheek.

"Ooh, Mums, don't embarrass me. Love you."

"Love you, too," Mai replied, but Natalia was already out of the car and skipping toward a knot of her friends.

This is my life now, Mai thought, dropping the offspring at school and fretting over a stranger's disapproval of her time management. Mai smiled at the principal as she passed her but muttered, "Fuck you."

22

AIFRIC BRENNAN-O'SAIDH

June 11, 1945

Fisher House
Knightsbridge, London

"How do I look?" Katherine Maitland asked.

She stood before a full-length mirror and turned to and fro, studying the ivory linen suit she wore. Not white. Good God, no.

The softly pleated skirt ended at mid-knee, and the only white she'd conceded to, the silk blouse, was almost blinding. The long-sleeved, buttoned-up jacket emphasized her narrow waist. A lapis-lazuli brooch Aifric had pinned to the right side lapel and a corsage of silk roses and baby-breath to the left side. A double strand of pearls at her neck. A pillbox hat the same shade of ivory as the suit.

Something old?

The pearls, her grandmother's.

Something new?

The ivory linen suit.

Something borrowed?

The brooch, from Freddie's mother's jewelry collection.

Something blue?

The brooch again.

Aifric had done her unruly hair in a simple, loose coil at the nape of her neck.

Everything looked perfect. It was her wedding day, all done hush-hush so Eithne O'Saidh wouldn't cross the Irish Sea to stop it. That had been Aifric's idea.

"Let it be a done deal when I tell her. I'll wait until after the honeymoon, so it's consummated and all," Aifric had said.

"Affie, it was consummated quite some time ago," Katherine had replied, making Aifric blush.

"Well, let's not tell her that." Behind Katherine, Aifric studied the reflection. "It's perfect, Cait," she said. "You're so beautiful."

"Will Freddie think so?"

"Of course he will. Don't you worry about that."

Katherine turned to Aifric and took her by the hands. "I'm sorry it's not a double wedding. I don't understand Johnny leading you on like this."

Aifric squeezed Katherine's hands. "He's not the bad guy here, Cait. He doesn't love me."

"Of course he does. All the attention he lavished on you, all the gifts, the time you two spent together. I thought you two had an understanding, and I am quite upset with him for not following through on that understanding."

"Cait, this isn't a Jane Austen novel. Besides, I don't love him either. He and I are great friends is all."

"I don't believe that. I've seen how you look at each other."

"Well, then, you missed how he looks at you."

Katherine withdrew her hands. "What do you mean?"

"Cait, you're the one he loves, but he's never said a word because he knows Freddie loves you, and you love Freddie."

Katherine laughed, but it sounded to Aifric more like a nervous titter. "Affie, that's ridiculous. How would you know?"

"What do you think it means that the four of us are together so often? Pretending to court me gave him an excuse to be close to you."

Katherine flushed, a hand coming to her mouth. "That can't be. That's . . . That's simply not right. It's not fair to you."

"I told you, Cait, Johnny doesn't love me. I don't love him. We're grand friends, but that's all. I'm with him for the same reason he's with me. To be with you."

Katherine scoffed at that. "You're with me anyway because your *mhaimi* wants you here."

"And you're twenty-five now. Per tradition, I could have gone home on your birthday, but I stayed not because I had to but because I want to."

Katherine smiled and hugged Aifric. "And I want to be with you. We're like sisters. You've always known that, and Freddie and I have talked. You're coming to live with us. He's remaining with British Intelligence, and he could be gone for long stretches of time. I told him I had to have you with me." With a smile and a blush, Katherine lay her hands on her flat belly. "And when the babies come, I'll need you even more."

Aifric's smile was weak, and she walked to the window. They were in the section of Fisher House not needing reconstruction from the Blitz. A month past VE Day, people had stopped taking to the streets to celebrate. Despite the damage still visible on the skyline, London had a feel of normal to it.

Aifric closed her eyes. Normal wasn't here in this room,

though; she wasn't normal. She had to be honest with Cait about that. Aifric turned around.

"Cait, I wasn't ever going to tell you this, but I don't want you to go forward into your life with Freddie upset with a man who is like a brother to him. Johnny does love you, but he'll never act on his feelings or tell you how he feels. Brit gentleman's code or some shite. I don't love him." She paused, fear making her hands shake, and she clasped them in front of her. "I can't love him."

Cait frowned and said, "Well, why not? He is rather handsome, and he's kind and respectful to you." Cait winked and added, "He's rich, too. Can't beat that combination in a man."

A deep breath, and Aifric replied, "Fine attributes all. *If* I wanted a man, but, you see, I don't want a man. Any man."

"Oh, you say that, but you'll find someone. If it's not Johnny, Freddie has plenty of other associates."

"Oh, Christ, Cait, don't make me say this."

"Say what?"

"Cait, I love you."

"And I love you, too, Affie. As I said, we're sisters. Maybe not by blood, but that doesn't matter to me. It shouldn't to you. We are sisters, and we love each other."

Aifric shook her head, forcing back her tears. "Cait, I'm . . ." Only the nasty, hurtful words came to mind, words Aifric didn't want to hear and, more importantly, didn't want to say.

"What is it? What's wrong?" Cait asked.

"I'm . . . I'm like Turing. Queer. And I *love* you. Johnny was with me to be close to you, and I went along with it because . . ." She swallowed the lump in her throat, straightened from the slouch the words had pushed her into. "Because he and I love the same person."

When Katherine shook her head, Aifric couldn't tell if it was from anger or denial.

"You and Johnny have . . . spoken about this?"

"Only after he confronted me about my feelings." Aifric smiled. "He does read people rather well."

"Obviously, I don't because the thought of either of you loving me . . . that way never entered my mind. Well, I knew you loved me, but I thought—"

"It was as a sister, yes. I tried to be so very careful, and I certainly didn't want to color this day, of all days, with this confession."

"Affie," Cait said, her voice low and gentle, "I love Freddie. I'm going to marry Freddie. I can't . . . I don't love you that way."

"Cait, I've always known that."

One hand fisted on her hip, the other at her mouth, Cait paced. "Oh, God, how awful you must feel. Oh, God!"

"No, Cait, I'm happy for you. All I've ever wanted is for you to be happy. I've always knew it wouldn't be with me, but I can stand with you today, sign the register, and witness your happiness."

Cait stopped pacing, standing before Aifric. "But . . . But you'll still come live with us? Or will that be too much?"

"I'll do whatever is best for you, Cait. If you want me with you and Freddie, I'll be there. My feelings won't change, but I can be what I have always been. Your companion and your loving sister. Until, of course, *Mhaimi* dies, and I have to take over the management of Maitland Enterprises."

Katherine Maitland studied her oldest friend's face, still a bit rattled by Aifric's revelation. Katherine really looked at her, as if for the first time, as if she'd never seen her before.

The mannish haircuts, the stolid, almost masculine cut of her suits. The way she smoked and drank. Like a man. And Katherine had never, ever thought . . .

"Have you . . .?" Katherine began but found she couldn't ask. She didn't know why she'd even think to ask.

"Been with a woman? Yes, but not since we've been in England. If I were caught . . ." Aifric shrugged. "They tend to overlook it in a woman regarding the law but not where the security clearance is concerned. So, I haven't. If I had, and they'd have forced me to leave Bletchley, I would have to tell Mam why. She'd disown me, kick me from the family business—and the family."

"I won't allow that. *That* will never happen," Katherine said.

Aifric smiled and said, "You know, I think that's true. You're the only person I know who can stand up to her." Aifric sobered quickly, looking away. "Cait, could this be our secret? Could you not tell Freddie, please?"

"I thought you said Johnny knew. If he does, Freddie knows."

"No, Johnny promised me he wouldn't say a word. He said he has friends whose lives have been ruined when their proclivities became known." Another brief smile. "He is a good man, like you said. He told me if anyone ever raised the issue about me, he'd marry me to shut them up. I understand the work Freddie and Johnny do, and I also know if someone were to find out about . . . me, it could make things difficult for them. And you. I won't have that, so I'll live like a nun. I once considered that anyway."

Katherine nodded. "Then, it's none of Freddie's business, is it?"

"A bad way to start a marriage, Cait. With such a big secret between youse."

"It's a confidence, Affie. Between sisters. Besides, given Freddie's work, he'll be keeping plenty of secrets from me. Fair's fair."

Aifric glanced at her watch. "Good God, Cait, look at the time! The car will be here any minute."

"Christ, yes. Affie, where are my gloves? I can't get married without gloves."

Aifric went right to them, in plain sight.

"Here they are," she said, smiling. "Honestly, Cait, what would you do without me?"

"I'd be awfully unhappy," she replied and tugged on her gloves. She picked up her matching ivory purse and slid her feet into the ivory pumps. "All right, *mo dheirfiur*, let's go marry me off. He's so rich, I think your *mhaimi* will eventually approve."

"You're right there."

Arm in arm, they went downstairs to the waiting car.

2002

Mount Vernon, Virginia

MAI SMILED and closed Aifric's diary. What courage to admit that to someone in 1945. Mai knew what had happened to Turing, the genius who'd contributed to the Allies' defeat of the Nazis, how the rejection from nearly everyone he'd worked with and the authorities' insistence on chemical castration had driven him to suicide.

But my mother, she thought, my mother accepted him and Aifric without a thought to it. Mai had plenty of reasons to be proud to be her mother's daughter, but this was the top of the list. She'd always loved her mother, rather, the memory of her, such as it was, but she loved her even more now.

Was such tolerance and acceptance, such altruism genetic? And Mai knew had her mother lived, they would have been close, that her mother would have been the one person in the world, perhaps more than Alexei, Mai could have turned to for anything, anything at all.

Mai was angry, too, for missing out on that. Once, when she'd been a prisoner of the Stasi, she'd focused on her mother, on the fact her mother hadn't broken under interrogation. Because her mother hadn't broken, someone had killed her, but that, in a way, was her legacy to Mai, an example of the kind of woman Mai could be and was.

23

ROUTINE

1991

Unknown Location

The room was close to what you'd have in a five-star hotel. A sumptuous bed with a thick mattress, over-stuffed pillows, high thread-count sheets, and a satin duvet. A sitting area with plush chairs and a sofa. A private bath with a walk-in shower that could hold a half dozen people, large, fluffy bath sheets, expensive soaps and facial creams, high-end shampoo and conditioner.

Even the view of snow-covered mountains topped by a cobalt blue sky was refreshing.

Except for the bars on the large, picture window and the fact she couldn't open the door from this side.

Men or women in scrubs but with no name tags brought her meals, which she had selected from a menu, and served to her on a small dining table with two chairs. The table was next to the large, picture window. An armoire opened onto a large television, but there was no service, only a selection of VHS tapes of movies, documentaries, or scenes of tranquility—fish swimming, a water-fall, rain in a forest, all very zen.

A nurse/guard had explained that a new set of tapes would be provided when she'd finished watching these.

No telephone or radio, of course. No control over the lights, which turned on and off on a schedule. Nor did she have a clock to determine the exact time, but she knew how to estimate that with some accuracy from the angle of the sun.

No paper or writing implements. No books, though she'd been told she could request them. No company except when she was taken from the room for X-rays, scans, or other tests or when the nurse/guard took her vitals twice daily.

Of course, the nurse/guard hadn't introduced herself as such, hadn't introduced herself at all, but she'd seen plenty of guards; she knew the type.

And she was a prisoner. No doubt about that.

She also understood what her interrogator was doing. Giving her a respite, allowing her to get comfortable in her new surround-ings, to trust him because he provided this comfortable space for her, all the while knowing he was also the one who could take it away. If he assumed she hadn't experienced this before, bad on him.

When she'd arrived, she was glad she'd been allowed to shower, though she was sure she was watched. Soft, warm pajamas had been laid out for her, and she was more than happy to see the shapeless, uniform-like outfit go. She'd even asked if she could watch it burn. The nurse/guard may have smiled at that.

She received fresh pajamas and a robe every morning. She wore her hair loose now; she was losing the strength in her arms to braid it, and when she brushed it each morning after rising and each night before bed, an old, old woman looked back at her from the mirror. She was seventy-one years old, wouldn't make it to seventy-two, and looked ninety.

The sunrises over the mountains were beautiful, and the reflected light of the sunsets on the snow were breath-taking. The moonrises were otherworldly. When the moon crested the mountains, it seemed close enough to touch.

All this made her think the window wasn't really a window but some gargantuan screen with a projection of reality on it. She'd touched it, felt the cool glass against her fingers. What she saw was real, as real as her being a prisoner.

She'd followed a routine for nearly thirty years and now stayed with it: rise, bathe, dress. T'ai Chi, which had always settled her, allowed her to escape reality, but even this slow exercise now left her exhausted. She could manage only five minutes or so a day, but she needed that time to center herself. The time was approaching when she'd be unable to get out of bed, when she would have catheters and adult diapers and lying in her own shite. She might as well prepare herself now for the inevitable.

In Fan's house in Beijing, her room had no windows. She had had comforts there, food, clothing, a purpose. She'd had Zhen until she'd left for university, and she had cared for Zhen as a mother would. Had she done otherwise, the reaction would be swift and unpleasant. At her lowest times, she considered shirking that duty in the hope the punishment would kill her, but another child shouldn't suffer because of her.

With Fan, she'd had comforts, yes, but not like this prison. At least here, Fan didn't make his daily visits to be serviced. She had thought his illness would have lessened his carnal desires, but he'd come to her even on the day he died.

Almost every day for twenty-eight years, he had raped her and called it love, and she'd learned the hard way not to fight that.

By counting the sunrises and sunsets, she knew she'd been here, wherever she was, for twenty-two days, in a gilded cage that was still a cage no matter how comfortable.

24

NO NEED FOR EXTREME MEASURES

1991

Unknown Location

Li Daiyu had taken two, perhaps three, spoonfuls of the creamy but bland soup when the door to her room opened. The nurse/guard entered, followed by the man Sergei. That likely wasn't his name. Interrogation protocol meant he wouldn't give his real one.

Without meeting Daiyu's gaze, the nurse/guard slipped the spoon from her fingers, lay it on the tray, and removed that from the small table in the room. The nurse/guard left, closing the door behind her.

"Was that necessary?" Daiyu asked her companion.

"You know how this works," he replied. "Consider yourself lucky we're not doing this in a cell."

"This, young man, is still a cell despite its cleanliness and creature comforts. We have no need for extreme measures. I will answer any question you pose."

He came to the table and sat across from her, unbuttoning his suit jacket as he did so.

An expensive suit. A handsome face. Striking eyes. The longish hair was a bit old-fashioned. His expression was bereft of humanity, as expected.

He brought out no notepad or pen. His hands rested on the table, the long fingers entwined with each other. The nails were not professionally manicured but well cared for. She tried to imagine him devoting attention to such grooming and found it difficult. A knuckle or two evinced he was capable of violence. That was on the right hand. Left-handed, perhaps. But his watch —a Rolex—was on that hand. Ah, he was left-handed but didn't want it to be an identifying clue to who he was.

An old scar bisected his left eyebrow. He wasn't a drinker or not much of one; no spider veins on his nose or cheeks. The crow's-feet at his eyes and the smooth skin elsewhere told her he wasn't yet fifty, but the eyes appeared older and had seen a great deal in his life.

"Tell me how you escaped from Taiwan," he said, barked like an officer giving an order.

"I am unable to relate that with much accuracy. I only know what I was told."

"Which was?"

"The summer of 1963, my husband and I were apprehended trying to board an aircraft home. We were taken to a Taiwanese prison. I was taken from that prison some weeks later—I don't know how many—under sedation."

"By whom?"

"Yazhu Fan. He took me to a reeducation camp near Beijing."

"Or you went with him willingly."

"Absolutely not. He came to me, claiming to be a Directorate asset. He said he'd received instructions to save either my husband or me. My husband was the preference. I told Fan, yes, save my husband for our daughter's sake. Then, Fan said he didn't want that. He wanted me for himself. I emphatically refused. I begged him to save my husband. The next thing I knew, I woke in the reeducation camp."

"What happened to your husband?"

"I hoped that he'd been spared, but Fan told me Freddie had insisted I be the one to live, again, for our daughter." After all these years, the emotion she felt, the pain she felt surprised her. She swallowed hard, closed her eyes, and added, "Fan told me he allowed Freddie to kill himself."

"Am I supposed to believe your husband agreed to have you become Yazhu Fan's mistress?"

Her eyes opened, and she leaned across the table toward him. He didn't react.

"Get this straight, me boyo," she said, noting the almost imperceptible widening of his eyes at "me boyo." She filed that away. "I was not Fan's mistress, except in his justification to himself that he wasn't a rapist."

No reaction. She leaned back in her chair, an abrupt movement that sent pain lancing across her chest. She struggled not to wince and show him her pain, likely the only thing she could control right now.

"I suspect my husband thought Fan would turn me over to the Directorate," she continued, "to be repatriated."

"Or your husband couldn't live with the knowledge you were willing to leave him to rot in a Taiwanese prison while you led a comfortable life in Beijing."

She raised an eyebrow. "Comfortable, was it?"

"Li Daiyu, Yazhu was a rising party star. He had a house commensurate with his status. He had a child to replace the one you abandoned."

"Do not call me by that name, and I did not abandon my daughter. Never."

A smile flickered on his lips. "You never tried very hard to escape, to get back to her."

"I was never let out of the house except under guard. This room we're in now, this was how I lived in Fan's house, except my room in Fan's house had no windows. An escape risk, you see. The only time I left the room was to bathe, feed, or dress Yazhu Zhen and then only under the watchful eyes of three armed guards. And every day, sometimes morning, noon, and night, Yazhu Fan came into that room and raped me. I always knew when he was out of town, though."

"How?"

"One of the guards would rape me."

"You've told me your first lie, and I don't like being lied to."

"What lie?"

"You were let out of the house to go to North Korea because you were a good interrogator."

"Only under Fan's supervision, and I botched that interrogation on purpose."

"Botched it? You amputated his arm."

"I could see he wasn't going to break. Those types of subjects are rare, but he was one. I wanted to look like a failure."

"To what possible end?"

She shrugged and looked out the window. "I hoped Fan would kill me because I'd failed. Or that he'd return me to a reeducation camp. I knew I could either escape from there or that a second reeducation would kill me."

"You were a highly trained operative; yet, you couldn't find a means of escape for nearly thirty years?"

She looked at him again. How odd were those blue eyes. Dark blue when he'd entered the room, but now the irises were pale, like glacier ice.

She must have stared too long.

"Answer my question." Another bark.

"The effects of my first reeducation took hold, a deep hold, but that began to wear off. I had to hide that. To survive, I had to appear compliant. I had to survive because all I wanted, all I thought about, all I still want and think about, is getting back to my daughter."

"Why would any daughter ever want to see a mother who abandoned her?"

"Is that what she was told?"

"No. When you left Taipei with Yazhu Fan, she was five years old. Her guardian told her you and her father died in an aircraft accident in Taiwan."

Daiyu buried her face in her hands but didn't weep. After composing herself, she looked at him again.

"You mentioned she had a husband. Does she have a family? Is she happy?"

"You expect me to believe that through three decades of *intimate* association with the head of intelligence for the People's Republic, you never tried to find out anything about her?"

"Of course I asked Fan. Offered him my body freely for just one tidbit of information about her. But he didn't want my body freely. He wanted to take it, and he did. While he did, he told me he would find her and kill her if I asked again."

His response was to rise and stride to the door. He knocked twice, and it opened inward. He slipped through the narrow gap and was gone.

"I NEED A SECURE LINE," Alexei said to the woman in charge of this place.

"Of course. This way."

She led him to her office and pointed to the gray phone on her desk. "I'll take a tray with some hot soup back in," she said.

"No. She can wait until morning."

"Alexei, she is a dying woman."

"She showed no compassion to anyone she interrogated, I'm sure. A taste of her own medicine is what she's getting. That is my instruction for you."

"Of course."

She left him alone.

Only after dialing a number did he realize it was the middle of the night where Nelson was. Nelson mumbled, "It's two o'clock. In the damned morning."

"The subject has indicated that Yazhu Fan coerced the subject's cooperation by telling the subject he knew where the daughter was and that he would kill the daughter. It could have been a bluff, but it did secure the subject's cooperation."

"Yeah, not a chance a parent would take. All right, I'll arrange some additional security. Shall I alert her, or do you want to?"

"If I call her, she'll ask too many questions," Alexei said.

"True. Okay, I'll say the country the subject defected from is making general threats and that I'm only being cautious. Let's hope she'll buy that."

"With Natalia at the condo, she'll buy it, and I've detected no suspicion from her. However, if she questions the security, get word to me. I'll risk reiterating what you've told her."

"I love it when a plan comes together," Nelson joked.

That drew a smile from Alexei, but he wasn't celebrating yet.

"Getting anything good?" Nelson asked.

"Right now, I doubt anything the subject tells me is useful."

"Well, we have to try and get our five million dollars worth."

"Ah, yes. Pile on the pressure. I work best under it."

A low laugh from Nelson, and he ended the call with, "I'm going back to sleep now."

25

AN ELABORATE RUSE
FOR AN ASSIGNATION

1991

Arlington, Virginia

Mai dropped a sleepy Natalia at school well before the cutoff time. When the principal spotted Mai's Toyota 4Runner, she checked her watch, checked it again, and stared at Mai, mouth agape in utter astonishment.

"Fecking screw," Mai muttered and managed not to flip the woman off. Mai gave her the royal wave instead.

On a morning as lovely as this—clear sky, moderate temperatures before the DC area's notorious heat and humidity rose—Mai usually walked to work. Most times it was quicker than driving in morning rush hour in Arlington. The school, however, was enough out of the way of Directorate headquarters that returning to the condo to drop off the car was backtracking.

She headed instead for the below-ground parking garage with

the mid-rise office building above it and the secret, World War II era bunker below it.

After entering the appropriate code on the keypad at the "Restricted Access" section, Mai circled down several levels to the spot marked "Reserved for Burke Financials," and pulled into it. Keeping her eyes on the move around her, she headed for the security checkpoint.

The guard on duty there, poked through her backpack, handed it to her, and said, "Mr. Nelson said for you to come see him when you got in. Not urgent, though."

"Thank you . . .?"

"It's Gary today, ma'am."

"Thanks, Gary."

Mai doubted it was an UNSECFOR protocol for the security specialists to use a different name daily, but Gary/Dave/Harry/Bob, etc., and his ilk seemed to revel in this minor subterfuge. Mai wondered which was his real name as she stepped into the elevator that would take her even deeper underground.

She was glad "Gary" had said, "not urgent." When she'd heard that Nelson wanted to see her, her first thought was something had gone wrong on Alexei's mission.

Granted, debriefing a mysterious defector wouldn't necessarily be dangerous unless it had been a trap or someone had inadvertently betrayed the location of the debrief. However, even she didn't know where it was. She hadn't thought twice about it until now.

She knew how this worked, of course, but that hadn't stopped a stray thought from intruding: Alexei wasn't with a defector at all; this was an elaborate ruse for an assignation with one of his stable of women assets. He'd sworn to her he'd passed them all to other operatives years ago, but despite that, she harbored some of the distrust his actions had created.

No. If he'd resumed his old habits, he'd have thought of something far more elaborate than, "There's a high-level defector from a signatory we haven't had any inroads into for a while, and Nelson wants me to debrief the subject."

She understood as well the mystery about the defector's gender. The less Mai knew about any of it, the smaller the chance something might slip out and derail the operation.

However, she couldn't ignore this "thing" with Alexei and women. Mai could be with him anywhere, and women would look. Those looks would linger, and there'd been an occasional licking of lips. At times, Mai had wanted to say, "Yes, he does taste yummy," but had stayed silent. He did a good job of ignoring them when in Mai's presence.

But Natalia had blown his cover.

"Whenever Popi picks me up from school, all the moms are at his car, talking to him."

Of course, he wouldn't turn them away because *"Dushenka,* that would be impolite."

No, he liked the attention. He was a man, after all.

Mai passed through Operations, where she was scheduled for remote monitoring of a black-bag job in Bulgaria. She headed for Nelson's private office since she hadn't seen him in Ops.

"Go on in," Nelson's assistant said. "He's expecting you."

That cheery greeting raised Mai's hackles a bit. If someone didn't have an appointment, the stickler-for-protocol assistant would make sure you understood that wasn't acceptable. Trying to shake off her unease, Mai opened the door after knocking.

Nelson looked up from his computer monitor. "Oh, I'm a priority?" he asked, smiling.

"Well, Alexei does say we have to let you think you're the boss. Is he all right?"

"Yes, he's fine. He alerted me of a threat associated with the subject he's debriefing."

"Against Alexei or the subject?"

"Not the subject specifically. A vague statement from the country the subject defected from, a reference to knowing where to find families. I sent a team to Natalia's school."

"Blue sedan, two men, and a woman?"

"Yes."

"I suspected they were school security. A couple of Congressmen's children attend."

Nelson nodded. "The San Fran station has worked a deal with NCIS in Hawaii to keep an eye on Peter on the Big Island. I'll put two guards at the condo, two more at the construction site. Alexei agreed when I suggested it."

But no one mentioned it to me except as an afterthought, Mai thought, her lips pursing to keep from saying it aloud.

"I don't want to alarm Natalia, so the ones at the condo must be discrete at all times."

"I will advise them."

"When Alexei will be finished with the debrief?"

"I have to be flexible with his time." He smiled at her again. Do you actually miss him?"

Mai shrugged and replied. "I might. On occasion."

"He'll be happy to hear that."

"Careful, Nelson, or someone might mistake you for a hopeless romantic."

"Never. Keep your eyes open, okay?"

She somewhat resented the warning. Given what he'd told her, of course she'd be more observant than usual.

"Will do," she said.

"Now, off you go to the exciting world of mission monitoring," he said.

Mai made a small circle with an upward-pointing index finger. "Huzzah!" she said.

Nelson's eyes narrowed at her. "Hire a nanny, and you, too, can be a spy again."

"Or, you could think of me first when something comes up."

Nelson's eyes narrowed further. "A child who's lost her mother shouldn't risk losing another. I'd think you, of all people, should understand that."

That brought her Irish up, but she again bit back the words she wanted to say. Instead, she said, "She also essentially lost a father, too, but you have no issue with sending Alexei out solo."

"I alone cannot change a sexist world, Mai. That black-bag job commences in . . ." He checked his watch. "Fifteen minutes." Then, he returned his attention to his computer.

Mai resisted the temptation to flip someone off for the second time that morning.

She left him and headed to Operations, stopping at the monitor's console. She dropped her backpack beneath the desk and sat. A technician linked her computer to the satellite feed, and she donned her headset, going through the radio checks.

Let the excitement begin, she thought and couldn't help but roll her eyes.

26

ARTISTIC LICENSE

1955

Uxfield Manor
Sussex, England

When Cait didn't come down for breakfast with Freddie, Aifric knew something had to be wrong. That, plus the fact they'd shortened their long weekend in London, confirmed it.

Freddie came into the breakfast room, looked over the offerings in the chafing dishes, and didn't pick up a plate. He had dressed to go riding instead of his usual "country squire" attire.

"Is Johnnie at home?" he asked Aifric.

"No. He rang yesterday and said circumstances would keep him in London this weekend," she replied.

He nodded, continued not to look at her, and headed for the door. She'd noted the hollow eyes, the dark circles, and the fact he hadn't shaved or oiled his hair.

Dabbing her mouth with a napkin, she rose and went to the drawing room. From the windows there, she had a view of the stables, and she saw him on the path to that structure, his shoulders hunched. In a few minutes, she saw him gallop away on his favorite gelding, an anniversary gift from Cait from the Maitland breeding farm in Ireland.

Frowning with concern, Aifric headed back to the breakfast room, though her appetite had waned.

Freddie and Cait could have had a disagreement, but those occasions were rare. They were so attuned to each other that the stimuli for arguments were almost nonexistent. They tended to resolve disagreements by talking through them.

That couldn't happen with one of them galloping over the English countryside.

Caitrin's lady's maid came into the breakfast room and dropped a curtsy to Aifric.

"Jesus Wept, woman, haven't I told you not to do that to me?" Aifric said, hoping she wasn't taking her reaction to Freddie's odd behavior out on the young woman.

"Sorry, ma'am. Habit. Shall I take a breakfast tray up to her ladyship? She hasn't rung for breakfast, but it's past the usual time she takes it."

Aifric was now sure something was wrong.

"For now, make a good-sized pot of tea. Two cups. I'll take the tray up to her and see if I can find out what's wrong. She didn't ring you to do her hair?"

"No, ma'am, not that neither. She usually dresses herself and rings for me to do her hair. It's past her usual time for that, too."

"All right. Only tea for now. Let me know when it's ready."

"Yes, ma'am."

She almost curtsied again but stopped herself.

LADEN TRAY IN HAND, Aifric climbed the main stairs to the third floor of the . . . Well, castle was the only way to describe the structure. Freddie insisted it was "merely a manor house, albeit an old one."

Aifric's steps were brisk, but she tried to slow down, hoping this wasn't an emergency in the making. On the third floor, she went down the long gallery lined with Fisher family portraiture from, oh, at least the last 400 years. The Fisher men were all handsome, the women, whether Fishers by birth or marriage, were stunningly beautiful.

Aifric gave an Irish snort. Artistic license, no doubt.

When she reached the earl's suite, she balanced the tray adroitly on one hand, knocked with the other, and went inside.

Cait had curled into a ball beneath the covers on the massive, four-poster bed, complete with bed-curtains because this whole place was almost impossible to heat in the winter. Even though the covers were up to Cait's eyes, Aifric could hear the soft weeping.

Aifric closed her eyes a moment. She suspected what was wrong. She set the tea tray on a table before the cold, ash-laden fireplace then sat on the edge of the bed, her hand on Cait's shoulder.

"Cait," she murmured, "tell me what's wrong."

Cait threw the covers back and sat up. Aifric caught a glimpse of red-rimmed, puffy eyes and a red-splotched face before Cait flung herself into Aifric's embrace and sobbed. Wracking, wrenching sobs that were more like wails.

"It happened again, Affie," Cait said. "I lost it. I hadn't even told anyone I thought I was pregnant, and I lost it."

"When, *acushla*?"

"T . . . Two days ago. Oh, God, Affie. Freddie and I have been married ten years, and I've had five miscarriages and so many false alarms. I can't bear it. I simply can't bear it."

"Freddie's not mad at you, is he?"

"No, God, no. He blames himself. Swears he'll never touch me again, that he's never going to put me through that again. That his father can go fuck himself and shut up about an heir. But I want his children, Affie. I want them so much."

Affie wondered if her mother, Eithne, was adding to the pressure. The Fishers needed an heir, but so did the Maitlands.

"All right, now, calm down. Did you lose a lot of blood like . . . Like last time?" Aifric felt Cait's nod. "Did you go to hospital?" Another nod. "Well, then, you need to calm down and not upset yourself. I brought up some good, strong tea. Do you think you can manage some of that?" Another nod.

Cait straightened and rubbed tears from her face. She sniffed and ran her hands through her tangled red hair.

"I'll . . . I'll go wash my face, brush my hair, and . . ." Another sniff, more tears. "And I have to change the damned sanitary pad."

"You'll feel better after that. I'll pour us some tea, *acushla*."

Aifric did so, feeling utter helplessness.

BY HER SECOND cup of tea, Katherine had composed herself. The red splotches faded, but her still-red eyes bespoke her grief. She and Aifric had moved to sit in the chairs before the fireplace.

"Where is Freddie?" she asked. "He got up and dressed without shaving and dashed out of here."

"He went for a ride on the gelding," Aifric said.

"Did he say anything?"

"Not really. He asked if Johnny was home, and I told him he had called yesterday to say he had to stay in London."

"Nothing else?"

"No, but it was obvious he was upset."

"Again, not with me, Affie. He was the same as he's always been. Comforting, loving, but he was angry. At himself."

"Most men are angry at the women over something like this."

"Not Freddie. I'm glad I hadn't told anyone. I was going to wait until I was well past four months. That's the longest I've gone. I thought if I got past four months . . ." She paused, looking at the cup of tea she held in her lap. Without looking up, she continued, "When Freddie called the doctor, he told Freddie to . . . save . . . everything and bring it to hospital. The doctor said I was between three and four months. So close. So fecking close."

"Cait, you're putting too much pressure on yourself. You want an heir for *Mam*. You want an heir for Freddie. Think about yourself for a change."

"I want a baby for me, Affie. I want to be a mother. I've always wanted to be a mother. I'm thirty-five. I'm running out of time." Elbow on the arm of her chair, Caitrin lowered her head to rest in the palm of her hand.

Aifric took the empty cup from Katherine's hand and sat both cups on the tray.

"Cait, do you remember my cousin Moyna, the midwife?" Aifric asked. Head still in her hand, Katherine nodded. "She's retired now, but she consults, as it were. I could ask her to come over and talk to you, perhaps even speak with your doctor. She was a midwife for over forty years, in good conditions and bad. She might be able to help."

Katherine raised her head but didn't let hope in. Not yet. "Midwives are for births, Affie. Not conception. Not carrying a baby to term."

"Not so, Cait. Out in the countryside in Ireland, midwives help women conceive and help them have successful pregnancies."

"And get rid of any the woman doesn't want, no doubt," Katherine murmured. "I mean, that's good work for those women, that they have a choice. I understand that." A soft laugh escaped. "Maybe I should have been a poor, country lass who had a baby a year until her womb fell out."

"Midwives also assist pregnant women all the way to birth. It wouldn't hurt to talk with her, would it?"

Katherine frowned; it wouldn't hurt at all unless cousin Moyna could do nothing for her.

"Let me speak with Freddie," Katherine said.

"Jesus Wept!"

"Affie, I'm not going to ask his permission. You know that's not him. He and I will discuss it and make a decision together, as we always do. Now, Moyna's not one of those drink this tea for thirty days and give yourself a daily enema charlatans, is she?"

"Not at all. She studied midwifery with a medical doctor and learned a great deal. Most doctors she's worked with have said she could be one of them. Mam consulted her to have Roisin. That's why we were eight years apart."

"All right. Freddie and I will discuss it. Did he say when he'd return from his ride?"

"No, Cait, he didn't."

Katherine turned to look out the window again, as if she sought Freddie's silhouette on the horizon.

"Thank you for the *tae*, Affie." She looked at Aifric and managed a weak smile. "And for listening."

"Of course, *acushla*. Always, and I am so sorry."

Katherine reached to squeeze Aifric's hand. "Thank you, *mo dheirfiur*." She held onto Aifric's hand, feeling as if she drew strength from the touch, then she released it and stood.

"I'm going to bathe and dress."

"Shouldn't you be resting?" Aifric asked, rising, too.

"I can lounge about in the library with a good book better than here. Will you tell Tilly to come up and help with my hair in an hour?"

"Sure and I will, but are you sure you shouldn't be in bed?"

"I'm to 'take it easy,' and I can do that without being in bed. Besides, I've wallowed long enough. Stiff upper lip and all that."

"That's Brit shite, Cait. Grieve your loss how you want to."

"I've done that, Affie, but I won't lose my sanity or my husband over it. I can't change the past, but I can look into the future. There, I see me and Freddie. And our child." Katherine took Aifric's hand and squeezed again, smiling. "And our child's doting Auntie Affie."

27

BONDED IN GRIEF

2002

Mount Vernon, Virginia

Mai turned the open diary face down on the sofa. That last entry was too close, too personal.

Mai knew her mother had had "issues with conception," as it would have been called then. Infertility now. Except her mother could get pregnant; she couldn't stay pregnant, until Mai.

Mai's issue had been slightly different. She'd easily gotten pregnant early in her relationship with Alexei, twice in two years, and she'd lost both. Then, years of nothing, despite the fact they fucked like bunnies. Finally, in 1992, everything had come together. She was pregnant with a child she wanted, Alexei's child. And she lost that, too.

After that stillbirth, Roisin O'Saidh had meant to console Mai by telling her of Katherine Maitland-Fisher's struggles.

"And she had you," Roisin had said. "There is hope."

For thousand of years, the inability to produce an heir was the woman's fault, when in reality the male DNA contribution determined gender. Annulments, divorces, and the occasional beheading or burning at the stake resulted. Mai was glad her father hadn't been a prick about it. Alexei hadn't either. Frederick Fisher declared he wouldn't "touch" his wife again. Alexei Bukharin had had a vasectomy after that last stillbirth without telling Mai until a few years later.

In 1992, she'd been thirty-four. She could have had another pregnancy. She could have taken to bed as her mother had.

Mai imagined her mother would have been there, with her, encouraging her.

"I got through it, Mattie. You can, too."

That first pregnancy, part of the reason for marrying Alexei, that poor unwanted baby, Mai would have given anything to have turned to mother and asked, "What should I do?"

Mai flashed back to Roisin's burial in the Maitland Mausoleum, to the plaque denoting her first and last pregnancies. She remembered the first one, the little boy Alexei named Ivan. The perfect features. All the fingers. All the toes. Tiny, perfect ears. The hint of Alexei's cheekbones, the shape of Alexei's eyes. Looking alive except for his cold, blue skin because as perfect as he appeared outside, his lungs were underdeveloped. He'd struggled only briefly, so she'd heard, to draw breath.

She and her mother would have bonded in grief over that shared experience, that shared tragedy.

Mai hadn't laid eyes on the little girl, the preemie born after a Serbian warlord had held Mai prisoner for three months. She'd been perfect, too, inside and out, so said the doctor. The umbilical cord had strangled her in the womb.

Mai hadn't wanted to know anything about that baby. She

hadn't known the gender except for the hints that Alexei had accidentally . . . No, that he'd deliberately dropped.

Mai could have wept about that on her mother's shoulder instead of internalizing her bitterness.

All the times Natalia had vexed Mai as a teenager, surely her mother would have had advice.

An epiphany passed through Mai like an electrical charge. If her mother and father had lived, likely Mai would never have run off to Amsterdam at fifteen. No Ian Flynn. No recruitment by John Stone. No Directorate.

No Alexei.

Many times, she thought that might have been best for them both. He'd stuck it out, which meant she had to, too. She couldn't let him win their personal war.

All those low times with Alexei. She could have leaned on her mother for support.

Had her mother and father had issues anywhere near what had plagued Mai and Alexei? Per Aifric, it seemed not, but that was the era when you didn't air dirty laundry in front of servants, who likely knew anyway. That was how the O'Saidhs had always thought of themselves—servants.

No, Aifric hadn't. She and Mai's mother were close enough that Aifric felt safe coming out to her and in the 1940s when homosexuality was still illegal in Britain. Even Roisin, despite her often obsequious behavior, had struggled with the relationship between the Maitlands and the O'Saidhs, at times wanted to assert her influence over Mai but agonizing over the "impropriety" of it. Mai was glad to see the daughters of Eithne O'Saidh were individuals each in their own way.

I should have liked to have known Aifric, Mai thought. She shook her head.

Too many "shouldas, couldas." No need to waste time on pointless speculation.

28

HER INTERROGATOR

1991

Unknown Location

Her eyes on the clouds moving over the mountain, clouds that coiled into balls like cotton candy, Katherine paid no heed to the opening of the door. It wasn't time for a meal or for having her vitals checked.

Her interrogator. Of course.

He again came to the table before the window and sat across from her. Once more, no pen or notepad.

Are we being recorded, videotaped, she wondered, or is his memory that good?

She'd never allowed for any of her interrogations to be recorded in any way. She couldn't risk someone recognizing her voice or seeing her picture. If that had happened, Fan would have killed her to hide the secret of how he got her.

Staying alive was the point of it all: enduring the reeducation camp, the rapes, the prison that was Fan's house. She had endured because that meant she had a chance to see her daughter again.

Her eyes still on the scenery, Katherine said, "You left yesterday in a rush. Was it something I said?"

He said nothing, so of course it was something she'd said. The last thing she'd told him was Fan's threat of knowing where Mattie was.

She looked at the man Sergei. "Is my daughter safe?"

"That is not your concern," he said.

"I'm her mother."

"You ceased being her mother when you began your life with Yazhu Fan."

"That was no life. I was in a jail in a room where I was raped every day."

"I am not here to talk about that, and I don't like repetition."

"Rape makes you uncomfortable. I can see that. Tell me, Sergei, how many women have you raped to get them to talk?"

Again, the transformation of his eyes from a deep blue to the color of glacier ice was startling.

"I have never raped a woman," he replied, his teeth clenched.

Score one for me, Katherine thought; that hit a nerve. She debated whether or not to tweak it again, out of perverseness, but she remained silent.

"I am not here to discuss the conditions of your alleged imprisonment," he said. "Give me details about the procedures supposedly used on you in the reeducation camp."

Alleged. Supposedly. Well, she'd react the same way if their positions were reversed. She let it pass.

"I'm not a sleeper agent, if that's what you think. The specifics remain vague, even more so with the time that's passed. They used drugs, but I don't know which ones. Deprivation of everything. Starvation. Physical violence. Rape, of course. I do remember they played Mao reading his Little Red Book constantly, without let-up. I was naked most of the time. I slept on a thin mattress on a cement floor. If I wasn't compliant enough they put me in the box. I'm sure I don't need to explain that. I was periodically tested to determine the extent of my reeducation."

"How?"

"I stood before a council of some sort. All women. I was naked, and I had to recite Mao's Little Red Book. If I missed one word, I was punished. Beaten. Cattle prod." Katherine's hand went to her throat. "Strangled." Her hand returned to the table-top. "They did use positive reinforcement on occasion. I got to wear clothing. Better food. I could bathe or allowed out of my cell to walk the grounds, trailed by two guards, of course. I think that was how I knew I was progressing, I guess you'd say. The punish-ment came less and less."

"Describe the grounds," Sergei said.

"Gorgeous. Tall stands of living bamboo, like an enclosure. I studied that as a potential escape route. They were too thickly planted. I'd have needed a machete. The walkways were not sand but tiny pebbles. Very Zen-like, relaxing. Other prisoners . . . Oh, my clothing was a monk-like robe, tan in color. I saw other prisoners, and I knew they were prisoners because they wore robes like mine and were followed by guards. Always one pris-oner, two guards with truncheons, sidearms, and a cattle prod. Several of the prisoners I saw were not Asian, but because we couldn't speak or look directly at each other, I have no idea if they were Americans or Europeans. I didn't recognize any of them."

Katherine paused for a moment. As she'd spoken, the memo-ries rushed back, and she needed to process them.

"Sometimes . . . Sometimes, lining the pathways, there were non-Asian observers. They weren't allowed to interact with us, either, but at times as I passed, I overheard them talking among themselves. Some spoke Russian. Others spoke Spanish. I . . ."

The memory seemed to explode in her head. She gasped, closed her eyes.

"Stop the drama, please," Sergei said. "I don't buy it."

"Give me a moment. I remembered something." Several deep breaths and with eyes closed, she continued, "One time, one of the Russians said something vile, something about sucking his dick, and I forgot and looked at him, called him a *sookin syin*. The guards used their cattle prods, and the reeducation process started again. From the beginning. That happened at least twice that I remember. The second time, I was so exhausted, so confused that when they put a bowl of broth in front of me, my bloody table manners kicked in. I asked for a spoon instead of picking up the bowl and drinking from it."

She paused again, trying to calm the memories and send them back into the dark part of her brain. Katherine opened her eyes, saw the emotionless face in front of her, so like her guards in the camp. Even when they beat her or punished her, their faces were like that. No anger, no remorse, no nothing.

She tried a smile. "I never did that again, I assure you." That got nothing from him. With a sigh, she continued, "During the harshest aspects of the reeducation, I would often wake in the camp's medical unit. I could hear the doctors talk about having to revive me. I'd have burn marks on my chest where they'd used a defibrillator. So, I must have died, several times. In a way, I think that was part of the reeducation, to show me I was not in control of living or dying. And . . ."

"And what?"

"Eventually, I complied with everything they had me do or learn. I blocked out who I was. It was too dangerous to remember. Even the training I'd received from the Directorate to resist interrogation they used against me. If I didn't answer questions, I'd be regressed in the process, and I usually woke up at some point in the medical unit."

"So, you did betray your oath. You answered their questions."

"No, I lied to them. Made things up."

"You expect me to believe that?"

"Sergei, I'm so tired I don't really care what you believe, but go do some research. If you do, you'll find no in-progress operations were compromised in a way that came back to me. I didn't tell the Taiwanese anything, and I didn't tell my re-educators anything."

"If you'd lied, they would have checked on what you'd given them and discovered you were lying."

"Of course. So, when they asked questions, I quoted Mao. The Little Red Book. His speeches that they played for me."

"The mere fact that you're alive, that you survived so long, tells me you sold out the Directorate."

"Ah, that would be the organization whose director ordered that my husband be saved and I be executed. I could have told them exactly where and how to find Nigel Hume, but I didn't because I wouldn't endanger other operatives. They kept up the relentless questioning, and I kept spouting Mao at them. Finally, they declared me reeducated. Nigel Hume has to be dead by now. He was more twenty years older than me. Tell me that's so."

"The Directorate has a new director now."

She smiled. "You're good at this. I am impressed."

"And I'm not."

"I want to see my daughter."

"No."

"What harm would it do?"

"More than you can imagine."

"Shouldn't she decide that?"

"I will answer that question, but ask another, and you won't be fed for a while. She can't decide whether she wants to see you because she will never know you're alive. She won't even know when you die. For her, you died a long time ago, and her husband wants to keep it that way."

Katherine stared out the window again. The clouds had accumulated, and the sky was almost obscured by them. A layer formed below the crest of the mountains, and she thought it might rain. Probably snow.

"My husband," she said, "was not a man of his era. He accepted me as his equal. He and I made decisions about our lives together, about our work, together. He'd never dream of making a decision for me without consulting me. Well, at the very end, he did. He decided I'd be the one to live, but I believe if he'd known what was going to happen to me, he'd have not been so quick to save me. It's disheartening to see that the world hasn't changed much, that some *man* made this decision for my daughter."

Sergei started to say something, and Katherine looked at him again, shaking her head.

"Don't bother to say it's in her best interests," Katherine told him. "It was still made by a man over her. I hope if she ever finds out, she'll give that husband of hers what for."

"Surely you were an equal in the Communist utopia of the People's Republic?" Sergei said, the sarcasm easy to discern.

"I'm sure it was the same in the glorious Soviet Union, Sergei. I've seen the propaganda posters. Women were equal to men as proletariats, but at home, she would still have to prepare the food, clean the house, service her husband whenever he wanted, take care of her children, and then serve the Union of Soviet Socialist Republics. I wasn't anyone's equal in Beijing. It's hard to think of yourself that way when you're rarely let outside a windowless room and when, every day, you're reminded that your only purpose is as a sex doll."

"Enough. Back to the reeducation," Sergei said. "You indicated you blocked the memory of who you were. You considered yourself Li Daiyu, then?"

"Yes. I pushed my true self so far down that even when I caught a glimpse of myself in a mirror, all I saw was a middle-aged Chinese woman, not the heiress to two fortunes."

"How long did the reeducation remain in place?"

"Too long. Years. Maybe a decade. Maybe more. I would have flashes of a different life, of a little girl who wasn't Zhen. I remembered at some point what I was seeing. My little girl, my daughter as the last time I'd seen her." Katherine smiled as that image returned. "A five-year-old little tomboy who could take two steps outside and be covered in grime."

"Stay on subject. Give me a specific date when your alleged reeducation faltered."

"God, man, I don't know. Let's see. 1963. That was when I was taken from Taiwan. Fan said I was in the reeducation camp for two years, so I would have left there in 1965 or 1966. I'd say mid- to late-seventies was when the flashbacks began."

"No one noticed?"

Katherine shook her head. "I made sure no one noticed. If anyone had, I'd have been sent back to the camp. Or executed. So, I repressed the flashbacks."

"If you cared so much for your daughter, why?"

"Ukrainian or American, whatever you are, you wield that sarcasm like a Russian."

"Why?"

"Because someday, somehow, I was going to free myself and find my daughter!"

The shout was loud enough and harsh enough that pain lanced from her lower left side up into her chest. She breathed hard, her lips pursed, but no reaction from her interrogator. Katherine ventured a deep breath, and the pain eased.

"I think the brainwashing fully slipped away when I interrogated the CIA man in North Korea. He said something to me. I don't remember what it was, but when he said it, everything . . . It was as if my whole existence popped back into being. It overwhelmed me, but I knew I had to hide it. I told Fan the CIA man wasn't going to break, that I felt ill, that I wanted to be home."

"Home? England?"

Katherine buried her face in her hands and sobbed, not caring how much pain that caused.

"No," she murmured, voice muffled. "Beijing. His house."

29

WARM AND TINGLY

From Aifric O'Saidh-Brennan's Diary

January 5, 1957

I am glad I went riding today. It was colder than usual, but I dressed warmly. The day was glorious, the scenery magnificent as always.

And I met The Honorable Virginia Cooper-Woodson.

When I started riding on the estate all those years ago when Cait and I moved here, Freddie had told me to be careful not to cross onto the Cooper-Woodson estate, which adjoined his.

Freddie had said, "Old Joe—he hates being called that, by the way, which is why I use it—is tetchy about people trespassing. However, he's not so careful about bringing his hunting parties onto my land. I don't care, really. Well, I do, but I want to stand in stark contrast to his pretentious arrogance. He's a jealous man, jealous of position and title, possessive of his few remaining acres. Not a good investor at all. He's had to sell off bits and pieces of his estate to pay his debts, but he strives to maintain his image of lord of the manor. I've offered to buy him out and give him a lifetime lease on the house, but his title is one that's tied to the land. No land. No Baron Cooper-Woodson."

But I wasn't the one who trespassed today.

I was most definitely on the Fisher estate when I saw a woman riding not far away and most definitely also on the Fisher estate.

Freddie and Cait are away. Again. But Freddie's always emphasized that I should report any strangers I see to the estate agent. What I noticed first was the horse. Beautiful animal. A bay with dark stockings, mane, and tail. Close to seventeen hands, I'd say.

Then, I noticed the rider.

A woman, early thirties perhaps, top-of-the-line winter riding gear. I felt a bit dumpy in my layers of denim, flannel, and wools, and my riding boots had lost their sheen years ago. Hers gleamed in the bright sun.

When she saw me watching her, she pulled up, waited a moment, then spurred the horse over to me.

"Good morning," she said. Her accent was that

affected, more than snobby Brit tone. Freddie talks that way when he puts someone down.

"Good morning," I replied.

Her cheeks were red from the chill, and I saw a blond braid trailing from under her riding helmet. Blue eyes like sapphires.

All at once, I was warm. And tingly. I hadn't looked that way at a woman for a long time. I'd stayed celibate for years, but this woman had instantly stirred me.

I knew I had to be careful. In Sasana, the homosexuality laws are focused mainly on men, but that would mean nothing to some. I reined in my rising lust.

"Sorry, have I crossed onto the Uxfield Estate?" she asked. Her smile was beautiful, her teeth surprisingly well-kept for a Brit.

"I'm afraid you have, yes."

"Oh," she replied, her smile brighter. "You're Irish?"

"I am."

"I absolutely love that accent. Always have. Where in Ireland are you from?"

"Dublin, but I've lived in Sasana . . . In England for some time."

"Do you work for the Earl?"

"No. I'm companion to his wife. She and I have been friends since we were children, like sisters."

"Oh, how lovely." The smile inverted, and she continued, "I'd have loved to have had a sister. All I have are brothers. Three of them. They ignore me, thank God." The smile returned. "I'm so rude. I'm Virginia Cooper-Woodson. The baron's my father. He ignores me, too, especially since I turned down all the rich men he hoped to marry me off to."

She laughed, sultry and inviting. My lust inched up a bit more.

"I'm Aifric O'Saidh-Brennan," I told her.

"Aifric? What an interesting name. Irish, I assume?"

"It is. It means pleasant."

"How lovely. I didn't know the Irish used hyphenated names."

"O'Saidh women don't like surrendering their names. A lot of hyphenations in the family."

Another laugh, low and sensual; I wasn't mistaking that. It sent a shock through my body.

"Does your husband live here with you?" Virginia asked.

Curiosity or a pointed question?

"I'm not married."

"Oh, sorry again. What you said about your hyphenated name . . . I assumed . . ."

"That's my mother's hyphenated name. I went by Brennan, my father's name, for a while, because he's a wonderful man. I decided I liked being an O'Saidh, too."

"Understandable. Do you ride often? I believe I've

seen you a few times."

That definitely sounded as if she might want another accidental meeting.

"Several times a month. The earl and countess travel a great deal. When they're away, I need to occupy my time."

"Oh, you don't travel with them?"

"On occasion. Sometimes they want to get away to themselves, have some privacy."

And, damn it, I took that moment to blush. This damned lust. My fault for suppressing it for so long.

"Totally understand," Virginia said. "My brothers and their wives are forever in the south of France, but I suspect that's more to escape my father's badgering them about heirs. God, Englishmen and their legacy obsessions. I'm quite tired of the badgering as well, though mine's about getting married. I'm stuck here with dear old pa. He's beginning to panic because, gasp, I'm thirty-one."

I hadn't actively pursued a relationship for so long I wasn't certain of the cue words to use to test if Virginia had any interest in me. I didn't want to be wrong and send her galloping back to daddy and tattling.

Now or never, Aifric, I told myself.

"It's quite colder than I anticipated," I said.

"That it is."

"Why don't we ride to the manor house for some

tea?"

She prodded her horse until it was parallel to mine. Our knees brushed, and she didn't move hers away. Her smile this time made me throb down below.

"I'd love to have some tea," she whispered. "Shall we ride on?"

I led the way and kicked my horse into a gallop, one that Virginia easily kept up with.

Virginia oohed and aahed at the great monstrosity of a house, the art on the walls, and the historical artifacts on display. Freddie always said the house was more suited as a museum than a home.

After tea and biscuits, I offered to give Virginia a tour of the house. She was the one who asked to see my room.

It was a cliche, but we shared a cigarette after.

"Does anyone know about you?" Virginia asked, expelling smoke before handing me the cigarette.

"Only two people. Both are trustworthy. Don't worry."

"For now, could we keep this between us? I know my father doesn't socialize with the earl. Rather, it's more the other way 'round. I wouldn't socialize with my father unless I had to, and I have to. I'd rather not risk . . . this. Losing this, that is."

"Why can't you live on your own?" I asked.

She took the cigarette back and took a long drag, staring at the ceiling.

"Aifric, I glossed over my relationship with my father. When I was seventeen, my father caught me and a maid together. Fired her, poor thing, even though I'd seduced her. No references. That bothered me, still does, because it was my fault. Anyway, my father took me to a psychiatrist, who diagnosed me with a sexual deviancy, meaning I was crazy. That's what it says in the medical books. Homosexual equals insane."

She smoked some more, and her eyes filled with tears.

"What happened?" I asked her.

"Dear old pater dispatched me to a loony bin. There . . . They did things . . . to me."

"Jesus Wept, what do you mean?"

"They'd make me watch pornography, men and women having sex, but that excited me because of the women. Next, they gave me drugs that made me vomit while they showed me pictures of naked women in suggestive positions, but I was still aroused. So, they'd give me electric shock treatments."

"Good God, I've never heard of such a thing."

"It's called aversion therapy, and it's something I never want to experience again."

She gave me the cigarette and turned on her side to face me.

"That's why I want to be careful, not because I'm ashamed. When I was finally discharged from that hellish hospital, it was on condition that I live on the estate with my father. I had to register with the police as a sexual deviant, but my father managed to suppress any scandal. So, to the world, I'm Baron Cooper-Woodson's old maid daughter."

I put out the burnt-down cigarette in the ashtray by my bed.

"I've never heard of this aversion therapy," I said, "but it sounds horrible."

"It is. It's mostly used on men. You see, in Britain, homosexuality is illegal only for men, not women. If you're a lesbian, you must be crazy and a sexual deviant. I guess I was somewhat of a guinea pig for testing whether that therapy worked on women. I did hear the doctors debating whether it would work on women."

"Obviously, it didn't work on you," I said.

"Oh, it did for quite some time. For years, actually. I can't help but think this is, you know, born into me, that I can't stop it. I don't want to stop it, but I also don't want to go back to that hospital."

"We'll have to be careful," I said, but I suspected what she really meant. "I mean, unless you want only this one time."

She embraced me. "Aifric, I want this to go on forever, but, yes, we'll have to be extremely careful."

"There are plenty of tenant houses on the estate. Cait—that's the countess—would let us use one of them."

"She knows about you?"

"For years now. She doesn't care about it, I assure you."

"Still, if my father caught me coming onto Uxfield Estate . . . We have an old hunting lodge in what forest is left on my father's property. He doesn't hunt anymore, and neither do my brothers. It's a bit run down, so he doesn't rent it. We could clean it up a bit, make it comfortable. We could use that. It's quite well-hidden. It'll be perfect."

"Freddie . . . The earl said your father was a stickler about trespassing."

"He is, but you can reach the lodge easily. It's only a few meters from a corner of Uxfield. I'll show you which direction to use so you'll be out of sight of anyone on either estate. There's even a small shed where we can hide the horses. This can work, that is . . . If you want to take the chance."

"Nothing will happen to me, but are you sure you want to take the chance? You're the one with every-thing to lose," I told her.

"But I also stand to gain a lot," Virginia said and kissed me.

2002

Mount Vernon, Virginia

Aifric had filled a diary a month between January through April of 1957. The entries in April ended with an abruptness that cued the analyst in Mai to speculate. She knew from Roisin that Aifric had died in late April of that year, but the diaries had given no indication she was ill. Indeed, she was deep in the bliss of love.

An accident, perhaps? A fall from the horse she liked to ride?

Not likely. From Aifric's mentions of riding with Mai's mother, it seemed Aifric was an excellent equestrienne.

Some sudden illness, then. A stroke or a heart attack? Men often had heart attacks in the midst of sex, but Mai didn't know the statistics for women. Knowing the sexism in the medical culture, she doubted if anyone had studied that.

Aifric had noted every one of her and Virginia's meetings at the hunting lodge. No steamy details, but it was apparent the two women were falling in love. What the diaries showed was utter, complete happiness.

Aifric had written in her final diary entry on April 28:

> I can't wait to tell Cait. She and Freddie are due back the first week of July, but I'll be long gone by then. I know she will be happy for me. She'll understand why Ginny and I are leaving to go far away and have a life together. I know she'll understand, and I know she'll keep our secret from Mam and Ginny's father.
>
> I have so much to look forward to at last. I've seen

Cait's happiness with Freddie. I hope Ginny and I can have half as much.

She'd put no details in writing—smart woman—but obviously, she and Ginny had done something other than have wild monkey sex in the hunting lodge. They'd planned their escape.

Such optimism and hope, only to have it end at Aifric's death.

Had Virginia backed out last minute? Had Aifric been so distraught that she'd . . .?

Fisher, she thought, you're a bleeding spy; you can find this out.

Ah, but Eithne O'Saidh was still Katherine Maitland's business manager in 1957, and Aifric was her older daughter. The answer lay in Eithne's diaries.

After they'd returned from Dublin, Alexei had taken the bulky wooden crates they'd secreted from Roisin's house down to the basement storage room. Mai hoped they'd be easy to find, that Alexei hadn't organized them there in some obscure spot known only to him.

For once he hadn't been anal about the storage room. The crates were against the wall to the left of the door. Four of Eithne's diaries covered 1957, and Mai took all four back up to the office and locked them in her desk drawer.

30

GOOD TO BE HOME

July 3, 1957

Uxfield Manor
Sussex, England

When her husband turned left between the massive stone pillars, Katherine Maitland-Fisher relaxed at last. They rounded the sweeping curve of the driveway, and Uxfield Manor in all its Tudor-Stewart-Georgian-Victorian-Edwardian hodgepodge hove into sight.

Katherine smiled. "Oh, it feels so good to be home," she said, laying a hand on her husband's thigh.

"Yes, nothing's quite like the sight of home, is it? We were away too long, I think. I'm going to insist on a bit of a break," said Frederick Fisher.

Perfect, she thought, but said, "The first thing I want right now is a decent *cupan tae*."

Somehow, she'd have to find a way to tell the butler to make hers mint tea to settle her stomach. She'd managed to hide the nausea from Freddie, and she didn't want to say anything to him until she could confirm what she'd suspected for a couple of weeks. Once confirmed, yes, she would insist, demand, require a break from the spy game for at least a year.

Freddie stopped the Phantom IV before the oversized, double front doors. He was out of the car at the boot when Tennyson the butler dashed from the house to assist. First, he opened the door for Katherine then took two of the larger suitcases from the boot.

"Welcome home, my lord, my lady," Tennyson said.

"Thanks, Tenny," Freddie said. "It's grand to be back. Everything running smoothly here?"

Tennyson's eyes flicked to Katherine, and he lowered his voice. "The estate is in fine shape. I'll ring the agent right away and tell him you're home."

"Not for a few hours, Tenny. I need to put my feet up for a while. Long flights, you know."

Katherine looked at the now-open doors, expected to see Affie any moment. God, she'd missed Affie. Katherine was the rare female operative, and though she seldom had trouble with her male colleagues, she missed the presence of women. Plus, she had this possible good news to share. Affie was like her sister, and Freddie would understand a sister, a woman, had precedence over a husband.

Eithne O'Saidh, dressed in black, though that wasn't unusual, stepped from the shadows inside into the sunshine.

Freddie came to Katherine's side as Tennyson and a couple of footmen lugged the suitcases inside.

"What is she doing here?" Freddie murmured.

"I don't know. Some slight of mine or Affie's, no doubt." She looked up at her husband and smiled. "Shall we find out or jump back in the car and speed off?"

"My little coward," Freddie said, kissing her forehead. "Let's go face the music."

Eithne had stepped aside for Tennyson to enter and now preceded Katherine and Freddie into the house. She stood in the foyer, grim and stark against the sumptuous decor there. Katherine frowned; she could make out Eithne's red-rimmed, exhausted eyes.

"This is a surprise, Eithne," Katherine said. "How long have you been here?"

"Since the first of May," Eithne said, reaching for the gloves and hat Katherine had removed and her purse.

"What? Since May. Where's Affie?" Katherine looked around and called out, "Affie, darling, we're home!"

Eithne winced as if in pain and said, "I need to speak with you. In private."

"Let's go into the library, then," Freddie said. He turned to Tennyson, who was always available when needed. "I'm bloody dying for some tea, Tenny. Bring tea for the three of us to the library, will you?"

"Right away, sir."

Freddie led the way to the library. As Tennyson passed her, Katherine murmured, "Mint tea for me, Tenny."

"Of course, my lady."

Eithne looked at Freddie's retreating back. "I said privately."

"Whatever you have to say to me can be said in my husband's presence. I've made that clear. Several times," Katherine replied.

Eithne took a rumpled handkerchief from a pocket of her austere jacket and dabbed at her nose. "Of course, Cait."

Katherine headed for the library, Eithne trailing her.

Katherine loved this room, the expanse of it, the ceiling so tall, you needed the rolling ladder to reach the top shelves, the floor-to-ceiling French doors that looked out on the English garden, and the smell of new books and old. She even liked the rusting set of armor tucked away in a corner, the set belonging to the first Earl of Uxfield. A telescope stood before one of the French doors, an antique one. She'd teased Freddie that his family must have appropriated it from Isaac Newton.

"Too bad it's too bloody hot for a fire," Freddie said. "I missed a good, roaring fire." He went to one of a set of love seats perpendicular to the fireplace and stood waiting for the women to sit.

Katherine sat on the love seat with Freddie, and Eithne lowered herself to the one opposite, perched on the cushion's front edge.

"Now, Eithne," Freddie said, smiling, "what's the news, as the Yanks say."

Eithne twisted her handkerchief around her fingers, her eyes on the floor. She said nothing.

Katherine's patience had ebbed. "Eithne, where is Affie?"

"Affie . . ." Eithne brought the handkerchief to her mouth but not soon enough to stifle a sob.

Freddie rose and went to her. "What is it, Eithne? You're white as a sheet. Shall I have Tenny call the doctor?"

"No, no," she said, waving him away. "Give me a second. Sit."

As he resumed his seat, Freddie and Katherine exchanged an inquiring look, and Katherine lifted a shoulder in a shrug. Freddie took her hand.

A dab at each eye, a deep breath, and Eithne seemed composed. When she happened to glance at the set of fireplace tools, she seemed to pale even more. She looked at Katherine.

"Affie . . . Aifric has left us," Eithne murmured.

"What?" Freddie said. "She quit?"

"No. She . . . She died. At the end of April."

Katherine squeezed Freddie's hand and took deep, quiet

breaths to calm her heart rate. She would not let this shock bring on a miscarriage.

"Eithne, what happened? Was she ill?" Katherine managed to ask and started to shake.

Unshed tears filled Eithne's eyes. "No. *Du'nmhara'iodh i'.*"

"What?" Freddie asked.

"She was murdered," Katherine translated.

Freddie's other hand closed over Katherine's. "Bloody Hell! Pardon me. Here? In this house?"

Eithne shook her head, and tears coursed down her cheeks. Katherine had never seen Eithne weep, and to see it now was unsettling. However, Katherine also needed to understand what had happened.

"Eithne, pull yourself together and tell me everything," Katherine said. "I need to how this has happened."

"I did, too, when Tennyson phoned me with the news. That's why I'm here. The investigation and the inquest took some time."

A knock, and the library door opened. Tennyson entered bearing a tray with two tea pots, one large and one mid-size, three cups and saucers, and milk.

Freddie squeezed Katherine's hand and rose as Tennyson set the tray on a table between the two love seats.

"Thanks, Tenny. I'll be mother, if you don't mind."

"Of course, sir." Tennyson pointed to the smaller pot. "Earl Gray for you, sir. Mint tea for the ladies."

"Yes, thanks, Tenny, and I'll need to speak to you later," Freddie said, an eyebrow raised.

Tennyson gave a knowing nod and said, "Ring when you're ready for me, sir." He left quickly, closing the door behind him.

Freddie poured the mint tea first, both women waving off the milk. He handed a cup to Eithne first then to Katherine. Katherine kept herself from gasping when Eithne's cup rattled against the saucer from the woman's shaking. Eithne braced the cup and saucer on her knees, holding them with both hands, and the rattling ceased.

Freddie sat close to Katherine again, with his cup of Earl Gray, white, in hand.

After a sip or two, Katherine said, "Eithne, please, tell me what happened. I insist."

Eithne looked away. "If only Aifric had controlled her . . . unnatural urges, this wouldn't have happened."

"What unnatural urges?" Freddie asked.

"Freddie, Affie is . . . Affie was a lesbian, remember?" Katherine said.

"You knew?" Eithne said, looking at Katherine.

"Yes. She told me years ago, and what does that have to do with anything?"

"It has to do with everything."

"Eithne, start explaining. *Now.*"

"She met a woman from an adjoining estate. Another . . ." Eithne's face screwed into an expression of disgust. "Lesbian."

"Not the Cooper-Woodson Estate?" Freddie asked. Eithne nodded. "So, the gossip from a decade or so back was true."

"I remember," Katherine said. "Not one of his servants?"

"No," said Eithne. "His daughter, Virginia. The two of them had been sneaking off to a hunting lodge on Cooper-Woodson's property for their . . ." Eithne's lips twisted, and she didn't finish the sentence. "That's where he caught them. In bed. Doing . . . things to each other, and he, and he . . ." A deep breath and Eithne straightened from hunching over. "He took up a poker from the fireplace and beat Aifric to death."

Katherine wanted to vomit and not only because she might be pregnant.

"I trust the bastard is in jail right now," Freddie said, his tone one Katherine recognized as angry.

Eithne shook her head. "The local constabulary did an investigation and had an inquest, as I said. They tried to make me use an English lawyer, but I informed them my law degree from Trinity was effective here. I questioned the bastard and his betraying daughter myself. But it seems that the daughter had been cured of her deviant condition some years before. A doctor testified and provided the medical records. The daughter testified that several months back, Aifric had lured her to the lodge and forced her to 'return to deviance.' The baron testified he was simply protecting his daughter, and his lawyer had his personal physician testify that his heightened emotions and obvious distress justified his actions. They found Aifric's death a 'justifiable homicide.'"

"What?" Katherine and Freddie blurted together.

"Bloody hell," Freddie continued, "what a time for class entitlement to rear its shaggy head. Old Joe likely bribed the coroner."

"The detective who investigated protested, and I said I would sue the Baron, so the coroner and his lawyer worked out that he'd spend thirty days on house arrest. His lawyer said that was punishment enough because Aifric was 'only an Irish queer.' He was also told to make restitution to me of one hundred thousand pounds immediately. I informed the coroner I'd be taking none of the bastard's English blood money."

Eithne's fingers were so tight on the tea cup, Katherine feared she might shatter it. She looked at Katherine, her eyes pleading.

"Cait, why? Why couldn't she stop herself from doing such disgusting things?"

"What do her diaries say?" Katherine asked. "Was this a one-time relationship, or were they serious about each other?"

"What does that matter?"

"It matters, Eithne. I won't have you slander her in this house. What did her diaries say?"

"That she was . . . in love, of all things. How is something like that even possible?"

"It's possible. What else?"

"It was obvious the girl was a willing participant, and Aifric and the girl were making plans to run off together."

"Girl?" Freddie said. "Hardly a girl. Virginia Cooper-Woodson is thirty or more. Is the bastard still on house arrest? I'm going to have a word with him. At once."

"No, Freddie," Katherine said. "Don't do that." She gave him a look she knew he'd understand: Not now but later. She looked at Eithne. "As for why, Eithne, Aifric was in love, and yes, that can happen. I learned from someone I worked with in the war that you don't choose to be homosexual. That person once said to me, 'Why would I choose a life of rejection and disdain? Why would I choose to love someone when it's a crime?' This is who Aifric was, and the real indignation here is that a man murdered her for being who she truly was. Not to mention her fecking murderer got away with it."

For now, she added in her thoughts.

"I trust you buried her here on the estate," Freddie said.

Eithne shook her head. "In her will, she indicated she wanted cremation, and I acceded to her wishes. I have her . . . I have her ashes with me. I will take her home when I go."

Katherine lowered her head, almost undone by knowing Affie would have no headstone, no place Katherine could go and mourn a beloved sister. Cooper-Woodson had taken Aifric not only from her mother but from Katherine, and too bad the baron didn't know Katherine was far more dangerous.

"Freddie," Katherine said, setting her empty cup on the tray, "why don't you go have your talk with Tenny? I'll sit here with Eithne a while."

"Of course, darling," he said. He kissed her temple and whispered, "I'm so sorry, darling. I know what she meant to you." He rose and stood before Eithne. "Mrs. Brennan, allow me to express my sincerest condolences and my deepest outrage for the brutal death of your daughter. She was an essential part of Katherine's and my lives, and she will be sorely, sorely missed. Should you require anything of me, madam, you shall have it."

He bowed his head to her and left.

When they were alone, Katherine came to sit beside Eithne, placing an arm around her shoulders. Eithne had drunk none of her tea. It was likely cold now, and Katherine pried the cup and saucer from Eithne's grip and set it on the tray.

"Eithne, I know it's difficult for you to understand who Aifric was, but I won't hear you blame her again. The baron did this, and despite what the coroner said, he's to blame for what he did. He murdered her from hate, from lack of understanding."

Eithne slumped again, and Katherine did understand the woman's grief. Each of her own miscarriages and stillbirths, Katherine had felt as deeply as the death of a fully formed child. She understood how Eithne felt.

Eithne sniffed, dabbed at her nose, and stiffened her spine. "Roisin is not quite ready to assume my duties, but I can send her here as companion within the week. She can finish her law studies here."

"No, no need to send her to me. Aifric stayed past my twenty-fifth birthday because I wanted her here. You need to go home, grieve with Aifric's father and the rest of your family."

"Mr. Brennan came over, you know," Eithne murmured. "Stoic he was during the inquest, but he cried like a baby here."

"Still, you need to go home. I need to grieve myself. Aifric was my sister in every way except blood, and I'll need time to accept I have to live without her." Eithne only nodded. "I should think some time next year, Roisin can come here. One more thing. How soon can Sister Moyna arrive?"

Eithne turned to face Katherine, a smile trembling on her mouth. "Is it . . .? Are you . . .?"

"I think so. I'm fairly certain, but I'd like Sister Moyna to confirm it. If I am, I'll take the advice she provided the last time and take to my bed. I would, however, like her here for the duration of the pregnancy. Dr. Coolley was quite impressed with her knowledge and would be glad to work with her."

"I'll have her here within the week," Eithne said, smiling broadly now. "Oh, Cait, I have a feeling about this one."

"Actually, I do, too, and within ten days would be better. Plenty of time to have rooms prepared for her."

And for me to take care of something, Katherine thought.

31

PLAYING THE GAME

1991

Unknown Location

Katherine Maitland-Fisher knew how this all worked. No set schedule of interrogations. The subject had to be kept off guard, insecure. She'd already decided she'd play "Sergei's" game.

Still, she was annoyed when he showed up on a day she felt absolutely awful. For two days, she'd kept little food down, almost the way it was when she was pregnant with Mattie. Of course, the only things growing inside her now were tumors that she could feel pressing against her stomach, her lungs.

She could tolerate the pain; it was no worse than what she'd endured in a Taiwanese prison or a Chinese reeducation camp. What she disliked was the general malaise and lack of desire to do anything except lie in her bed and die.

In a way, Sergei's unannounced entrance was a welcome break

in the monotony. By her calculation, uncertain as it was, he hadn't been here for three weeks.

"Ah, Sergei," she greeted him. "I trust you had a pleasant journey to wherever we are. I'm debating whether it's the Alps or the Rocky Mountains."

No flicker of recognition in the unyielding expression. He was good; she'd give him that.

"I'd offer you some tea, like a proper hostess, but, as you can see, I don't have the means to do that," she continued.

He said nothing and studied her in that disinterested way he had.

Katherine tossed her covers away and sat on the side of the bed. She was constantly cold, even though the room's temperature should have warmed her, and she'd slept in her robe. She pushed her feet into her slippers and rose, slowly so she wouldn't feel light-headed, another recent annoyance. She took the few steps from the bed to the table, managing not to lose her balance. After she sat, Sergei came to the table and again sat opposite her.

"I was told you demanded pen and paper," he said.

"I made no such demand. I *requested* pen and paper. I was told no."

"Why did you want that?"

"I thought if I began to write down what I remembered, along the line of the questions you've already asked, I'd have to see less of youse. After the nurse/guard refused, I offered to dictate, but that's not allowed either. So, I now assume that you returned because you enjoy my company so much."

Again, nothing.

"I simply thought it would be more efficient if I wrote down or dictated useful information, though after all these years, its usefulness is questionable. We are on a short timetable."

"How so?" he asked.

"I'm dying, and today I'm not feeling particularly chipper. I may have to lie down again in a bit."

"You can talk lying down."

"You are a fecking cold bastard, aren't you?" There. A flicker of something in his eyes. She'd hurt him with that, though he'd covered it well. "That bothered you," Katherine said. "Didn't it?"

He didn't move; his face remained expressionless. "Let's review the scant detail you have provided thus far on the procedures at your reeducation camp," he said. "You mentioned drugs. What were your physical reactions to those drugs?"

"Ah, I see. You think you can identify them from the effects. Let me back up a bit. They didn't use drugs at first. At the very beginning, they treated the injuries from my torture in Taiwan and allowed me to recover. I had to take a pill twice a day with food, and I suspect that was a course of antibiotics. I'd had a fever when I arrived. I don't recall any particular effects from the drugs, other than my fever abated and several of my wounds, which had shown signs of infection, had cleared."

Katherine's eyes narrowed as she looked out the window, deep in thought.

"They did all the usual things to soften me up for the 'curriculum,' as it were. Fed me plenty of nourishing food. Let me sleep. Gave me water, soap, and towels. Clean clothing. I'm not sure how long that went on. Long enough to lull me into a sense of complacency. So, it was a shock when they changed the process."

"Describe that."

"Why should I? You're obviously a seasoned interrogator. You know exactly what they did."

"Indulge me."

"Really, you are becoming rather tiresome, but very well. I was stripped naked. Not allowed to sleep. Food and water withheld. Over-stimulated with discordant noise. Sexual assault. You must have an awfully good memory. You haven't taken a note of anything I've said. Or, are we being recorded?"

"You know better than to ask," Sergei replied.

"You forget, I've had the same training as you to evade answering questions. You should expect these abrupt changes of subject."

"And you should expect to be punished for that."

"And I could give a fuck, me boyo."

"Did you answer the questions put to you at the reeducation camp?" he asked.

"We've already discussed this."

"Answer my question."

"I responded to them much in the same way I'm responding to you. That's why I was there so bloody long, long enough I decided to stop resisting. When I started to regurgitate Mao, things changed, became better. That's when the drugs started. No injections. No more pills, so I suspect my food, what I got of it, was laced. I would eat, and within minutes, I felt detached from my body. My surroundings would spin. One time, I thought everything around me was melting, disintegrating. I do remember at the time I thought it was LSD. I recalled that the CIA had experimented with it some years before. Were you KGB-trained?"

"Stay on subject," was Sergei's reply. "How often do you think they gave you mind-altering drugs?"

"It seemed like weeks and weeks, but later Fan told me it was only days. I didn't believe him, though. I was in a constant state of un-reality for a long time. The doctors, my interrogators, the guards, Fan, none of them looked human. They were monsters, nightmares, but I could always recognize Fan. He was always there, suggesting things, telling them to change my therapy. That's what they called it. Therapy."

"How long did they continue the LSD therapy?"

"I just told you, it felt like weeks, but I have no idea how long it was. I had no concept of time."

"Women have ways of measuring time," Sergei said.

"You mean menstruation? Sergei, I'd always had irregular periods. By this time, however, I was forty-three and in early menopause. I had no way to measure how long the drug therapy lasted. Again, it could have been days, like Fan said, but it could also have been weeks, months. I do know I had flashbacks."

"Any other mood-altering effect you can remember?"

"No, I . . . Wait. Yes, I remember they did give me an injection one time. I felt . . . It's difficult to describe. I felt compliant, obedient, that I'd do anything asked of me. Yes, yes, one of the doctors told me to hop on my left foot with my right arm raised, and I felt compelled to do that, that if I didn't do it something awful would happen. More than compelled. I wanted to do it."

The rest of the memory rushed in: Fan telling her to fellate him, telling her to masturbate, all with the doctors watching to see if the drug worked.

"What?" Sergei said. "What are you remembering?"

No, she could not share that with him. The humiliation would be too much.

"Sergei, I need to lie down," Katherine murmured.

"Go ahead."

"Please. Help me to the bed."

He laughed, a mocking sound, like the doctors and guards and Fan had.

"And have you attempt an attack? Stop playing the femme fatale with me," he said.

"This is no game, you bastard. I'm fecking dying. I can't keep down food. If I try to walk to that bed, I'll drop."

He rose, went to the door, and knocked, a different pattern this time. The door opened, and Katherine heard him murmuring with the nurse/guard. Their voices were muffled, as if they spoke through layer after layer of wool.

Katherine used the table to lever herself to her feet. Her vision tunneled, white at the edges. Then red. Then black.

EVEN THOUGH HE took the woman's unconscious body from the floor, Alexei had to be convinced she wasn't faking it. From the doorway, he watched as the medical team assessed. They started a saline drip for dehydration. A heart monitor, blood pressure cuff, and an oximeter were attached, and a monitor rolled in to show her vitals, erratic as they were.

Once Leana, whom the woman had referred to as the nurse/guard, was satisfied the woman was stable, she and Alexei left for Leana's office. Neither a nurse nor a guard, Leana was a doctor trained in handling special prisoners.

Once inside, she turned to Alexei and said, "This is progressing faster than I anticipated."

"Or she's faking."

Leana shook her head in frustration. "She's not. The emesis has been nearly constant now. This isn't the first time in three weeks we've had to put her on an IV. The next step would be a feeding tube and anti-nausea medication, but the feeding tube would only prolong her death, not her life."

"Is she making herself throw up?"

"No! I monitor her visually, per your instructions. She is deteriorating rapidly. I suggest you get what you can out of her soon. She may last only one or two more sessions. Perhaps not even that before she's in a coma she won't emerge from. Alexei, what you're getting from her is outdated, useless. What is the point of this? Why are you being so . . .?"

"So what?"

"Mean to her, so cruel."

"She could be an enemy agent, given the fact she's been in Communist China for nearly thirty years. She has quite possibly betrayed the Directorate," he replied. "We have to determine the extent of the damage. And I'm treating her no different from how I've treated any other enemy agent."

"Surely any betrayal would have revealed itself thirty years ago in compromised operations?"

No response.

"Alexei, this so-called interrogation seems like punishment to me," Leana said. "I know of Nelson's charm and yours, but I also know you both have a mean streak, especially you. An enemy agent kidnapped that woman—"

"So she says," Alexei interrupted, though he knew Leana was right. He, after all, was aware of Yazhu Fan's missive to Nigel Hume, but Fan and Katherine Maitland could have cooked that up between them.

He could see as well Leana's distress for a patient.

"Leana, she could have gone willingly with him, leaving her husband to be executed and abandoning her child. You can't convince me she resisted questioning for twenty-seven years. She betrayed something. It could be small and insignificant but have serious ramifications later. That's the point of this."

"No, the point is you're reacting much like the KGB officer you were. You're using her as an example."

"No, she won't be marched in front of our new recruits and executed, Leana."

"She's dying. Why imprison her here? Why badger her?"

"Before she dies, she will understand what her defection did to the people she left behind."

"Alexei, you don't know she defected."

"And you don't know she didn't."

"If that's the case, what will happen to her?"

"That will be my decision."

"I'm a doctor. I will not participate in murdering my patient."

He looked at Leana. He'd known her a long time, shared a bed with her once years ago. But that was the past.

"I accept that," he said. "It doesn't have to involve you, but you're right. The sooner I get this over with, the better. Let me back inside."

"No. I will not let you back in there to kill her. She may be a traitor to the Directorate, but I am her doctor."

"All I want to do is sit with her until she wakes, and I can resume the questioning."

Leana took a step closer to him, hands on her hips.

"I'll be watching."

"No. You know the rules. No monitoring while I'm with her. Don't worry. I'm not in the habit of killing old women."

32

FILLING A NEED

Katherine opened her eyes but slowly. She heard a soft beep, beep, beep and realized it synched to the pulse she could feel at her neck. Pain in one hand also throbbed in time to her pulse, and she raised the hand that felt as if it weighed a stone.

An IV needle, held fast with surgical tape.

She let her hand fall to the bed, and she closed her eyes.

"No, no," she murmured.

"No, what?" said a man.

A familiar voice. Not Fan, thank God. Not Freddie, unless ghosts were real. Ah, yes, of course. Sergei, her interrogator.

She opened her eyes again. He sat at the foot of the bed in one of the chairs from the table. His legs were crossed at the knee, left over right. His clasped hands, long fingers intertwined, rested on his thigh. That damned blank expression stared at her.

"Oh, it's you," she said. "Do you play piano? If not, you should take it up. You have the hands for it." Nothing. "I could always tell a KGB agent. It's those damned, soulless eyes," Katherine said.

"I'm not KGB. There is no KGB anymore."

"Perhaps not now, but you were." She smiled at him. "You slipped, finally. You gave me personal information."

"Not personal at all," he said. "Let's say, it was merely a professional acknowledgement."

"Did you like the KGB?"

One shoulder lifted in a shrug. "I suppose I did. Everything was clear cut, black and white. No gray areas. Why did you say 'no' when you woke?"

"The IV. I thought I was in the reeducation camp."

Damn. She'd given him an opening. Dying was a damned, inconvenient thing.

"Yes," he said, "you mentioned you'd have done anything not to return there. How far did you go? Did you bargain with Yazhu Fan? Save me, and I'll tell you everything?"

"No. I have explained this before, though I understand it's interrogation protocol to cover old ground. He removed me from Taiwan when I was sedated. I had no idea what had happened until I woke, and he told me I was in the People's Republic."

"Do you expect me to take your word for that?"

She laughed, stopped when it became painful, and replied, "If our roles were reversed, Sergei, I certainly wouldn't. Is that your real name?"

"How did you go from captured Directorate operative to one of the mainland's top interrogators?"

"Hardly the top interrogator. I filled a need. You see, the Cultural Revolution led to many arrests, lots of prisoners to interrogate before lots of executions or permanent exile to a reeducation camp. The Ministry of State Security was short-handed, and since Fan was the head of State Security, he used what resources he could find. Soldiers, former soldiers, me. He had to talk the government into it, stressing it would be safe to use me on 'graduates' of the reeducation camps to make certain they were loyal again. All under strict supervision."

"Fan's idea? Or yours?"

"I did not offer my services but took the opportunity."

"Why?"

"It would allow me time out of my house-prison, and by then, I had begun to have memory flashbacks. I needed a way to hide that I was remembering. I had to let them continue to think I'd absorbed every scrap of propaganda they'd fed me and that I still believed it. And in the beginning, I did believe it. They'd convinced me I was a tool of the capitalist elite to oppress the proletariat. I'm sure you were taught the same."

"Yes, but with a few differences. I never had to be reeducated because I'd never been a capitalist, and I left that world. You embraced it."

"Not of my free will."

"Again, so you say."

"Look, you insufferable bastard, my husband and I were married thirteen years before I had a successful pregnancy. Nothing except miscarriages and stillbirths before that. Do you honestly think, after all that pain and blood, I'd willingly abandon the child I worked so hard to have?"

He uncrossed his legs and leaned toward her, elbows braced on his knees.

"That's exactly what you did," he said, his inflection flat but damning, nonetheless.

"Not willingly!" she shouted.

Various alarms and alerts blared from the medical monitor. Katherine tried to sit, pain lancing from low on her left side. A tumor must not have liked being disturbed, but she didn't care. In the end, all she could raise was her head.

"I loved that child and her father more than my own life. I would have done anything to get back to her! Anything!"

"Yes, that's the point of all this. However, not once in almost thirty years did you try."

"I planned. I plotted. A few of those plans might have succeeded because I visualized them down to the tiniest detail. I had no opportunity to put any of them into motion. Fan made certain of that."

She rested her head back on the pillow, her eyes on the white ceiling. A memory made her smile.

"Mission planning brought Freddie and me together," she murmured. "When he was in SOE, I planned an operation for him. I didn't know it was him, of course, but after, he came to Bletchley to thank the person who'd delivered such a meticulous plan. He was pleasantly surprised to find the planner was a woman. He asked me to dinner, and we were rarely apart after that." She smiled at the memory.

"That ended badly for him, though," Sergei said. "Dying as he did in that Taiwanese cell."

"He chose to die. To save me. Fan had offered me that same choice, first. I begged him to free Freddie, that I would gladly die if it meant Freddie could return to our child."

Thirty years of anger, frustration, humiliation, and debasement pushed to be released.

"Fan saved me and let Freddie die!" she screamed. She kept screaming, pounding the mattress with her fists, the alarms on the medical monitor adding to the cacophony.

Sergei sat there, unmoved, unfazed. Uncaring.

Exhaustion and pain quieted her, and she lay panting until the pain eased and her heart rate returned to normal.

"Tell me," she murmured. "Tell me one thing, one small thing about her. Please."

Sergei stood, looming at the side of the bed. That expressionless face, she realized, was probably the last thing a great many people had seen before he'd killed them. So, do it, she thought.

"She needed her mother," he said and moved to leave.

"How could you possibly know that?"

He stopped, turned to look at her once more. "She told me."

"Why? Why would she tell you of all people?"

He smiled at her, that smile crueler than any Fan had given her, worse than Fan's smile when he'd raped her.

"I told you her husband decided that she didn't need to know you lived."

The realization grew in her thoughts. "Yes," she whispered and held her breath.

"*I decided* that."

He went to the door, pounded on it this time. When it opened and he slipped from the room, Katherine tried to call to him, but she had no voice.

ALONE IN LEANA'S OFFICE, Alexei once more called Nelson on the secure line.

"It's the middle of the night here. Again," Nelson answered.

"I may not have been the right person for this," Alexei said.

"Why?"

"I let her get to me, make me angry. All that simpering about missing her child and how she plotted and planned to return to her. It was too much. I slipped and told her I'm Mai's husband."

"Well, that could work in our favor. Use Mai as a dangle."

"No. We agreed she'd know nothing about this."

"Dangle her, but that doesn't mean you have to produce her."

After a moment's consideration, Alexei said, "Good point. However, the subject's physical condition is deteriorating faster than expected, per Leana."

"Yeah, pancreatic cancer is that way. My father had it. He'd be fine for weeks then crash. The final crash, he went in days, well short of the time the doctors had predicted. Okay, honest opinion time. Are we getting anything useful from her? Because my read of your reports says no."

"Not really. Leana brought this up today. If the subject had betrayed any Directorate operations after her capture or after arriving in the People's Republic, the organization would have known almost immediately. Now, she's been out of the loop for decades. She remembers only the vaguest of details about the reeducation camp, and everything she has told me is so far out of date as to be meaningless."

"All right, take a break and come home. You and I will discuss the end game for this. It might be useful to know if she interrogated any other westerners besides Terrell. To ensure her cooperation, give her something small about Mai. A photo maybe."

"I don't know . . ."

"Alexei, the woman's dying. Show her a picture of her adult daughter and be done with it."

A sigh and Alexei said, "Leana accused me, and you, of punishing the woman. Is that what we're doing?"

"If you're one hundred percent convinced she left with Fan willingly and defected to the Chinese, she deserves to be punished. However, showing her what she had and perhaps willingly gave up I would think would be punishment enough. Don't you?"

Nelson hung up.

33

WELCOME TO THE DUNGEON

1991

Directorate Headquarters

Alexei Bukharin shook himself from his distraction when someone knocked on his office door. He looked up to see Mai, and Katherine Maitland's face at the same time. The resemblance was unmistakeable, as Terrell had said.

He smiled at her and said, "A bright spot in my otherwise dreary and dull day."

She rolled her eyes but laughed. "I was wondering if you wanted to pick Natalia up from school or shall I? I thought you might since you have to leave again tomorrow."

"Yes, I'll get her." He looked at his watch. "I won't have to leave for at least an hour and a half. We've both been in briefings all day. Sit and chat a bit."

She sat at the chair beside his desk, facing him, her expression somewhat wary.

"This trip will be my last session with the subject," he said.

"Milked him for all he's worth, have you?" she asked.

He hadn't corrected her when she'd first used a male pronoun for the nameless subject.

"Pretty much."

"Have you encountered an impasse with him?"

"Why do you ask?"

"Because you've been rather distracted since you returned from the last session."

"No problems or impasses. I'm bored with the process. I'd rather be home, in *our* house, with you and Natalia."

"Yes, well, don't overdose on domestic bliss. You'll come to find it confining."

"Confining," he echoed. "What do you mean?"

"Hearth and home. Raising a child." She lifted an eyebrow. "Fidelity. Eventually, you'll feel trapped."

"If that's the trap, snare me in it."

"Don't joke, Alexei. I'm being serious."

So she was, but this damned insecurity of hers—never about her work, always about her life, their life together. The fear that someone else she cared for would leave her or stop loving her.

More of Katherine Maitland's doing.

"Mai, I want this," he said. "Our home, Natalia. Maybe, soon, a baby of our own. I've never had my own home, and I embrace what we're establishing."

"For how long?"

"Forever. Hold me to that."

She nodded, looking away for a moment then back.

"After you finish this defector's debriefing, the priority is to find a nanny. I'm tired of analyzing, tired of monitoring ops, tired of you being away so often," Mai said.

"I know. Break down and have Roisin send a nanny."

"No, I'd like to do something on my own for a change where she's concerned. So, when your debrief mission is over, we, as in, you and I, start to research. We know people in other intel agencies who have children. Maybe a spies' nanny agency is out there somewhere. However, I must insist no attractive young women."

Alexei smiled. "Why would I want that when I have you?"

"Ah, on cue. The renowned Bukharin charm."

"How much will I have to use to induce you to have us work on making that baby tonight before I leave?"

"A spectacular send-off for your business trip is a possibility."

They laughed at that together. That had happened more frequently lately, and he liked that, too.

She rose from the chair, and he stood, too.

"So," she said, "I have to go monitor yet another operation. Be still, my heart."

"I'll see you at home. I'll practice being charming."

Her crooked smile was endearing, and she kissed his cheek before she left.

He checked his watch again. Yes, he had plenty of time to take care of something.

ALEXEI BUKHARIN WAS a rare visitor to the Directorate's Information Technology domain. Nathan Hempstead, head of InfoTech, always considered him a welcome one. Unlike some older operatives, Alexei had embraced computer tech in espionage and was a quick learner.

When Alexei darkened the door of Nathan's office, Nathan greeted him with, "Yo, my man. Welcome to the Dungeon."

Nathan's hackers and coders referred to their space as the Dungeon, an appropriate name since the Directorate was underground and InfoTech was on one of the lower levels. Alexei thought it was more likely because of the ongoing *Dungeons and Dragons* game that took place there.

"What can I do for you?" Nathan asked when Alexei said nothing."

"Are you familiar with a Sony Mavica video recorder?"

"Sure am. Sony sent me a couple of prototypes a year or so back. I had a station test them for covert work. Good quality video, but even though it's hand-held, still too big and too conspicuous. Why?"

"Mai and I got Natalia one for her birthday."

"Uh, isn't that, like, not advisable, dude? A video recorder in a spy's house in the hands of a mercurial teenager?"

"Not quite a teenager yet, except in attitude. We had a talk with her. She's mostly recorded the final stages of the house construction and the day we moved in so she could show her father. I'd like to transfer that from the diskette to a VHS tape."

"No problem. I got the equipment here."

"This isn't a Directorate matter but a personal one."

"So?"

"Nathan, I don't want to take anyone's time away from a Directorate project to do this."

"Do you pick and choose which internal rules to follow?"

"Yes."

Nathan had to laugh. "I can walk you through the process if you want to do it."

"That would be acceptable." Alexei remained standing in Nathan's office.

"Oh," Nathan said, "you mean now."

"Yes."

"Come with me."

None of the half-dozen stations in the video room was in use. Nathan headed for the one farthest from the entrance.

"Okay, turn the computer on and let it boot. Insert the diskette and open the video player. This icon, then turn on the video recorder."

"That looks like the one I have at home," Alexei said.

"I got ours on a bulk deal from Circuit City. Hit Record on the recorder, wait a couple seconds, then play the video on the computer. Then, wait for it to finish. That's it."

"What if I want to edit something out?"

"Ah, do that first on the computer. Open this program." He pointed to another icon. "Make a copy of the original—always do that, by the way—and save it. But make your edits on the copy, save that under a different name, then do the procedure I explained before."

Nathan grinned at Alexei and winked.

"Admit it, man. You're editing your and Mai's home porno."

"Of course, that's it exactly," Alexei said, his tone bland. "Is the video editing program straightforward?"

"Let me give you a demo."

Nathan opened the editing program and brought up a file he'd recently worked on. He talked Alexei through the edit and made sure he restored the original file.

"Got it?" Nathan asked.

"Yes."

"Cool. Let me get you a fresh VHS cassette."

Nathan went to a cabinet and returned with a cassette still wrapped in the manufacturer's packaging.

"Another bulk deal from Circuit City?" Alexei asked.

"No. CompUSA."
"Thanks, Nathan."
"And this never happened, right?"
"Stands to reason," Alexei said.
"Cool, man. Have fun."
Nathan left him alone.

34

THIS IS SUFFERING

1991

Unknown Location

The next stop after clearing security was always Leana's office. She would update Alexei on anything that had happened with Katherine Maitland in his absence. This morning, upon his entrance, her expression was grave.

Maybe, he thought, this is over.

"I need to prepare you," Leana said.

"Prepare me for what?"

"Her condition is considerably worse. She stopped eating and drinking, but because you indicated she needed to remain alive, I inserted a nasogastric tube. She protested to the point I had to sedate her to do it. She begs me to remove it and let her die. Alexei, this is suffering."

"This will be the final session, per Nelson's orders," he said.

"Thank God," she replied, sagging in relief. She nodded to what he carried in his hand. "What is the video tape?"

"A reward if she answers my final questions."

"She is weak, Alexei. Too much of a shock could cause a cardiac event."

"You tell me this as if I should care."

Leana pursed her lips and shook her head. "I've always known you were cold, Alexei, but you were never a bastard until now."

"My parents were married, Leana, but if you mean my behavior, I've always been this way. You wanted this to be the final session. I've told you it is. I suggest you cease moralizing and let me start."

"I can't believe I let you fuck me all those years ago," Leana said, like a hiss between clenched teeth.

He conceded that with a shrug before heading for the subject's room.

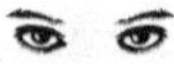

Katherine Maitland's sullen expression matched Leana's, and Alexei had seen a similar one from Mai far too many times. The older woman's resentful eyes followed him as he walked to the foot of the hospital bed that had replaced the regular one.

The feeding tube was clear for now; he knew the nutrient-rich liquid was transmitted with a large hypodermic-like device. The tape that held it in place on her cheek had irritated the skin there, leaving it inflamed. A smell of stale urine and feces pervaded the room, a hint that death was near.

Her eyes were so narrowed that he thought she might be asleep, but she blinked.

"I understand you want to die," he said.

"If you offer to kill me, I shan't give you the satisfaction," she said, barely above a whisper.

"I could never do that to her. I'll watch you die, yes, but I won't be her mother's killer."

Katherine stared at him. "Why did she marry *you*?"

His smile was stingy. "She likes me."

"But, I don't understand how could she have ever come to know someone like you?"

"We encountered each other on several occasions. We had definite chemistry."

"Met her? How?"

"Through John Stone."

"Since you dropped your bombshell last time, all I've been able to think about is what you and she could possibly have in common. I hope it's more than mere chemistry."

"Why did you want to be with your husband?"

"I loved him."

"There you have it," Alexei said.

"Love is the most human of emotions, and you are the least human I've ever seen. Not as inhuman as Fan, I'll give you that."

He said nothing and made sure his anger at the comparison didn't show.

"Freddie and I," she said, "shared our work. We had a common interest in providing a peaceful world for our child, for all children. What do you and she share that . . .? Oh, no. God, no. She's an operative, isn't she? Who recruited her? You?"

"No. John Stone."

"And I thought he was our friend. How could he do that? We trusted him to be her guardian in all things."

"She was headed for the life of a spoiled, rich brat, which she can still be on occasion. He explained her true legacy but left the choice up to her. She chose to follow in her parent's footsteps."

"But is that truly what she wanted to be?"

"Yes."

"Is she good at it?"

"The best. Now, I have an offer for you. Answer all my questions today, no matter how long it takes, and you won't have to see me again. However, you will get to see this."

He held up the VHS cassette. Her eyes fixed on the cassette, something like sadness and hope shining from them.

"You wanted to see her," Alexei said. "This is the only way you can. Take it or leave it."

"Ask your questions," she said, tears on her cheeks.

He walked to the table and put the cassette on it, where she could see her incentive.

"May I ask something first?" she said.

"Go ahead," he replied, settling in his usual chair.

"After I've answered your questions and seen what's on that cassette, can I please die?"

His pause was more for effect than contemplation. "I'll have the doctor remove the NG tube," he said.

She closed her eyes, and her "Thank you" was barely audible.

"You said you saw westerners at the reeducation camp. Did you ever interrogate any westerners besides that one CIA officer?" Alexei asked.

"Only one other," was the reply.

"His name?"

"I only heard him referred to as Wilson. He was British. Yorkshire, I'd say."

"When was this?"

"Perhaps 1978 or '79. Whichever, it was early in the year. He was British intelligence."

"What did he tell you?"

Her smile was as thin as his could be. "He was a clever boy, I'll give him that. Because he was British Intelligence, I approached him in a way he'd understand and perhaps appreciate, but he was still quite a challenge. Fan lost patience eventually and shot him in the head."

"He gave up nothing?"

"I didn't say that. My approach was working. You know, establish a rapport, find common interests, things you didn't bother to do. That's how I knew you were KGB."

"Actually, that's more *Spetsnaz* than KGB. That's why I didn't bother. What did he tell you?"

"He gave up three KGB assets in the People's Republic, but after Fan confirmed that and took care of them, Wilson stalled, gave us false information. Fan wasted time trying to verify it. That's when Fan lost patience and shot him."

"Or you did."

She laughed, winced, coughed. One thin, skeletal arm emerged from beneath her covers and reached for a plastic cup of water with a straw on the hospital tray next to her bed. Though her hand shook as she brought it to her mouth, she managed to get a good bit down.

She cleared her throat and said, "Do you honestly think that the man who'd kidnapped me and raped me daily would have let me near a gun with him in the same room?"

"Who else did you question?"

"A number of people in government who confessed to being moles for various intelligence agencies."

"Names?"

"I was never told their names. They were given a number, and I called them by that number."

She went on to speak for three more hours, an interval punctuated by other coughing spells, each leaving her weaker.

"Last questions," Alexei said.

Her eyes, sunken in a skull-like face, brightened. That disturbed him so deeply, he had to force himself not to shake. He made himself remember he was fifteen years older than Mai, who resembled this woman too much, and that he would never see this happen to her.

"Did you amputate the CIA's officer's arm?" he asked.

She sighed and said, "I knew right away he wouldn't break. Sometimes, you just know those who will never give you anything no matter what you do to them. I tried to tell Fan that, but he'd promised the NKs results and didn't want to lose face. And the CIA man made me angry. He told me he'd slept with my daughter and said salacious things about her. When Fan handed me the amputation saw, I used it, even though I knew it wouldn't change anything. Indeed, all it did was harden the man's resolve. I told Fan it was no use, if he didn't talk after that, he wasn't going to. To my surprise, he agreed. He told the NKs we'd 'softened' him up, and we left, returned to China. I was certain I'd either be sent back to a reeducation camp or executed. I would have preferred either over being his prisoner."

"How long did you serve as an interrogator?"

"Only a few more years. Fan retired from State Security—or he was purged, who knows?—in the late 1980s, I believe, and the ministry no longer requested my services. However, because Chinese state security operatives watched me conduct those interrogations, I likely 'trained' a generation of them. I assume the NKs executed the CIA officer?"

"No. They continued to torture him, but we rescued him before they could execute him."

"Ah, yes. I recall you said he cued you to my existence."

"And you're sure he told you nothing useful?"

"Absolutely nothing. He'd been a U.S. soldier, apparently. Name, rank, serial number, and a great many vulgar insults. He reminded me of Freddie in that regard."

Alexei recalled the only photos he'd seen of Frederick Fisher. A typical, effete British nobleman. A good cover but an immense contrast to the rough and tumble, crass Edwin Terrell.

"Freddie didn't break either," Katherine said.

"The Taiwanese tortured him in your presence?"

"No. The Taiwanese weren't as incompetent as the mainland thought. They knew if we'd been tortured in each other's presence, we would have given them too much false information that they'd have to expend resources to confirm. No, near the end of World War II . . ." Her weak smile came again. "Pardon me, the Great Patriotic War, the SS captured Freddie after he'd finished an SOE operation. He lured the Germans so Johnny—John Stone—could escape. Fortunately, British Intelligence had an asset in the prison where he was taken, but it took him nearly two weeks to get Freddie out. The commandant was about to kill Freddie because he hadn't told them a single thing."

Her smile lingered, and she seemed lost in reverie. Or was taking a break. Alexei let her but cleared his throat when he decided it was enough.

"What? Oh, yes," Katherine said. "This . . . Now, what was his name? Something amusing. Ah, Snake. From a racy tattoo he had, a naked woman with dice for breasts, the dice rolled to snake eyes. Yes, Snake reminded me a great deal of Freddie."

Tears pooled again in her eyes, coursed over her cheeks, and dripped from her jawline and chin.

"Freddie," she murmured, her gaze far away. "I loved him so much. When Fan told me how he died, I wanted to kill Fan for making that bargain. I plotted all sorts of ways to kill him. While he violated me, I'd close my eyes and imagine killing him. Now, are we done?"

"I have no more questions."

"Did I perform well enough for my reward?"

Alexei rose and retrieved the cassette. He turned on the video player and the television. He inserted the cassette, but Katherine spoke before he could press play.

"Sergei?"

He turned to her.

"Do you love her? Truly love her?"

They stared at each other, and Alexei saw Katherine's cold op face, one he'd seen too often on Mai. He realized Katherine—and Mai—was only reflecting what she saw in him.

"Yes," he said, "more than you ever did."

"Never, me boyo, never."

He pressed play, went to the door, and knocked.

35

CAMERA ANGLES

The camera angle was from the backseat of a vehicle toward the front seat. The most Katherine could see was the profile of her interrogator, who drove, and a glimpse of the back of a woman's head, a chestnut-haired woman in the passenger seat.

When the car turned left onto a driveway bordered on both sides with trees, the woman remarked, "We'll need better security. Harden the gate. Perhaps a fence hidden by the trees."

English accent. Almost the same cadence as Freddie's.

"All in the works," Sergei replied.

"Mums! Close your eyes," said a child. The voice was not that of a teenager but not a small child. either.

Was this . . . Was this her and Freddie's granddaughter?

"Nat, I know what the house looks like."

"But you haven't seen it all finished. Close your eyes. Please, please, please!"

"I don't see why—"

"Mai," Sergei spoke again. "Indulge her."

Mai? Who was Mai? Did she no longer call herself Mattie?

Of course not. That was a child's name. Mai? Taken from Maitland, perhaps?

"All right. My eyes are closed."

"Are they, Popi?"

A low laugh and, "Yes, they are."

The trees appeared to part, but Katherine realized that was a trick of the curve of the driveway. A large, red brick house more Georgian than anything else loomed into view. A three-car garage connected to the house with a short breezeway. A view of a large lawn lacking any sort of shrubbery, a river beyond that. Stately double doors for the main entrance. A paved, circular driveway.

The car stopped, and the video was jumbled, erratic as the child exited the car.

"Isn't it awesome, Mums?" the girl asked.

Katherine now saw only the back of a woman standing by the car. Form-fitting trousers, a tweed jacket, brown leather ankle boots, shoulder-length hair. Katherine could only see a sliver of a profile as the woman looked at the house.

"Jesus Wept," the woman said, "what a monstrosity. I didn't realize it was so huge. We must have a sign done, declaring this The Monstrosity."

"Don't you like it, Mums?" the child said, this time in a little girl's voice.

"Of course I do. It's rather large, is all."

Sergei came around the car to stand beside the woman. He was at least a head taller. Katherine had estimated he was six-two or six-three. Her daughter was at least five and a half feet. She had a strong build, and her posture was equestrienne perfect.

But Katherine wanted to see her face.

"Natalia, go open the front door, but do not film the key code," said Sergei.

"Yes, Popi, I remember. You've only told me, like, a couple thousand times."

The child did film her approach to the door, but she held the camera toward the ground as she entered the key code. In the background, Katherine heard her daughter's voice.

"What are you doing?" she said, presumably to Sergei.

"It's our first house together," he replied. "I'm carrying you across the threshold."

"Good God, no."

The child turned the camera on them. Sergei carried Maitland Katherine Fisher in his arms. And he smiled at her. With adoration. With love.

Katherine's sob caught in her throat. She had last seen her daughter's face when she was five years old. Now, Katherine felt as if she looked in a mirror at her younger self. Except for the eyes. The dark brown eyes were Freddie's.

The child filmed as Sergei carried his wife through the open doors. The child followed them inside, still filming.

"We're inside," Mattie said. "You can put me down."

"You have to kiss me first," Sergei said.

Katherine shook her head. This couldn't be the same man who had badgered her for weeks, not this loving and doting man.

But, the KGB would have taught him how to mimic emotion when he needed to.

They kissed, not a perfunctory peck, but a deep, lingering kiss that ended when the child said, "Ewww! Yuck!" Sergei put Mattie on her feet.

Hands on her hips, Mattie looked around the circular foyer. Katherine recognized most of the artwork, some from Maitland houses in Ireland, some from Freddie's manor house.

"Very nice," Mattie said, "all my favorites." She looked at

Sergei. "You realize I'm going to test the security system. I don't want anyone walking off with the art."

"And I will make it a challenge for you."

Another woman's voice broke in. "And, of course, they're all your favorites." An Irish accent and a voice Katherine hadn't heard in a long time.

The woman came to stand with Sergei and Mattie. Roisin O'Saidh. Jesus Wept. What a businesswoman she'd become. Dressed to the corporate nines. Hair in a French twist. Muted makeup, barely any jewelry, oozing a no-nonsense attitude.

"Well, if this is an example of the rest of the decor," Mattie said, "I think I shall be more than pleased."

Before Roisin leaned to kiss Mattie's cheek, she gave Sergei a glance that could kill.

Ah, you consider him a bastard, too; good eye, Rosie, Katherine thought.

"Shall we have a tour?" Roisin asked.

"Yes! Yes!" said the child, bouncing up and down, as did the camera, making the scene rather chaotic.

The video went black, and Katherine's mood blackened, too. Not enough. It wasn't enough. A few seconds later, a new image. By the windows in the background, it was evening. The glow on Sergei's and Mattie's faces had to be from a fireplace. The scene was out of focus then it snapped to clarity. Both Sergei and Mattie sat on a sofa, some space between them, glasses of wine in hand.

"Got it!" came the child's voice.

The child's approach to the sofa blocked the camera for a bit. She sat between Sergei and Mattie. She had bright, red hair, very curly. From Mattie? The ice-blue eyes, high cheekbones, and wide forehead with a widow's peak, the hint of Mongol ancestry in the shape of her eyes were Sergei's.

"Hi, Daddy, it's Natalia," the child said. She waved at the

camera and smiled. "What did you think of the new house? It's so totally awesome. Did you see how huge my room was? And, like, I have my own bathroom."

Katherine watched the interaction with an analyst's eye. Mattie looked at the child with affection and tenderness but not like a mother who'd endured blood and pain to bring that child into the world.

Sergei's child by some other woman? No, the girl—Natalia—had greeted "Daddy" in the film. Sergei's grandchild perhaps, because of the strong resemblance.

Sergei's eyes never left Mattie, and his mouth had quirked into the semblance of a smile. Again, his eyes weren't hard and icy, but soft and warm.

Easy on, Katherine warned herself, it could still be an act.

In the film the girl sobered with a startling abruptness.

"I wish . . .," she said. "I wish Mommy could see it."

The girl started to sob. She turned to Mattie, almost climbing into her lap, her face against Mattie's neck, her shoulders heaving.

A tragedy, then. The mother had died?

Mattie handed her wine glass to Sergei and embraced the child, stroking her hair and murmuring softly to her.

Mattie might not have given birth to this child, but she did love her.

Katherine smiled. She was watching her child be a mother.

Mattie looked at Sergei and nodded toward the camera.

The film "jumped." Something more had been edited out. For Katherine's sake or the father's?

The three of them were on the sofa again, the child seated closer to Mattie, with Mattie's arm around her.

"I'm sorry," Natalia said, looking up at Mattie.

"Don't ever be sorry for missing your mum," Mattie said. "That's perfectly normal."

"Do you still miss your mum?" Natalia asked, and Katherine held her breath.

"Of course I do. Not every day, perhaps, but certainly when something important happens in my life," Mattie said.

Katherine's chest constricted, a sharp pain stabbing at her left side.

"Like . . . Like moving into a new house?" Natalia asked.

"Yes. Or when I've done a good job at work. I'd love to be able to pick up the phone and call my mum and da and tell them about it."

"Like . . . when you married Popi?"

Sergei and Mattie looked at each other. If anything, Mattie's face was neutral, noncommittal. Sergei raised an eyebrow.

"Yes," Mattie said, her voice flat, uninflected like Katherine had heard from Sergei. "Like marrying Popi."

Natalia turned to look at Sergei. "Do you miss your dad?"

"I do. Remember, he died in a war not long before I was born. I never got to meet him, but, yes, I miss him. Like Mums said, for the big things in life, and the little things, too. Right, Mai?"

Natalia's head swiveled to look at Mai again.

"That, too," Mattie said. "In some ways, the little things can be more significant than the big things."

"How do you mean, Mums?"

"Oh, like, asking my mother's opinion about an outfit or what I should wear to a party. I remember she always dressed so perfectly. I wish I could wear clothes the way she did. And other things, like, should I cut my hair or wear it in a different style. Going shopping together."

"I love shopping," Natalia said, smiling again.

"I know. So do I. These are the things girls and women do with their mothers, and we both lost that at a young age. So, it's perfectly all right that we miss our mothers."

"But," Natalia said, "you'll be here for me to ask about an outfit or my hair or—" A big grin. "To take me shopping."

"Of course."

Sergei's arm was on the back of the sofa, and he moved his hand to rest on Mattie's shoulder. His fingers brushed her neck, a gesture so intimate, Katherine almost looked away.

"What would you say to your mother if you could?" he asked.

The bastard. This was her reward? To hear her own flesh and blood rebuke her?

"What would you say to your father?" Mattie countered.

"I'd thank him for fighting the Nazis even though he had to sacrifice himself in the process. I'd tell him how proud I was of him. That I loved him."

Mattie nodded, but she frowned. Natalia looked up at Mattie, her face expectant.

After a sigh she said, "I'd tell my mother that I probably would have disappointed her and my father with some of my decisions and that I might have made better ones if she and my father had lived. But they were trying to build a better world, not only for me but for every child. That was all the inspiration I needed. I keep that in mind in my work, that I'm living up to my parents' superb example. And . . ."

For some reason, Mattie looked toward the camera and smiled.

Katherine felt her heart stutter at that smile. Freddie's smile.

"That I loved her and always will."

The film ended there, but the image of her smiling daughter stayed on the television.

Katherine began to sob, wracking and wrenching sobs, her back arching against pain and iciness spreading out from her chest.

And then she was very cold, and it was very black.

36

NO EXTRAORDINARY ATTEMPTS

When Katherine Maitland's medical monitoring alerted a cardiac event, Alexei held up a hand to Leana.

"I'll go in first," he said.

"Why? I'm her doctor."

"Security, Leana. Wait here."

Alexei strode into the room, headed directly for the television, which still showed Mai's face. He shut the television off. The steady whine of the monitor told him what he didn't need to see. Flat lines on heartbeat, respirations, pulse.

Leana bustled in with a nurse and a crash cart. Again, Alexei held up a hand.

"Leana, remember what she wanted," he said.

Leana looked at her patient, her shoulders slumping. To the nurse, she said, "Per the patient's directive, which I noted in her file, she wanted no extraordinary attempts to revive her. Her condition was terminal."

The nurse nodded.

Leana fingered Katherine's pulse at her wrist anyway. She donned her stethoscope and listened for a heart beat, lung sounds. She removed her stethoscope and looked at her watch then Alexei.

"Time of death, 1813 local time."

He nodded and ejected the tape, leaving the room with it.

"All right," Leana said to the nurse. "Detach the monitoring equipment and remove the NG tube. Have someone bathe and dress her in a clean nightgown. Then, seal the room until I learn what the arrangements are."

"Yes, ma'am," said the nurse and got to work.

Leana looked over the body, peeling off her latex gloves. She headed for her office.

Alexei Bukharin was there, pouring a drink from Leana's stash of whiskey, but he turned and handed the glass to her.

"I thought you might need this," he said.

She took the glass from him and took a long drink. "Did you know that would happen?" she asked him.

"Leana, I'm not a doctor. How would I know?"

"What did you put on that tape that induced a heart attack? Because that's what it was."

"Nothing that would have done that. You said she wanted to die. She asked me for something. I provided it, and she died."

"That simple?"

"Trust me, if I'm going to kill someone, I wouldn't do it in such a roundabout way. She answered all my questions to my satisfaction, and I let her see the video. I thought it would be a comfort. Nothing more sinister than that."

"What was on that tape?"

"Leana, it's too dangerous for you to know that."

Her eyes narrowed at him, and she downed the rest of the whiskey, setting her glass on her desk with a thud. She unlocked and opened a drawer, removing a business-sized envelope, which she held out to Alexei.

"What is that?" he asked.

"A letter for you. I know you said no paper or writing implements, but she was my patient. I determined it was in my patient's best interest to let her write a letter."

He made no move to take it from her.

"I was in the room with her while she wrote. She didn't hide the pencil I provided," Leana continued. "I brought in two sheets of paper; she used only one, and I brought the unused sheet out along with the pencil. She sealed the envelope herself."

For a moment, his eyes showed her sadness, but Leana doubted that, too, was in his repertoire.

"Leana, please tell me, swear to me you did not see what she wrote," Alexei said.

"I did not, but if she said you're a heartless son of a bitch, I'll sign my name to it, too."

He took the envelope from her and slipped it into the inside pocket of his jacket.

"Leana, I apologize that Nelson and I couldn't tell you all of it. It was highly sensitive, compartmentalized information. It had to be this way, and again, I apologize for having to say this." He stepped closer to her, and she was surprised his scent was still familiar after all these years. "If, at any time, I get the slightest hint that you lied to me about listening in or seeing what she wrote, someone will come here, and that won't be pleasant. Is that clear?"

"It's clear. I haven't lied to you. I followed your instructions and my protocols for prisoners here. However, if you think you've received some sort of hint otherwise, I prefer you do the unpleasant thing."

He shook his head. "I don't kill women."

"You killed the woman in that room, but let's not debate

semantics. I repeat, I followed your instructions and my protocols to the letter."

"Not to the letter," he said, "but I accept your obligation to your patient."

They stared at each other for a long time, and the whiskey emboldened Leana.

"For a weekend two decades ago, we were the most important people in each other's lives, but that ceased on the Monday morning you left. Now . . . Now, I wish it had never happened." She waited for a reaction but wasn't surprised when she got none. "What arrangements have you made for the body?" she asked.

"Have it cremated. When you've made the arrangements for that, send the particulars to my hotel. I'll accompany the body to the crematorium and take possession of the ashes."

"Why? To make sure she's dead?" Leana said, sneering at him.

"Something like that. Thank you, Leana, for being a good doctor. It was good to see you again." He smiled at her. "For me, that memory is a fond one."

"Get out," she said. "Don't come back."

AT HIS HOTEL, Alexei ordered room service and thought about asking for a bottle of vodka. He decided two Heineken would be better than getting blackout drunk.

He ate at the small table in his room, looking out at the night skyline, and the letter lay on the table with his dinner.

Katherine Maitland-Fisher had written "Sergei" on the front of the envelope, and on the reverse side, she'd signed her name on the edge of the flap, so the signature was half on, half off the flap. No one had tampered with it, he could see. He was glad of that.

Leana had worked for the Directorate almost as long as he

had, and she would have known better than to be curious. She was a good doctor. Her patient might have been Adolf Hitler, but she would have provided him excellent medical care. That, Alexei could admire.

He finished his dinner and opened the second Heineken. After cleaning the knife with his napkin, he slit open the envelope. He unfolded the single sheet of paper and read.

Sergei—or whatever your name is—I don't know exactly what you are to my daughter. Her husband, apparently, but there are many different types of marriages—convenience, financial, political, and for love. What I've seen of you, I don't believe you are capable of caring for her, but I am her mother, regardless of what you believe. I understand the need to protect her. However, if she is anything like me, I suspect she resents any sort of overt protection. If I'd been around when you married her, I'd have protected her from you, and she never would have realized it.

Now, I realize you sincerely believe I cared nothing for her and left her behind with ease. That is far beyond the truth, but I know I will never convince you of that truth. All that matters to me is that I know what my feelings for my child are. I love her more than my own life. For whatever report you prepare, I want that on the record.

When my husband and I were taken into custody at the Taiwan airport, my first thought was of Mattie and that I would do anything to return to her. When I discovered that wasn't likely to happen. I wished Fan had killed me or that I'd died in the reeducation camp. Upon waking each day and every night before I slept, I thought of her. In my mind, she and I said her bedtime prayers together; I read her countless books in my head. Until my dying breath, I will long to see her again.

I am aware that if that were to happen, my reception likely wouldn't be what I expected or imagined, that it was a definite possibility she would reject me. I understand that, but a dying woman hopes that at the end of her life, she can have some peace after living nearly three decades without the two people she loved most in the world.

I'm also aware I'm in no position to ask anything of you—you've reminded me of that with an annoying frequency—but I request that at some point when you think she can handle this reality, tell her what happened to me and that I loved her and never stopped loving her. I might have raised another man's child, but I only ever loved my Mattie.

I fought to stay alive for that longed-for reunion. That won't happen. Because of you and your male arrogance that you know what is best for her. You are the one who will have to sleep next to her for the rest of your lives together, knowing you were the one who ultimately kept her from her mother. I hope that keeps you awake.

Yours truly,
The Countess Uxfield, Lady Caitrin Maitland-Fisher

Alexei wished Katherine Maitland had lived long enough for him to tell her he'd sleep well next to Mai for the rest of his life.

He finished the second Heineken, took the letter and the envelope into the bathroom, burned them over the toilet, and flushed the ashes away.

37

A CULTURAL THING

1991

General Post Office
Dublin, Ireland

Roisin O'Saidh paused in her purposeful stride when she caught sight of the tall man standing before the commemorative plaque in the GPO. Even though his back was to her, she recognized him. The shock of white hair brushing the collar of a black cashmere coat was a giveaway. His posture was always tense, on edge, as if he suspected everyone around him was an attacker.

She walked on, but before she could call to him, he turned to her. He wore a suit and tie, unusual for him. A plaid, wool scarf hung about his neck, and he held a pair of soft leather gloves in his right hand. He looked like a businessman, which is what he claimed to be, though Roisin knew better. She also knew better than to talk about it.

What disturbed her now upon this meeting was he was alone.

"Roisin," he greeted when she was close. The accent was slight but enough to mark him as a *sasanaigh*, a foreigner, and, therefore, not to be trusted.

"Mr., well, I suppose it's Mr. Burke, isn't it?" Roisin said.

"Yes, please." He looked again at the plaque and back to her. "I didn't realize the GPO was destroyed during the Easter Rising."

"That happens when an army lobs bombs at it."

"Such a long time to rebuild. Thirteen years."

"The Brits wouldn't provide the funds, and it took the Republic a while to work it into the budget. I'm surprised you even know of the Easter Rising."

"Only what Mai has mentioned." His skimpy smile was brief. "Were there any O'Saidhs among the martyrs?"

"No. Nor Maitlands, though Maitland Enterprises donated plenty of construction material and helped to rebuild."

"Of course."

"Excuse me," Roisin said, "are you trying to make small talk?"

"It's a cultural thing I'm not very good at. I need to speak to you about something."

"Is there a problem with the new house?"

"No, not at all. It's perfect. We've settled in quite nicely."

"Then, I can't imagine what you and I have to talk about."

"I assure you, you'll want to hear what I have to say, but this is too public."

"Well, me boyo, you're the one who suggested it."

"To meet, yes," Bukharin said. "I'd prefer to talk someplace more private. I've always wanted to see The Long Hall Pub."

"Being a public house, it, too, is a public place."

"This time of afternoon, it'll be busy. Background noise will cover our conversation. Shall we walk there?"

"It's too cold and not in these heels."

His eyes dipped to her feet. "Lovely Ferragamos," he said.

"Aren't you full of bourgeois surprises?"

He looked away, a muscle pulsing at his jaw. When he looked at her again, his face didn't betray the annoyance she saw in his eyes. She'd seen that odd reaction before: His dark blue eyes became lighter, like pale blue glacier ice.

"Roisin—Ms. O'Saidh, you know I wouldn't ask to speak with you unless it involved something important," he said.

Aye, that was certain. The two of them had no like for each other. "My car is outside," Roisin said. "Come with me."

WHEN HE ENTERED The Long Hall Pub, Alexei felt as if he'd stepped back in time, from the late twentieth century to the middle of the Victorian Era. He spotted engravings of Tsar Paul I meeting with Kosciusko, the Polish patriot. Prints of the paintings known as "Gainsborough Ladies" added to the Victorian air, along with the dark wood.

But over the entrance to the toilets were stained glass windows in an Art Nouveau style. An eclectic mix of art and decor, but it somehow worked.

"Wait here," Roisin ordered in a tone that almost made him snap to attention.

She headed for the bar, and the publican came from behind it to speak with her. He gave her a certain deference, hunched over as if bowing, not meeting her eyes, nodding at everything she said.

Roisin returned to Alexei and motioned for him to follow her. She led him to a door well past the doors marked "*Na Fir*" and "*Na Mna*"—the men's and women's toilets.

The inside of the room Roisin had entered was decorated much like the main area of the pub. Similar decor and atmosphere, but it contained only a single, round table with six chairs.

Roisin unbuttoned her coat, and Alexei stepped up to help her out of it.

"Here, then, what are you doing?" she asked.

"Being a gentleman," Alexei replied.

"That must be difficult for you. I'm perfectly capable of managing me own coat."

"I suppose, then, that holding the chair for you is also out of the question."

"You'd suppose right." She shed her coat and tossed it over the chair to her right. She seated herself and asked, "Do you take coats and hold chairs for herself?"

Alexei lay his coat and scarf on a chair and sat next to her. "No," he replied. "When I've tried, she has said much the same as you did."

"Good to see I've had some influence on her, then. Where is she? Why isn't she with you?"

"She's at home with my granddaughter."

"Ah, you've put her in the place where you've always wanted her, have you?"

"Roisin, I long ago accepted nothing I do or say will change your mind about me, but putting Mai in a place she doesn't want to be will never happen. Get that straight."

"Mind who you're talking to."

"I'm speaking with my wife's employee."

Roisin had opened her mouth to speak, but someone knocked on the door. A man in dark trousers, a white shirt with sleeve garters, and a bow tie entered.

"Ms. O'Saidh, a pleasure to see you again," he said, with a smile and another near-bow. He turned to Alexei, dropped his smile, and said, "Sir." Back to Roisin, he continued, "Will you be having your usual, ma'am?"

"Yes," she replied. She looked at Alexei. "Do you like beef?"

"Yes."

"Try the beef stew in puff pastry."

"All right, I'll have that."

"Two Guinnesses," Roisin said.

When they were alone, Alexei asked, "What's your usual?"

"Shepherd's pie in puff pastry. Now, what is this important thing you need to discuss with me?"

"First, you and I did not meet. I was never here in Dublin, and we did not have lunch together. We never discussed what I'm about to tell you. When you hear what I have to say, I think you'll agree it's best Mai know nothing about it."

"I'll be the judge of that."

"If you do say anything to her, I'll deny it, and I'll have plenty of proof to back my story. Understand?"

"Oh, I understand, 'Mr. Burke.' I've always understood the underhanded aspect of you. Say what you have to say. Being in the same room with you will sour my stomach for good food."

"Fuck you, Roisin."

She smiled and said, "Ah, the unrefined peasant comes out at last. It *is* hard for you, isn't it, to act like a gentleman?"

"Best to step down from that high horse, Roisin. You may manage one of the biggest business conglomerates in Europe, perhaps the world, but it's not yours. It never will be. Now that we've pissed in all the corners, let's talk."

"You called this meeting."

"I have to inform you that the People's Republic of China has returned the body of Katherine Maitland-Fisher."

A sharp intake of breath, and she paled so much, she was ghost-like against her black suit. He thought she might faint.

"What are you saying?" she whispered.

"In 1963, a Communist Chinese operative, who had infiltrated the Taiwanese police, became obsessed with a prisoner in custody. Katherine Maitland. This infiltrator removed Miss Maitland from the prison before she was to be executed."

"Took her where?" Roisin's voice was still barely above a whisper but hoarse from the tightness of her throat.

"To Mainland China. There, he subjected her to so-called treatment in one of their reeducation camps for two years. She did not survive. Because of his obsession with her, he had her buried with respect. Recently, he became fatally ill, but he was of such a position in the Chinese government, they fulfilled his request to have her body exhumed and returned to her family."

"No plane crash, then?"

"No. That was something John Stone thought would make her and her husband's deaths more palatable to their families."

"The bastard. Of course, he would think that. What about Fisher? Was he taken to China, too?"

Alexei shook his head. "The Taiwanese secret police executed him as a spy."

"Where is Caitrin . . . Her remains now?"

"Somewhere secure." He paused and pinned Roisin with a stare most people found intimidating. "Mai does not need to know this."

"Then, we have found one thing you and I agree on. I'd like to see Katherine."

"Roisin, twenty-eight years in the ground, no embalming, there were only bones. I decided it was best to have the remains cremated. I have the urn."

"Then, how could you confirm it's her from bones? This man could have assuaged his conscience with anyone's body."

"DNA comparison with Mai."

"How did you manage that without her knowing?"

"I live with her, for God's sake. Her DNA is everywhere in the house. It's on me."

Another knock on the door, and the waiter entered with a tray. He placed the food and drinks before them and hurried away, closing the door.

Roisin picked up a fork and broke the crust of the pie. Steam and a wonderful smell emerged from it, but she returned the fork to its place on the table.

"This is unbelievable," she said and held up a hand when Alexei started to speak. "No, I believe what you've told me. As the Scots would say, it's beyond my ken. Why did the Chinese return the body to you?"

"They didn't specifically request me. They negotiated with my boss, and he sent me to take custody of the remains."

"And Mai has no inkling?"

"No. I've been careful."

"Where does she think you are?"

"Attending to some old business in Moscow. Roisin, for Mai to learn that her mother survived when her father didn't, that her mother was subjected to horrible torture in a Chinese reeducation camp would be devastating. In some ways, she's still recovering from that bomb in Lifford, and—this is classified, by the way—a couple of years ago she was briefly a prisoner in East Berlin, a prisoner of the East German *Stasi*."

Roisin's eyes glistened with tears. "And she was tortured?"

"Yes, and she survived because she focused on her mother, took strength from her mother's example. She can't have anything bring her down, understand? She wants to have a baby, and I'm doing my best to assure that for her."

Roisin rolled her eyes. "I'm sure you are. That aside, as I said, I agree with you. She doesn't need to know this. Not now. Not ever. Why aren't you eating?"

"Because you're not. It would be impolite."

First, an eye roll, now a snort. She picked up the fork again and ate from her pie for a bit. Alexei did the same.

"What do you plan on doing with the ashes?" she asked.

"Well, I can't take them home, can I? My intention is to give them to you."

"I see, and I suppose you want me to . . . What? Hide the ashes of a woman who was like a sister to me?"

"Roisin, you and I both understand the importance of being buried in your homeland, with your family. My father's bones ended up in a mass grave in Stalingrad, not among his family. I want you to inter Mai's mother in the soil of her land."

Roisin ate some more. "How much did you have to pay? I've had business dealings with the Chinese. They never give anything out of a sense of philanthropy. There's always a price."

"Five million dollars."

"You do not have that much money, me boyo. I'm well aware of that. You're comfortable, but, trust me, you don't have five million to spare."

"No, I don't, but my organization does. All I'm asking of you is to have her buried and to never say a word to anyone about it."

"Again, you and I agree on that. It will be done."

"How?"

"Well, now, lad, you're not the only one who can keep secrets, are you?"

"No reports to the corporate board?"

"Of course not. It's a personal matter not a business one."

They ate in silence, finishing almost at the same time.

"I saw plenty of tables free in the main area of the pub," Alexei said. "How did you manage to get this private room?"

"More small talk?"

"Indulge me."

"EuroEnterprises owns the building, though the publican's license belongs to him who served us. It's a special room that few have access to. I'm one of them."

"What's so special about this room?"

"The Fenians have held secret meetings here for a hundred years or more. Plenty of plots and plans hatched here. Appropriate, then, for our lunch and the topic of our discussion."

She lay her fork across the empty plate, her napkin atop it.

"By the way, 'Mr. Burke,' you're buying lunch. It's the gentlemanly thing to do."

38

REUNITED AT LAST

December 1991

Lough Neagh
Northern Ireland

To draw no attention to herself, Roisin O'Saidh had not taken a company jet to Belfast. She'd taken a commercial flight, coach class, from Dublin to Britain and on to Belfast. For "security" reasons, flights couldn't go from Dublin to any airport in Northern Ireland.

Dressed in sturdy boots, a warm coat, and corduroy trousers, she shouldered a hiking backpack on both legs of the trip.

At Belfast airport, after clearing Customs—in her own country—she rented an older Land Rover and drove to Antrim and through the town to Castle Road. A few miles down Castle Road, she turned the Rover down a dirt track and parked amid some trees but with the lough in sight. She looked in all directions.

No one could see her from the road. No boats on the lough. No hikers nearby.

It was bitter-cold and windy, the chop on the lake more like small waves. Roisin was glad for the insulated coat and trousers, the thick, cable-knit Aran sweater. She was warm everywhere except her face, and she told herself it was the wind that made her eyes water.

For a moment she stood by the lake and studied it. She preferred the origin myth that the giant Fionn mac Cumhaill had grabbed a fistful of earth and hurled it at a Scot who'd angered him. The huge clod of earth had fallen into the Irish Sea and become the Isle of Man. The hole left behind filled with water and became Lough Neagh, the largest lake in the British Isles.

That myth had flair to it, not like the other origin story of fleeing lovers reaching Ulster after a long ride and one of their horses pissed so much, a spring appeared. The lovers took it as a sign they were safe. They capped the spring and built their house nearby. For years, they hid from the king the woman had married from obligation. At night, one or the other of them or their families, were supposed to cap the spring, so the deep depression they lived in wouldn't fill with water.

One night, someone forgot to cap the spring, and the depression filled with water and drowned the lovers and most of their family. With no way to cap the spring now, the flooded area became Lough Neagh.

Yes, Fionn mac Cumhaill was preferable to horse piss.

Roisin loosened the straps on the backpack and lowered it to the ground. She knelt beside it, opened it, and removed two crematory urns. She placed them on the ground, side by side, a hand resting on the bronze one, Grecian in style with squarish handles. The metal already felt cold from the air.

This urn had been in her mother's possession from Aifric's

death to her own, eight years later. Then, it had become Roisin's responsibility and had sat in a niche in Roisin's bedroom in her Dublin house ever since. Until this morning. Twenty-seven years. She'd extinguished the candle, the last in a long succession of them, and put the urn in the backpack with the newer one.

The bronze one weighed nearly two stone. Back in the fifties, cremation had caught on in Britain, not so much in Ireland, where the Church insisted the body remain intact to rise from the grave when Christ returned. However, Eithne had agreed with Aifric's will and had her cremated. Roisin always felt it was more the sight of her daughter's horribly battered face that convinced Eithne to allow the cremation.

Two years before Aifric's death, the mother of a young Black man murdered by white men in the south had insisted upon an open casket so people could see the horrific way those men had treated him. All because a white woman alleged he'd whistled at her.

Roisin could appreciate that mother's gesture to highlight injustice, but she suspected her mother hadn't wanted Aifric to be a symbol of injustice afforded homosexuals. That had to remain a secret. Even retainers to an established family had to maintain an image of propriety.

Things had changed. In England, where Aifric had been murdered, ten years after her death, the law changed to allow homosexual acts between consenting adults. Because the Church presided over everything in Ireland, it was still illegal, though activists were pushing for change.

Either way, changing laws now wouldn't help Aifric, wouldn't have changed the scandal had anyone known the real reason why she'd been murdered. Eithne had let the family believe Aifric's body lay buried beneath a headstone in the O'Saidh section of a cemetery in Belfast.

The shiny aluminum urn was much lighter and less ornate than the bronze one, and though she'd had it from Alexei Bukharin for only two weeks, she'd burned candles for it, too.

Eithne, Roisin believed, had started dying when she'd learned of Caitrin's death. Eithne had held out hope that the plane crash that had killed Caitrin Maitland and her English husband had been an error, that Caitrin had survived, perhaps with amnesia, like in a movie, and that she would miraculously reappear.

But movies were fantasy, and reality was harsh and final.

Still, the O'Saidhs and the Maitlands and, she supposed, the Fishers had closure now, even if they could never know about it. No happy reunion with her family, no chance for the child Caitrin had left behind to see her again. That child, now a woman, thought her mother had died in a plane crash, and it was best left that way. The Irish knew if you stirred the shite, you'd be wearing its stink in the end.

Every night for two weeks, Roisin had stared at the two urns, pondering what to do with them. She'd die someday, after all, and Mai would outlive her. Roisin didn't want her to learn this secret Bukharin had imposed on her when Roisin was no longer around to explain.

Caitrin should, by rights, go in the Maitland Mausoleum in Glasnevin, but that would involve sextons, stonemasons, and official documentation.

No one must know that Caitrin didn't die almost thirty years ago.

Two nights ago, Caitrin and Aifric came to Roisin in a dream about a picnic Eithne had had one summer near Lough Neagh. Caitrin and Aifric were thirteen and sixteen respectively, trailed and annoyed by eight-year-old Roisin. In the dream, Roisin saw the two girls, holding hands, wind blowing their long hair. They exclaimed again and again about the beauty of the water, the sky, the sand, the grass, the rocks, everything.

When Roisin woke, she knew they should rest in Lough Neagh. Together.

It was a fitting place. Five of the six counties of Northern Ireland touched Lough Neagh, and Caitrin had always felt more at home in the North than in Dublin. And wherever Caitrin had gone, Aifric went, too. First, only as an obligation on Aifric's part, as a companion to the Maitland heiress, but always friends.

And sisters.

This was fitting.

She took the plastic bag of Caitrin's ashes from her urn and carefully added them to those in the bronze urn, making sure the breeze carried nothing away.

Roisin pulled on the waders she'd rolled up and stuffed in the backpack. The wind picked up, lashing at her. The heavy bronze urn was a burden, but she waded several meters into the water until she was mid-thigh in it. She murmured a Hail Mary for each woman, opened the bronze urn, and up-ended it.

The wind caught the fine ashes, swirling and intermingling them before spreading them on the churning water. Though her arms ached from holding the heavy urn, Roisin stood fast until she was sure the urn was empty.

The ashes would eventually filter down to the lough's silt, but silt was *ithir*, soil, only wet.

Roisin, like most Irish, north or south, considered all the soil of Ireland sacred. Caitrin and Aifric might not be in coffins in a consecrated cemetery, but their bodies, reunited at last, would rest in peace and become part of that sacred ground together.

Aifric O'Saidh-Brennan and Caitrin Claire Maitland-Fisher were home.

39

RESTRICTED ACCESS

December 1991

Hong Kong Directorate Station

Harry Thompkins rubbed his eyes, picked up his coffee cup, but put it down again when he saw it was empty. Somehow without a caffeine kick, he'd have to finish reviewing Gary Clifford's report. Gary's mission reports went well past detail and beyond minutia, to an almost second-by-second description of the operation. In a previous report, Gary had noted how many puffs on his cigarette before he tossed it away.

Harry rubbed his eyes once more and resumed reading.

When someone interrupted him with a knock on the door, he didn't care who it was; he was going to kiss him or her.

Susan Chan from Communications. That would be far more pleasant than, say, Gary's appearance to ask if Harry had any questions. Given the difference in their ages, though, Susan felt barely legal to Harry.

"Hey, Suze, what's up?" he asked.

"A secure video conference from Headquarters. Whoever it is, is waiting."

"You don't know who it is?"

"Screen's blacked out, voice disguiser engaged. They sound like a robot with a sore throat."

"Okay, let me put this away."

Thank God, he thought and locked the report in his desk. He snagged his suit jacket and pulled it on, re-buttoned the top button of his shirt, and tightened the knot of his tie.

He bared his teeth to Susan and asked, "Do I have anything?" He pointed to his teeth.

She peered at them. "No, but the resolution will suck anyway with all the scrambling involved. It wouldn't matter if you did."

He followed her down the hall, up two floors in the elevator, down another hall. Why hadn't she called him instead of coming in person? Well, for one, they didn't get secure calls from Head-quarters often.

They walked past a series of identical doors and stopped before labeled "Secure Room 7 - Restricted Access."

Harry brought the proper code to mind and punched the numbers on the key pad. A series of clicks told him the multiple locks had disengaged.

"You know the drill, Haru," Susan said. She never called him Harry, preferring, as she said, his ethnic name, though she never asked anyone to use hers. "Don't hit the Go button until all the lights are green."

"Good thing I'm not color blind, isn't it?" he said, winking at her.

She rolled her eyes. "You need a new line, Haru. That one's as old as the Great Wall."

"I'll work on it."

He pushed the door open and entered alone. He closed the door, reentered his code on the key pad inside, and listened as the locks reengaged, sealing the room from eavesdropping.

Harry shook off his discomfort at that, fearing that an electronic glitch would lock him in one of these rooms forever.

The room was no more than a medium-sized closet with a table, chair, and a large monitor. A cable ran from the monitor to a bank of equipment along one wall. A keyboard and a mouse were plugged into the monitor. Harry sat, entered a password on the keyboard, and studied the row of red lights on the monitor. One by one, they changed to amber then green. A box labeled "Go" appeared on the monitor, and he used the mouse to click it.

Now that he was behind who knew how many firewalls, the monitor showed him the big boss himself, Nelson.

"Nelson," Harry said and calculated the time difference. "Good afternoon. Yesterday."

"You're at work early. It's what, 0400 there?"

"Yes. I sometimes take the night shift."

"Good man."

Harry had known Nelson a long time and was a good reader of body language anyway. Any other time, he and Nelson would have shot the shit, but today, from Nelson's narrowed eyes and lack of a genial smile, Harry could see this wasn't one of those days.

"Sorry to barge in unannounced, Harry," Nelson said, "but the matter you confirmed for me earlier this year is closed out. We do, however, have a loose end that has to be snipped."

Well, shit, Harry thought, I haven't had to do something like that in a long time.

"I gather you'd like me to take care of it personally."

"Yes. The target may be a problem for you."

"How so?"

Nelson stared at the screen, not speaking for nearly a minute. If not for the man blinking, Harry would have thought the video feed had frozen.

"The target," Nelson said, "is Li Zhen or Yazhu Zhen, whichever name she's using right now."

"Hard to say," Harry replied, trying to will his face not to sweat. "She changes names like she changes shoes."

"You have a way to contact her?"

"Yes. As I said, we don't have regular meets. We use standard tradecraft signaling if we have something for the other."

"All right. It needs to be done as soon as possible. Discretely, needless to say. I don't want China raising an issue at the U.N."

"Of course, sir, but she rarely responds to my signals immediately. It could be a couple of weeks before I can arrange a meet."

"When it's done, place an ad in the Asian Wall Street Journal for a housekeeper for Mr. Hooper."

"Yes, sir."

"I ask again, will this be a problem?"

"No, sir. She and I traded misinformation mostly. It was a game between us more than anything. Not a problem."

Nelson's eyes narrowed again, and Harry realized the man was determining Harry's truthfulness.

"I'm sorry it has to be you, Harry."

"I get that. It's all part of what she calls the Great Game."

"Don't let her lure you into a trap. Get to the meet before her. Any questions?"

"Do I need to know why?"

"No, but I'll extend that courtesy. She has leverage. That's all you need to know."

"Understood. No worries, sir. It'll be done."

"Good. I'm counting on you, Harry, and I'm certain you understand this conversation never happened."

"Of course, sir." Harry ventured a smile. "Nice not talking to you, Nelson."

Harry's spine relaxed when Nelson laughed. The video call ended at Nelson's location. Harry knew the specific shut-down procedure on his end, but right now it eluded him.

He didn't care for Zhen, didn't love her, sometimes didn't even like her, but what he'd been tasked to do . . . He'd never killed anyone he knew well enough to know how she preferred her coffee, which side of the bed she slept on, that she wore only coral lipstick at the beach and bright red all other times.

They weren't a couple. Far from it, and he knew if she were tasked to eliminate him, she'd cut his throat without hesitation.

So, then, how to do it in a way that he wouldn't get himself killed, too?

"Keep it simple, stupid," an old Army buddy would say.

Straightforward, then. No elaborate seduction scene. No poison. No knives. Meet her. Shoot her with a silenced throwaway gun, and walk away.

Don't overthink it, he told himself; don't overcomplicate it.

He congratulated himself on not having looked at the information Zhen had given him for Nelson. If he had, he'd have the same leverage as Zhen had. That could bode well for him in terms of promotion, but no doubt the first time he would use it, he'd be dead, too.

He was glad he didn't know what this was all about.

And he was sad that Zhen was in the middle of it and would have to pay the price.

Harry knew people who wouldn't make it quick and clean, and he owed that kind of death to Zhen.

For the good times.

The shut-down procedures came to mind, and he followed

them precisely. Susan would be happy. He unlocked the door from the inside and exited.

Susan had waited. She'd go inside and ensure he'd shut everything off properly.

"You okay, Haru?" she asked, frowning.

"Yeah, why?"

"You look like you've seen a ghost."

He hadn't seen one, but he had to go make one.

40

THE GREAT GAME

January 1992

Marco Polo Hotel
Hong Kong

The room Yazhu Zhen had selected in the Marco Polo was simple but elegant and had a wonderful view of the skyline and the harbor. The *feng shui* extended to the expensive furnishings and the sumptuous, decadent bathroom.

Harry Thompkins had hesitated when she'd suggested a hotel because that's what she usually booked when their meets led to sex. He wasn't sure he could make love to her then kill her, but he'd have to overcome that. If he'd refused the meet, she'd have been suspicious.

He'd expected a suite, and he hadn't expected to see a scattering of children's toys, appropriate for a toddler. That shouldn't surprise him; Zhen wouldn't be above using a child as a safety net.

He'd bypassed the room's lock and now sat in one of the

comfortable chairs, where he could keep an eye on the view and another on the door.

He didn't have to wait long.

When he heard the electronic lock cycle, he slipped his hand beneath his jacket, resting it on the butt of his gun in his shoulder holster.

Zhen smiled when she saw him, and she carried a sleeping child. She made a shushing motion and brought the child to the bed.

"Would you turn back the covers?" she whispered to him.

Overcoming his shock, Harry rose and complied. Zhen lay the child, a girl, on the bed, slipped off the tiny, patent leather shoes, and covered her to her chin. Zhen straightened and smiled again at Harry.

"I gave her a little something to make sure she sleeps," Zhen said. "There is no need for her to have nightmares about anything she might witness here."

"Who is she?" Harry asked, smirking. "A prop from a nearby orphanage?"

Zhen's smile dropped, and her stiffened body bespoke her anger. "Of course not. She's my daughter."

"Right."

"Harry, you're such a cynic. I am allowed one child, you know, and here she is. Oh, by the way, she's also yours."

"Bullshit. I was married twice, no birth control, no kids."

"I suspect your wives quickly deduced you'd be as shitty a father as you were a husband and took care of that themselves. You got lucky with me, and I think you've matured enough to take on the responsibility."

"And I should take your word for it?"

Zhen unslung a messenger bag from her shoulder and handed it to him.

"Everything you need is there. Birth certificate. Vaccination records. Results of a DNA test." Her smile came again. "Over the years, you certainly left enough of your DNA for the results to be credible, but by all means, conduct your own."

Harry took the messenger bag and peered into it. A file folder, perhaps an inch thick, was inside. He let the bag drop to the chair he'd vacated.

"Don't be upset, Harry. When I knew I'd be dealing with Nelson and Bukharin, I knew how this would end. I mean, Bukharin's Russian, for God's sake."

"Ukrainian."

"Even worse, and it's all right. I've always known this was a possibility when playing the Great Game, though I was certain at first if this were to happen, it would be my own government. My father made sure I understood that when I started to play the Game. I was surprised it was you. Nelson must not have known about you and me."

"Oh, he knows, but he also knows I'm a company man, something you can understand."

"Quite well. However, even though I can accept the outcome, I can't accept leaving my daughter to become a ward of the state, of having her end up in a state orphanage and adopted by strangers, maybe even American strangers. When I got your message and in case this was my swan song, I took the measures to ensure that won't happen to her. Among the papers is one giving you full custody of Yazhu Jun." She smiled again. "But I call her Ichiko."

Harry blinked, his chest tightening. "Ichiko? That's my mother's name."

"I know."

"I never told you that."

"True, but I know. I have taken great pains to hide who her

father is from my government. They were aware of my several regular partners, and around the time she was conceived, at least three others could have been her father. I let my government think her paternity was unknown after I eliminated all except you."

"How could you manage that?"

"I saved the condoms. I got the idea from a recent movie with the delicious Harrison Ford, *Presumed Innocent*."

"Let me get this straight. You saved semen from your lovers?"

"Yes. Surely, Harry, I have no need to explain leverage to you."

Harry shook his head in denial. Perfectly logical but also gross. He'd assumed her trips to the bathroom after sex were to empty her bladder, not to retrieve his condom from the trash can for a . . . science experiment.

"For the others, it would have been leverage, I should say," Zhen added.

"For me, too, I expect." He narrowed his eyes at her. "Unless? Did you deliberately make me the father, with the child the biggest leverage of all?"

"Oh, the male ego. No, it was a complete accident, Harry. I could accuse you of the same thing. Obviously, one of your condoms was defective. I tested Ichiko's DNA against all the possible fathers, and you won. If it had been any of the others, yes, I would have used her as leverage. However, I wanted her to be with someone I could trust to do the best for her. That's you. The money I wheedled out of the Directorate? Not for me. Like I said, I knew how this would end. I put it in a trust for her, a trust you'll manage. That'll be picked up in the next sweep of your finances the Directorate will conduct in about two months, so I'd advise them as quickly as you can. All the paperwork for that is in the bag, too. The bank has strict instructions on how it can be spent, which is only for her. Best schools, good clothing, organic food, that sort of thing. No yachts, no villas in Capri or Bali for you."

Harry turned away from her, hands on his hips. "Zhen, I need time to process this," he said.

"Not too long, Harry. I gave my daughter something to help her sleep, but I took something that should kick in soon."

Harry whirled back to her. "You did what? Why?"

"I didn't want Ichiko's father to carry the guilt that he'd killed me, and I knew you would have completed your mission because, yes, you are a company man who follows his instructions to the letter. You know, I think I need to sit down."

He tried to go to her, to help her sit in the matching chair, but his feet felt glued to the floor.

"Oh," she said, "while I can, I suppose I should ask about the disposition of my mother."

"I know nothing about your mother. I didn't want to know."

"Smart man. I hope it was peaceful. She deserved that after all my father did to her. Did she ever see her real daughter?"

"Again, I don't know, and I don't want to know."

Zhen smiled again, her lips trembling, her eyes a bit glassy.

"A warning, Harry. Where Bukharin is concerned, your being a fellow operative won't stop him from assuring that every person connected to that spy exchange I facilitated is silenced. That's another reason I gave Ichiko to you. He will think twice about depriving a young child of her only parent. Because of his experience with that. One of his weaknesses. You're sure neither he nor Nelson told you who the woman was."

"No, they didn't."

"You didn't look at the material I gave you to prove her identity nor my report on the results?"

Her hands now gripped the arms of the chair, her knuckles white. She had broken out in a sweat, rivulets of it streaming down her face.

"I didn't look at any of it."

"You're sure?"

"Yes, Zhen. I know how the game works, too."

"You're a smart man, Harry, and a good spy." She looked at him, turning her head an effort. He thought he saw fear in her eyes. No, that had to be a trick of the light, a flash from one of the boats in the harbor. "You're smart enough to figure out who Bukharin was protecting," she said.

"I haven't a clue," he said, "and I'm going to forget everything about it."

"Say that and keep saying that, no matter what. Okay, time is running short, Harry. Some of my loyal employees will be here within an hour to clear all evidence of Ichiko from the room and to deal with my unfortunate and unexpected death from an undiscovered, congenital heart condition. You need to take her and go before then, and . . . Thank you, Haru."

"For what?"

"For Ichiko. She was a complete accident, and my initial thought was to have an abortion. However, I decided motherhood was something I needed to experience. Li Daiyu was a good mother, and that left an impression on me. I was Ichiko's mother for only two years, but it was the only time I felt like a human being instead of a cog in a machine. It was worth it for that. Take her and go. Please."

Instead, he sat on the bench at the foot of the bed, close to the chair where Zhen sat. "You shouldn't be alone," he said.

Maybe she nodded. He could never be sure, no matter how many times he relived it. In his memory, it was a nod.

Her hands relaxed on the chair, and he and Zhen looked into each other's eyes until she could no longer see anything. Harry waited a few minutes longer, watching the relaxed, serene face and remembering each time they'd been together.

Finally, he rose and lay two fingers on the pulse at her throat.

Nothing. Her pupils were dilated so much that her eyes looked black. He waited five minutes, ten. She was definitely gone.

He picked up the messenger bag and the sleeping child. Maybe his sleeping child; he'd prove that to his own satisfaction.

Without a glance backward, he left the room.

This was going to be one helluva report to write.

41

RATHER CLINGY

2002

1789 Restaurant
Washington, D.C.

Mai Fisher was already seated at a table in the corner of the Middleburg Room at the restaurant named for the year Washington, D.C. was founded. Her back was to a wall full of prints of the history of D.C., and she faced the room's entrance—pretty standard tradecraft for a spy.

As Grace Lydell approached the table, she took in the surroundings. She'd always wanted to eat here but had been too busy with work. Within seconds she knew she'd like it. Rich, deep red and gold carpeting; thick wooden beams in the ceiling, which was covered in planks of hardwood. The walls and wainscoting were an elegant, pearl-like cream, the tables set with replicas of eighteenth-century china and tableware, a bowl of fresh flowers on each. So many flowers, the room smelled like spring.

The maitre d' had escorted her, and he pulled out the chair next to Mai at the round table. After Grace sat, he flicked the napkin with a flourish and lay it across her lap.

A bottle of wine with a napkin around the neck chilled in a bucket on a stand next to the table, and the maitre d' picked up the bottle.

"Wine for madam?" he asked Grace, showing her the label, which meant next to nothing to her.

"Yes, thank you."

He poured for her and refreshed Mai's glass.

"Do you wish to order now?" he asked Mai.

"Give us fifteen minutes and have the server bring menus," Mai replied.

Grace lowered her head to hide a smile. Mai used what Grace called her "Buckingham Palace" British accent, and the maitre d' had almost bowed before he retreated. Amazing how Americans reacted with such obsequiousness to that.

Grace glanced around the dining room again. She and Mai were the only diners.

"Did you buy out the room for little old me?" Grace asked.

"No. I picked a time later than the usual lunch crowd, but I did ask that no one be seated here unless it was necessary. Alexei and I have dined here many times, so the maitre d' knows I tip well for good service. How's the wine?"

"White and cold. Perfect."

Mai smiled and said, "My God, you enjoy acting the Philistine, don't you?"

"We have all the fun. So we have our stories straight, does Alexei know you're meeting me for lunch?"

"Yes, he does. He tried to invite himself along because it's you, but I told him that every now and then I need the company of women. He's probably concerned I'm grilling you for gossip about him."

"The gossip would be that he has lunch with me almost every day in the commissary because you're undercover in the CIA. He misses you."

"Yes, he's been rather clingy since we returned from Afghanistan."

"Is that behind you both?"

Mai shrugged. "We both still have nasty dreams. About 9/11."

That Mai indulged in small talk showed some evolution in her attitude. More often than not, she would have cut to the chase, and social niceties be damned.

"I hope that eases off soon. Bukharin is mighty cranky when he doesn't get enough sleep," Grace said.

"You're telling me? He's cranky at the slightest thing lately. Most of the time, it's amusing. Other times . . ." Another shrug, then, "What do you have for me?"

Small talk done.

"I'm sorry it's taken months to get back to you. I've only been able to work this in my spare time, but that's scant post-9/11. I tried to free up my time by turning some things over to Elizabeth Drake, but that's gone to her head. I'm sure she's using one of those computer programs to see how to place furniture in my office when the space is hers. Which still won't be for a while. This war horse has a few battles left in her."

Mai smiled at that, but it disappeared quickly. "What were you able to find?" she asked.

"A motherlode of information. A transcript of the inquest and a copy of the police file for Aifric O'Saidh's killing. They'd been digitized, so I was lucky. In reviewing them, I had to remind myself it was forty-five years ago, and things were different."

"How so?"

"'Unnatural' was the word that cropped up a lot in reference to Aifric at the inquest. What I learned from that file matches what was in the diary. The coroner pointed out for the record that The Honorable Virginia Cooper-Woodson had been 'mildly sedated' for her testimony because of the trauma she'd suffered. She did give damning evidence against Aifric."

"Poor Aifric," Mai said. "She thought Virginia was in love with her. Instead, she saved her abusive father from prison."

"Don't be so sure of that. Let me finish. Oh, and I have everything on a thumb drive for you to look over at your leisure. So, the police definitely wanted an indictment on the Baron. In the detective inspector's report, he wrote something to the effect that this was the worst crime scene he'd ever encountered, that the victim was unrecognizable as a woman. Per the autopsy report included in the transcript, in addition to beating Aifric's face and chest in, the Baron almost flayed her skin from her and . . ."

Grace stopped and took a sip of her wine.

"And?"

"He raped her with the handle of the poker."

"Dear fucking God," Mai said. "Her mother never said anything about that in her diary."

"Would you?"

Mai conceded that with another shrug. "Go on," she said.

"I found the allusion to Virginia's having been 'cured' of her 'deviancy' interesting, so I dug deeper. In 1941, Virginia was admitted to a psychiatric hospital, a private one that specialized in aversion therapy on homosexual men. One of the doctors wrote a paper afterward about how the techniques used on men—emetic drugs combined with pictures of the same sex—didn't work on women, at least not on Virginia."

"It didn't work on men, either," Mai said. "It was torture. Virginia told Aifric about it, which was in the diary I gave you."

"Yes. Whether men or women, if nothing else worked, they resorted to electroshock therapy."

"Per Aifric's diary, Virginia told her that, too."

"So, shortly after the killing, the Baron admitted Virginia to a different hospital, again private and one whose therapy consisted of keeping patients full of sedatives. She was allowed out under medical escort to attend and testify at the inquest."

"Grace, I really don't give a fuck about Virginia, considering what she did."

"Again, hang on for a minute, and let me lay out an interesting timeline for you."

"It's about time for the server to arrive with the menus. Hold onto that."

Seconds later, the server did appear, waiting patiently as the two women examined the selections. They both ordered appetizers and an entree. He refilled the wine glasses again and left.

"All right," Mai said, after drinking some wine, "tell me all about this timeline."

42

AN ACUMEN FOR BUSINESS

Mai saw the hesitation in Grace's eyes and waited for her to overcome it. A generous drink of wine did the trick.

"Okay, on July 3, 1957, your mother and father returned to Uxfield Manor after an extended mission of nearly five months. I cross-checked the mission logs for that year."

Mai smiled. "Quality time with Mr. Zamora, was it?"

"Ugh. Not quality at all. Anyway, your parents had been in Taiwan, the Philippines, Australia, and New Zealand for—"

"Those details don't matter, Grace."

"Sorry. You know me and detail. Well, some of this you likely know from Eithne O'Saidh's diaries."

"It's pronounced Enya."

"Ah, okay. Eithne was waiting for them and delivered the news about Aifric. The inquest had only ended ten days before their arrival, so Eithne had stayed to tell your mother. The next day, July 4, Eithne goes back to Ireland, and on July 5, your mother goes to see the DI who'd investigated Aifric's death. He's no longer alive, but he attached a memo about her visit to the main report. Your mother asked to see the police report and the crime scene photographs. Per the memo, she pulled rank on him by reminding who she was married to, and he gave her the file to review but only at the police station. Again, per the memo, she 'perused it thoroughly and spent an inordinate amount of time on the photographs but didn't show a visible reaction.'"

"If it had been me, I'd have snuck a Minox in and photographed it," Mai said.

"Oh, do you think she would have done that?"

"Doesn't matter. Go ahead."

"On July 7, Virginia Cooper-Woodson disappeared from her asylum. Big search, lots of coverage in the regional press. She was never found, and the police eventually concluded that she'd wandered away and died from exposure or killed herself. However, the newspapers reported rumors that a 'mysterious female visitor' had come to the asylum the day before to see Virginia. A tall woman with black hair and blue eyes. The name on the visitor's log was Dolours O'Saidh."

Mai paused after lifting the wine glass. "Dolours O'Saidh? You're sure?"

"Yes. Why?"

"My mother used that as a cover name on occasion. I saw that when John Stone gave me her official file."

"I wondered if it might have been her."

"My mother had red hair, much redder than mine, but from what I understand from her file, she was good at disguises. Go on."

"Five days after his daughter's disappearance, July 12, Baron Joseph Cooper-Woodson was found dead on his property, shot in the head."

"Suicide?"

"Only if he could shoot himself in the back of the head with a high-powered rifle that was nowhere to be found. The inquest for his death concluded it was likely a poacher who was too afraid to come forward. The police searched the houses of known poachers in the area as well as surrounding estates, including Uxfield, with no result. But that DI, remembering your mother's visit to him, came to Uxfield Manor on July 13, only to be told that on July 12, your mother had taken to bedrest because she was a bit more than two months pregnant with you. Doctors' orders said no visitors, enforced by your father. The DI made a note on the Baron's case file to follow up, but he was transferred. The DI who took over his cases didn't follow up. In January of 1958, the Baron's sons sold the estate and went on to live rather scandal-free lives. Care to guess who bought that estate and at an excessive price?"

"I'd have no way of knowing, Grace."

"Your father."

"What?"

"Yes. Not long after the sale was settled, he had an estate sale of the interior furnishings the family didn't want. Only days after that, he had the house, all the outbuildings, and the hunting lodge where Aifric was murdered razed."

"What are you saying?" Mai asked.

"You're as good an analyst as I am, Mai, but hang on. I have more. In October of 1957, a Saoirse O'Saidh left the Dublin offices of Maitland Enterprises, as it was then called, to head up a marketing branch in the Boston office of Maitland Enterprises. However, she didn't sound Irish but English."

"That means nothing," Mai said. "Roisin could sound more British than I when she needed to."

"Granted, but Saoirse matched the description of Virginia Cooper-Woodson. She developed quite an acumen for business and eventually—"

"Wait a minute," Mai said, frowning. "I've met her. She was the head of the Boston then New York office. She oversaw the expansion and the move to New York. Roisin and I talked to her on several occasions."

"No doubt. She didn't retire until ten years ago. She'd become an American citizen at some point and now lives with her wife on Cape Cod, where she paints delightful little seascapes and sells them to tourists."

Mai set the wine glass on the linen tablecloth and leaned toward Grace. "What exactly are you trying to say?" Mai asked, voice low and edgy.

"That your mother helped Virginia Cooper-Woodson escape from a loony bin and set her up with a new life in America. And that your father sought to eradicate the existence of the place where his wife's dearest friend was murdered."

"Why would my mother do that for the woman whose testimony set Aifric's killer free? Why would my father buy property he clearly didn't need?"

"All I have are guesses, Mai. I have a question for you. Is there anything in the diaries about when Eithne packed up Aifric's belongings at Uxfield Manor?"

"Yes, Eithne had packed all of Aifric's clothing, diaries, etc., almost as soon as she arrived in England, but she stayed for the inquest, apparently. When she did return to Ireland, she was in a hurry. My mother had asked for a family midwife to come and supervise her bedrest. Eithne accompanied the midwife to the estate then when she returned to Ireland, she had Aifric's effects with her."

"Would your mother have had time to read Aifric's 1957 diaries in that interval?"

Mai raised an eyebrow. "In between grilling a DI, freeing a

woman from an asylum, and killing a Baron, which is what you're saying, yes."

The server came with the appetizer and left after asking if they needed anything.

"That rather sums up my conclusions, Mai, and I dug deep on this. I think your mother killed the Baron because he'd bludgeoned Aifric to death. She'd had the training. She was more than capable of it."

"No."

"Why? Because she's your mother?"

"Yes, damn it. She is . . . She was my mother, the mother who loved me, not a cold-blooded killer. Like me."

"You don't have to take my word for it, of course. Review everything I loaded on the thumb drive and decide for yourself."

"My mother did not kill a man in cold blood."

"Okay. Maybe your father did it for her."

"No."

"I understand you want to believe that."

"Because it's true!"

"Mai, you're reacting like a daughter, not an operative trained the same way your mother and father were."

Before Mai could respond, the maitre d' appeared to inquire how the appetizers were, likely noticing they hadn't been touched.

"I find I'm needed back at the office," Mai said. "Please have the appetizer and my entree boxed."

"Of course, madam. Was there something wrong with our service, madam?"

"No, not at all. Something rather urgent at my office came up. My friend, however, will finish her lunch here."

"Very well, madam."

"Mai, don't," Grace said, when the maitre d' had left with

Mai's appetizer. "Damn it, why did you ask me to look into this if you didn't want to face what I might find?"

"I don't know. I wish I hadn't opened any of those bloody diaries. Where's the thumb drive?" When Grace hesitated again, Mai said, "Grace, I'm not angry at you. I knew you would be thorough. I'm angry at myself for thinking it would be all hearts and flowers. I should have known better. Nothing in my life has ever been simple."

Grace took the thumb drive from her purse and lay it on the table. "I found Saoirse's current address and included it. Should you want. Look, if you're going to leave, I'll have them box my lunch, too."

"No. Lunch is paid for. You always said you wanted to eat here, so eat."

Her movement deft, Mai plucked the thumb drive from the table and put it in her pocket. She lay her napkin on the table and left the Middleburg Room.

43

THE SHE-BEAR EMERGES

2002

Mount Vernon, Virginia

Alexei walked from his workshop to the house and found, to his surprise, Mai's car in the garage and the door to the home office locked and the keypad lights indicating, "do not disturb."

For some reason after her lunch with Grace, Mai hadn't returned to the CIA but opted to work from the secure home office. She did have a cover to maintain, whereas he'd had enough of Directorate bureaucracy and taken the day off.

This mission of Nelson's to put her undercover in the CIA was now the mission she hated the most, but she understood the need for a direct line from the Directorate into the Arbust Administration. She hated the mission, but, as usual, she gave it her all.

He went to the kitchen and snagged a Heineken from the refrigerator. After uncapping the bottle, he drank nearly half the cold liquid. It was after five somewhere in the world, and wood-working always left his throat dry despite the respirator.

In the refrigerator, he'd noticed a carry-out bag from 1789 and peered inside. It seemed Mai had brought her lunch home instead of eating at the restaurant as planned.

Some CIA crisis she needed to address? Not likely, if she opted to come home. He had his Directorate cell phone with him and had received no notice of any significant issue.

No need for concern, then. She'd tell him when she came out of the office.

Alexei set the bottle on the counter and assembled what he needed: clean microfiber cloths, some steel wool, and a bottle of olive oil. He lined them up in order of use, along with his latest creation, a large salad bowl he'd turned on his new lathe.

He'd never been good at turning wood. Building with wood, yes, but his early attempts at making decorative table or chair legs were amateurish, uneven, and nonidentical. He'd decided to give it another try, starting with simple objects. Like a bowl.

He was pleased with the result. He'd exposed the grain perfectly. A single flaw marred the outside bottom of the bowl where he'd hesitated and gouged a divot. No one would see it unless they turned the bowl upside down, but he'd smoothed it as much as he could. However, he knew it was there. It was functional, though, and that was what mattered.

Over the next hour and with the help of another Heineken, he worked the steel wool over the entire surface, wiped the bowl clean with a damp cloth, dried it, and rubbed in a coating of olive oil. He let that soak in, wiped away the excess, and applied another coat of olive oil.

He was on the third application when the office door opened and Mai appeared. Her forehead was creased in a frown, and her bloodshot eyes showed strain.

"Ah," he said, "the she-bear emerges from her cave."

She blinked, looked at him, as though surprised to see him. Then, her expression blanked and became noncommittal.

"What are you doing?" she asked, coming to the counter.

"I made a bowl. I'm conditioning it so I can serve salad in it."

"Made it on your lathe?"

"Yes. First attempt." He held it up for her to inspect. If she spotted the flaw, she said nothing of it.

"It's beautiful," she said, if a bit distracted.

"Thank you. What's up?"

"Why would anything be up?"

"You brought your lunch home, you came home instead of returning to your office. What's up in the halls of the CIA?"

She sat on one of the counter chairs, her arms crossed on the counter's surface. The frown returned. Was she contemplating whether to tell him or whether she could tell him?

"The CIA churns along as the bureaucracy it is," she said. She looked up from contemplating her hands. "I may have become too tangled in those diaries."

He kept his own mask in place as he wondered if she'd found something he'd missed.

"Oh?"

She nodded. "Aifric's diaries ended rather abruptly in the spring of 1957, so I dug out Eithne's. Roisin had always said, 'Aifric died,' or 'Aifric passed away,' or whatever euphemism she chose for being dead. It turns out she was murdered."

With her usual phlegmatic delivery, she told him about the circumstances of the brutal murder. He'd only read Eithne's diaries from 1963 and '64 and didn't know.

"But," Mai continued, "Eithne didn't supply any details. I asked Grace if she could find anything. A personal favor, but you know how thorough Grace can be."

He did indeed, but how deep had she gone? Alexei and Nelson were the only ones alive who knew the reality of Katherine Maitland's death. Alexei hoped Grace Lydell, his friend almost as long as Nelson had been, hadn't added herself to that short list.

Mai outlined everything Grace had told her. As she did, the knot of uneasiness in his chest unwound.

When Mai finished, he contemplated what she'd told him for a moment and said, "Let me see if I understand this. Grace believes that your two-month pregnant mother sprang a woman from an asylum, killed that woman's father, gave the woman a new life, and took to her bed for seven months to make certain you were born?"

"Essentially. Or it could have been my father. However, according to the diaries, my father was friends with Aifric but not to the depth he'd kill in cold blood for her. I've reviewed everything Grace found for the past three hours. She put it all on a thumb drive for me. As much as I don't want to, I keep coming around to Grace's conclusion. My mother, the trained operative, took revenge for the murder of a woman she considered her sister. And, yes, I acknowledge the irony. Like mother, like daughter."

Alexei set the bowl aside to let it finish absorbing the final coat of olive oil. He cleaned the counter and washed his hands in the sink. He returned to the counter but went around it to sit beside her. She turned to face him.

"Mai, your mother was a trained operative, as you say, for almost twenty years. You know at times she and/or your father had to use extreme prejudice," he said.

"I get that because, hello, had the same training."

"Easy. Don't shoot the messenger." Her eyes widened. "Sorry. Poor metaphor."

"She was my mother. All I remember of her is that she was a loving and kind woman, who read to me and played tea party with me and tucked me up at night with kisses. I understand who she was beyond that domestic aspect, but I never thought . . ." Mai shook her head and looked away from him. "I should have trashed those damned diaries. I never should have opened the first one."

"Tell me, did you learn positive things about your mother you didn't know?"

"Yes."

"Like what?"

She looked at him again, a hint of a smile on her lips.

"She was an unrepentant flirt with my father. She loved him fiercely, and he, her. She accepted Aifric's homosexuality even after Aifric confessed that she loved my mother more than as a sister. In 1945, that was bloody remarkable. She went to visit the woman responsible for Aifric's murderer getting off, and the next day killed him. That one's not so positive, I suppose."

She looked at him with an expression he rarely saw from her, one of need.

"You know my father was a sniper at the Battle of Stalingrad. From what I was told, before he was conscripted in his forties by the Red Army, he rarely picked up a gun, except to put down a sick or injured animal on the collective. That didn't stop him from becoming one of the Red Army's top snipers, along with my brother and sister, in Stalingrad. The three of them accumulated more than 150 kills. Their comrades called them Death Bringers. I was proud of that, for his killing an enemy that needed to be killed like the sick animal it was.

"When I joined the Army myself, even though there was no hot war, I knew the possibility I'd have to kill existed, but it was only that. A possibility. When I joined the KGB, I knew I would have to kill. That was a certainty. I told myself my father found a way to do it, and I would, too.

"Maiya, *dushenka*," he said, tapping her temple, "you've always known here your mother could have killed people." He tapped her chest over her heart. "But here, you wanted to believe, because you only knew her for those few years, that she couldn't. You could believe that your father, the man, dealt with the violent aspect of this work, not your mother.

"I know all these years, you've looked to her example for strength, for resilience, for resistance. You've never broken under questioning because you knew she and your father didn't break. Your mother was and can still be that example for you. She was a human being, like you. She was ruthless when she needed to be, like you. She was also kind and loving and humane, like you. You are, have always been, and will continue to be the best part of her.

"Through those diaries, you have learned more about her than you could ever know in the scant five years you had her. That was a gift from Roisin O'Saidh, who loved her and you."

She stayed quiet, her eyes on the floor. When she looked up at him once more, he read some emotion in those eyes, but he couldn't identify it.

"When I did what I did after the Kansas City bombing," she murmured, "I was in the darkest place I'd ever been, but she wasn't. She was pregnant at last and happy to be that way. She was happy with my father, with her life. I wasn't. I know why I was able to kill a man in cold blood. How could she?"

"Because sometimes, people deserve to die."

"That simple?"

"Yes."

He cupped her cheek in his hand, his thumb rubbing. Another surprise: She leaned into his touch.

"Or," he said, "you can dismiss Grace's findings as if from an overactive imagination."

She smiled at that, taking his hand from her cheek but gripping his fingers.

"I hate it when you're right, Bukharin," she said.

"*Dushenka*, how long have I lived with you? I am more than aware of that."

"All right, you go have a look at the contents of that thumb drive and tell me what you think."

"I can do that, but what if I agree with Grace's conclusions?"

She released his hand. "Then, I suppose, you'll be right again."

WHILE MAI ATE her belated lunch from 1789, Alexei went into the office and sent Nelson a lengthy text about what Grace had done for Mai. Nelson's reply came at once:

> Let me know, soonest.

Alexei studied the contents of the thumb drive. Yes, Grace had been her usual, thorough self, and Alexei came to the same conclusion as Grace. Thankfully, Grace had found no hint of anything to suggest Katherine Maitland had survived beyond 1963.

Alexei brought to mind a Muslim prayer of thanks, "Praise be to Allah, who has guided us to this. Never could we have found guidance, had it not been for the guidance of Allah."

Alexei had killed for Mai. People who'd hurt her, and that was another of his secrets. He didn't mind keeping any secret that might harm Mai. He was her partner, her husband, and he was "old school," as she often teased him. It was up to him to protect her when she wouldn't protect herself.

When he finished reviewing the contents of the thumb drive, he again texted Nelson.

> All clear.

Thank God.

When he left the office and returned to the kitchen, Mai turned from loading the dishwasher, the look on her face one of expectation, perhaps some hope, a touch of fear.

He nodded.

Distress appeared for only a second before neutrality returned. She nodded to him and resumed her work.

44

THE BURN ROOM

1992

Directorate Headquarters
Somewhere near Washington, D.C.

As soon as he received confirmation from Harry Thompson that Yazhu Zhen was no longer an issue, Nelson went to his office safe. He removed a file folder with a single sheet of paper—the copy he'd made of Yazhu Fan's letter to Nigel Hume nearly thirty years ago, along with the diskettes Harry had given him, and the recordings of Alexei's interrogation of Katherine Maitland.

He put everything in a burn bag and headed for Archives.

Mrs. Zamora was on duty, her son at a desk nearby, textbooks before him. When the younger Zamora looked up, it was with the surly expression of a teenager.

"My, young Master Zamora is becoming quite the handsome lad," Nelson said to Mrs. Zamora, aware women liked to have their children acknowledged. Young Zamora's face was a crimson morass of inflamed flesh and pimples, shiny with either facial oil or his acne medication.

Mrs. Zamora nodded, a smile coming and going. "I estimate he'll be ready to begin his training in six months," she said.

She was rather a plain woman, her hair prematurely gray. She wore dresses with high collars to hide the evidence of Mr. Zamora's continuing fetish of auto-eroticism. Nelson had never seen a real smile from her. He supposed being married to a man like Zamora would cause that.

"No rush, Mrs. Zamora. Let him enjoy some of his life first, and Mr. Zamora is in good health, after all."

The boy's expression lost its sullenness and showed hope instead. At the mention of Mr. Zamora's good health, Mrs. Zamora became even more sullen, if possible.

But Nelson was in no hurry to have Mrs. Zamora and her progeny take over the Archives. Unlike Mr. Zamora, Nelson had no leverage over them.

Yet.

"I'm retrieving something from the Director's private archive," Nelson explained.

Mrs. Zamora's eyes lingered on the burn bag, but she nodded. Like the mistress of a castle, Mrs. Zamora wore her keys on a chatelaine attached to the leather belt on her shirt-waist dress. She slipped the key ring from the belt, bypassed the door for the main archives and opened a door marked "Restricted Access." She didn't enter but returned to stand behind her desk.

Only a few items resided in this room, the most sensitive information on various operations and world events. As always, when Nelson passed the shelf labeled "11/22/1963" he longed for a peek at what was in those boxes. However, he'd controlled himself every time. As Director, he could look inside them, but some things were best left alone.

He went to the shelf that contained the only remaining items associated with the late Nigel Hume: the original of the Yazhu Fan letter and the file with the fabricated evidence that Katherine Maitland had been executed in Taiwan. He put both in the burn bag and returned to Archives' reception area.

Mrs. Zamora came from behind her desk again and relocked the door.

"Mrs. Zamora, do you know who is working the burn room this shift?" Nelson asked.

Without consulting anything, she replied at once, "That would be Mr. Morton."

"Thank you for your time, Mrs. Zamora. Sorry to have disturbed you."

Nelson nodded to young Zamora and left for the burn room, also on this level.

Burn room.

A misnomer now. It had started out as a literal place to burn items and papers that were too sensitive to archive. Venting the smoke had caused too much curiosity in the area around the Bunker. Now, items were "burned" in vats of acid or by acid baths. A crew of four men working six-hour shifts staffed the Directorate's burn room.

When Nelson made a rare appearance in the burn room, it was a happy occasion. It meant the man on duty could take a break. Nelson preferred to do his own disposal.

In an outer area sealed off from the burn room, Nelson stood before a security camera and pressed a button on the wall. The thick glass in the door's window distorted the hazmat-suited man who stopped his work and stepped into the airlock separating the burn room itself from the outer area. A spray of sodium hydroxide neutralized any acid on the protective suit before Mr. Morton entered the outer area.

"Good day, Mr. Nelson," Mr. Morton said, his voice metallic from the small speaker on the front of his suit.

"Good day, Mr. Morton. Fifteen to thirty minutes should do it," Nelson said.

Without another word, Morton removed his protective suit and placed it in a hazmat bin.

"There's a clean one there, sir," he said, pointing to a cabinet along one wall.

Nelson nodded his thanks, went to the cabinet, and selected a suit. He carefully pulled it on over his business attire, and Mr. Morton checked all the seals after Nelson settled the hood in place. Morton then donned a pair of gloves and held open a large bag made from a material that would enhance the effect of the acid bath and make sure nothing remained.

Nelson dropped his burn bag inside. "The commissary is serving Salisbury steak for lunch today," Nelson said, smiling behind the Perspex of his hood. "Your favorite."

"Indeed it is, sir. Thank you for letting me know. A half-hour, you said?"

"Yes. Enjoy."

Mr. Morton hustled away.

As with Mr. and Mrs. Zamora, it was an unspoken rule that if Nelson took something from the Director's personal archive and used the burn room himself, he'd never been in either place.

After putting himself through the airlock routine and double-checking he was sealed inside the burn room, Nelson put the bag in something that looked like an outsized wall oven and engaged its seals. He set the timer for fifteen minutes. When a green light on the "oven" flashed, he entered a code on the keypad beside it.

The oven filled with a liquid, which Nelson could see through another thick window in the oven's door. The bag began to bubble and boil. When the timer expired, the cloudy goo slowly drained away, but Nelson set another timer for ten minutes and repeated the process. After that was done, he opened the oven door and checked for any trace.

Nothing.

After his weak base "bath" in the airlock, Nelson removed his hazmat suit and hood and put them in the same bin Mr. Morton had used. Empty-handed, he headed back to his office.

Nothing remained to show Katherine Maitland had lived twenty-seven years beyond her "death."

👁 👁

2002

Directorate Headquarters

AFTER READING Alexei's first text about what Mai had had Grace do, Nelson's first emotion was annoyance. He thought this was all over with years ago, and now it might raise its ugly head yet again.

He'd personally eradicated every aspect of that particular secret—any paperwork, any recordings, the people involved.

He was a spymaster, and he knew secrets were a burden. Sometimes that burden could be too much to handle. Five years after Katherine Maitland's death, Dr. Leana Burgess had killed herself with a morphine overdose. Not because of that one secret patient but all of them she'd treated. That had overloaded her conscience.

As he had many times over the last decade, Nelson also wondered if Haru Thompkins had told the truth about not knowing this secret. Thompkins didn't act like a man with leverage over his boss. He'd retired six months after taking custody of his daughter, who now attended a pricey private school in San Francisco while Thompkins cultivated rare orchids. Periodic checks of his finances, mail, computer activity, and phone calls, plus occasional surveillance, indicated Harry had left the covert life behind completely.

Nelson sent a quick email to Nathan Hempstead and to the head of UNSECFOR to increase Thompkins' monitoring.

Nelson accepted some secrets had to be kept. He knew why. Mai Fisher's parents, both of them, had given their lives for the Directorate. Mai herself had given it two-thirds of hers thus far. She'd give even more. He had a plan for that.

What she did not need was for this secret to ruin the rest of that life. That was why this secret had to be eradicated. Two people knowing such a secret shared its burden, making it easier to bear. A time would come when Alexei would bear that secret alone, but no man or woman alive could hold onto a secret tighter than Alexei Bukharin.

The burner phone in his hand vibrated. Nelson's trip down memory lane and his introspection had lasted longer than he realized. It was Alexei texting him again.

All clear.

Thank God.

Nelson put the burner phone in his burn bag. He was satisfied that secret would die with him and later Alexei Bukharin.

A long time from now.

45

WHY DID MY MOTHER KILL
FOR YOU?

2003

Near White Crest Beach
Wellfleet, Massachusetts

Mai had debated this with herself for months. She told herself nothing would change, nothing would come of it, but her curiosity won.

She'd flown herself to Cape Cod Gateway Airport, rented a car, and driven to the address Grace Lydell had provided. From the street and a few doors down, Mai had watched the house until a vintage station wagon left the cottage. Mai followed it to the small parking area for White Crest Beach. She watched the woman who'd driven the car gather supplies from the rear then head to a well-worn path that cut across the grass-stabilized dunes.

From three-quarters of a mile away, Mai watched the woman set up her easel, a small folding table for her paints and water container, and a folding stool.

The winter wind was brisk, the white-capped ocean dark beneath gray clouds.

Mai left her car and crested a dune to study the ocean. She understood why people were drawn to it. It was powerful and unforgiving of the ignorant. It was the source of life.

Ireland, not to mention England, was an island, surrounded by ocean and seas and channels. To be Irish was to understand the ocean, from which every living creature had evolved.

President John F. Kennedy, almost as Irish as she, had been born not far from here. He had once remarked that the percentage of salt in human blood matched the percentage of salt in the ocean. Maybe that was why he'd joined the Navy, so that if he were killed at sea, which he almost had been, he'd return to the ocean.

It hadn't worked out that way for him. It was his son who'd been buried at sea.

Staring at the beauty of the ocean didn't quell Mai's inner debate about whether or not to encounter the woman with the easel. Mai doubted it would alter what had bounced about in her head for weeks, invading her free time.

Mai had always wanted to get to the bottom of anything that had intrigued her. What she'd learned from Eithne's and Aifric's diaries and Grace's research, had intrigued her far too long.

The thought that her mother had murdered a murderer in cold blood had more than intrigued her; it haunted her.

She'd come here on a lie, to the CIA and to Alexei. Best to get it over with and be done with the matter once and for all.

She turned up the collar of her cashmere coat and cut across the dunes to the path the other woman had taken. Mai's Beretta was buttoned up beneath the coat, but Mai knew from practice she could get to it when she needed it. This was a nearly eighty-year-old woman she would confront, but you never knew.

Mai patted the pockets of her coat, confirming that what she'd brought with her was there.

The crash of waves on the shore overcame the whooshing of the wind, and both covered any sound of her approach. She stopped several yards away from the artist and observed.

The woman wore sturdy, mannish boots, corduroy trousers, several layers of jumpers over which she'd buttoned a paint-smeared cambric shirt. On her hands were fingerless gloves. Her all-white hair was in a single braid and trailed down her back and below her waist by several inches. Her spine was ramrod straight. No stooped old woman here.

Why, Mai thought, did my mother kill for you.

The woman mixed some colors on her palette, loaded her brush, and added a shadow to a cresting wave she'd painted. She'd captured the color of the sky and the sea perfectly. The winter-faded sea grass she'd rendered as if it grew at the height of summer, and she'd added items that weren't there today: shells, starfish, people in bathing suits on the beach.

The painting was good. Not spectacular, nothing Mai would look at twice. It was something Mai supposed in her snobbery an average family would hang in a guest bathroom or the family room. Nothing like this would ever join the artwork Mai owned.

When the woman turned her head to study the scenery, she caught Mai in her periphery. Frowning, she turned on her stool to look at her interloper.

Mai pushed her sunglasses onto the top of her head and walked closer. "A lovely afternoon, isn't it? Virginia."

The erect shoulders sagged a bit as if in relief, as if she'd waited a long time to be found out and was glad of it. She put her brush in a container of water and the palette on the small table.

She wore glasses, old-fashioned ones, and her face was a web of fine lines indicating she'd spent far too much time outside. It was, however, a kind, grandmotherly face. Overall, this portrayal of her was a deep contrast to the woman Mai had met no more than a half-dozen times in the 1980s. That woman had been decked out in a severe business suit, her hair maintained as ash blond by an expensive salon, long painted nails, high heels, and hair cut in a page boy.

Did she know even then who Mai was?

"I haven't heard that name in a long, long time," the woman said, her aristocratic English accent faded. She sounded more American than anything else. "I've been Saoirse longer than I was Virginia. You look like your mother. The same hair. Same build. Your mother was taller, though. I thought that when Roisin introduced you and me, oh, nearly twenty years ago."

"Did Roisin know who you were?"

Virginia shook her head. "All she knew was that your mother bypassed everyone to help out an obscure cousin."

"Roisin didn't know you were instrumental in her sister's killer going free?"

Virginia's sigh could be heard over the waves and wind.

"If she did, she never let on. How is Roisin?"

"You don't know?"

"I don't keep up with the company. Not my concern anymore. Don't get me wrong. I'm grateful, but I moved on."

"Roisin died in 2001," Mai said.

"Oh, I am sorry to hear that. She was always tough but fair. What happened to her?"

"She had a heart attack while trapped in the debris of Number Two World Trade Center," Mai said, pushing the images of that day away.

"Oh, my God! Why on earth was . . . Oh, of course. Even before I retired, she spoke of eventually needing more space."

"Yes, she was looking at a potential venue that day. I was with her, but I got out. By the time rescue arrived, she was gone."

"Well, I am grieved. She was always supportive of my plans and suggestions. I suppose that does mean she didn't know who I was." Virginia looked Mai over again. "What is it I can do for you after all this time, Countess Uxfield?"

"Answer my questions."

"If I can."

"Did you really love Aifric O'Saidh, or were you using her to escape your father?"

Another smile and a glance at the real seascape.

"At the asylum, your mother asked that question. Almost the same wording." She looked at Mai. "I'll tell you what I told her. I loved Aifric like I'd never loved anyone before. We were . . . I guess the cliche is soulmates. Everything about us meshed. The four months we were together were the happiest of my life."

"Was it your idea to run away together?"

"No. When Aifric first suggested it, I was too frightened of my father to even consider the possibility. But she plotted and planned it in such detail, she convinced me it could work. It was going to mean several weeks away from each other, but I wanted one last afternoon together. It turned out to be the last one forever."

Her voice caught at the end, and she looked at the ocean again.

"It took years to erase the image of what happened that day from my every waking thought," Virginia said. "In my nightmares, it was like a movie on a loop, over and over again. The fireplace in that old lodge was massive, the tools for it an according size. The spike and the hook on that poker were the size of a pike you might carry into battle. After his first blow, it was a frenzy, like he couldn't stop stabbing and slashing. I tried to scream at him to stop, but I had no voice. Shock I suppose. I fainted or went into a fugue state or something. When I came to my senses . . . Well, I never really came to my senses for weeks because he drugged me, even before he let me talk to the police. Then, he drilled me, rehearsed me on what I was to say to the police and at the inquest. When I testified, it felt as if someone else spoke from my lips. In a way it was. It was my father's voice." She looked at Mai again. "How do you even know about this? You weren't born yet."

"Eithne's and Aifric's diaries, as well as Roisin's personal papers, came into my possession last year. I did some digging of my own. I've read the inquest's transcript and the police file."

"But why would you want to delve into that?"

"Initially, because I thought I'd learn more about my mother. She died when I was five, and Eithne and Aifric knew her best. However, I learned a lot more about her from my research into Aifric's murder."

"Like what?"

"Like, after she freed you from the asylum your father sent you to, she killed him. Your father."

The smile that touched Virginia's mouth angered Mai to the point where her fingers curled as if she held the Beretta.

"Are you often wrong, Your Grace?" Virginia asked.

"Not a duchess, and hardly ever."

"Well, you got that one wrong. Yes, your mother came to me at the asylum, using a fake name. She'd also read Aifric's diaries, and she challenged me much in the way you have. I told her everything, more than what I'd told Aifric, more than what you found in her diaries."

Virginia stood for the first time, and Mai prepared herself to get to the Beretta.

"When I was sixteen," Virginia said, "my father caught me with a maid. He fired her and sent me to a psychiatric facility where aversion therapy was practiced. Aversion therapy is—"

"I'm aware. Go on."

"The doctors pronounced me cured of perversion but told my father to reinforce the therapy they'd used. Bastard that he was, he put his own twist on it. He'd invite friends, male friends, from London for a weekend of shooting, after which they could use me, show me what the proper kind of sex was, to convince me I wasn't homosexual. Your mother asked if that was likely to resume when I was released from the asylum. I told her it was beyond likely. It was a certainty. She asked me again if I truly loved Aifric, and I told her what I told you. More than anything.

"To my shock, she offered to get me out of the asylum in secret and into a new life away from my father. I told her she didn't understand. He'd find me, no matter what she did. He had well-placed friends. In Scotland Yard. In British Intelligence. He'd find me. She told me not to worry. She'd take care of everything, and she did. A new name. All the paperwork. A job. A different life. A safe one."

Virginia took another step closer to Mai.

"But your mother didn't kill my father. I'd hunted on his estate, too, all my life. I knew the guns poachers used. I knew where they hunted, close to property lines. They'd shoot into someone's woods, hoping to drag the game out without being caught. I explained all this to your mother, and then I asked her for one more favor. She wanted to know if I could do it, and I said after what I saw him do to Aifric, it would be as easy as brushing my hair.

"She procured an unpapered rifle and gave it to me, and I shot him. That was the best feeling I'd ever had, seeing his blood and brains fly, like how Aifric's . . . He'd killed Aifric and gotten off. He'd debased me, but now he'd never do that again. I felt bloody good. Your mother did dispose of the weapon and assured me it would never be found. She gave me that new life, and she gave me advice. Work the job she arranged long enough to build a nest egg, then go do something I wanted to do. But, she'd rescued me, saved me, and I stayed on to honor her, to thank her for forgiving me.

"Your mother was exactly as Aifric or Eithne likely described her in their diaries—noble, compassionate, just. When I heard of her death in a plane crash, I was devastated, but I dedicated my life to Maitland Enterprises then EuroEnterprises. I even impressed Roisin O'Saidh with my work ethic."

The two women stared at each other, the symphony of waves and wind swirling around them. Mai, feeling her pulse pound in her ears, had rarely been at a loss for words, but at this moment, she had none, none that were correct to say. She knew she should thank Virginia for this knowledge, but even that wouldn't form.

"Goodness," Virginia said with another smile. "I hope I haven't shocked you mute. Shall I expect to see the police soon?"

Mai shook her head and cleared her throat. From her coat pockets she took four leather-bound books. The leather had been white when new, not a dingy cream as it was now, no dull patina, no fading gold lettering. On the cover of each, though, 1957 still stood out.

"You might want these," Mai said from a tight throat. "They're Aifric's final diaries. In them, she writes about you, your first meeting, how she felt about you, about the plans you'd made, and the future she was looking forward to, with you."

Mai held the diaries toward Virginia, who didn't hesitate to take them and hold them to her breast.

"The apple didn't fall far from the tree with you," she said to Mai. "You're as good and kind as your mother."

"Not by a long shot," Mai replied, "but thank you."

Mai lowered her sunglasses, turned, and walked back to her car.

46

EPILOGUE

MOTHER AND DAUGHTER

Three months later . . .

Mount Vernon, Virginia

Alexei opened the front door for Moira Pearse-O'Saidh, and Mai was not far behind him in greeting her.

"I'm steeping some tea," Mai said as Moira stepped into the foyer, "and Alexei's gotten rather good at scones. Shall we have some in the library?"

"I'd love some. The Concorde got me here with its usual speed, but that trip from Dulles to here, not so fast."

"I've heard it'll be taken out of service soon, the Concorde," Mai said.

Moira set aside a rectangular, slender box as Alexei took her coat and hung it in the foyer closet.

"I've heard that, too," Moira said. "Bad publicity from the accident in France, and AirBus doesn't want the liability or the maintenance costs anymore." She smiled at Mai and wagged a finger. "Now, don't be telling me to buy one. Not a good investment at all."

"Unless I were to donate it to a museum," Mai said.

Moira considered that. "Well, then, I'll crunch the numbers, as they say, and let you know."

Mai headed for the library, and Moira picked up the box before she followed.

They lingered, chatting, over the tea and scones, and an hour into it, Moira checked her watch.

"I've got to catch a flight out of National to New York. We're signing the lease on the new space this afternoon. I did send you a copy," Moira said.

"I saw it. I didn't have any issues, that's why I didn't respond, and I've been busy here," Mai said.

Moira reached for the box and handed it to Mai. "This came to the Dublin office a few days ago, a gift for you from a former employee of EuroEnterprises."

"For me?" Mai asked.

"There was a note with it asking me to thank you for a gift you gave her and that she wanted to return the favor."

"What is it?"

"I've no idea," Moira said. "It's addressed to you."

Mai laughed and replied, "You do know Roisin would have opened it?"

"I know she would have. I loved *An Roisin Dubh* dearly, but I'm not a busybody."

"Who was the employee?" Mai asked, mostly for Alexei's sake since he didn't know about her trip to Cape Cod.

"I never met her personally, but I looked into her personnel file. She was the manager responsible for our growth in the U.S., but she's been retired for more than a decade. Saoirse O'Saidh. Again, though, I've never met her."

Mai was aware of Alexei's scrutiny. He'd reviewed the material on Grace's thumb drive; he'd have seen Saoirse's address.

"Roisin and I met with her a few times."

Moira must have noticed Alexei's frown and misinterpreted it. "Not to worry, Alexei," Moira said. "It's been scanned and X-rayed and sniffed by dogs. It appears to be a painting."

Moira rose, and Mai set the box aside. Alexei immediately picked it up and examined it.

"I'll open that, me boyo," Mai said to him.

He smiled and winked at her. "I'm not a busybody either."

She almost laughed at that, knowing he was trying to figure out a way to open the box, see what was inside, and fix it so she wouldn't know.

Mai walked Moira back to the front door and retrieved her coat from the closet.

"Thanks for making time for me," Moira said. "When I got the package, I thought I'd bring it with me since I was coming for the lease signing. Two birds. One stone."

"Thanks for going out of your way," Mai replied. "I'm rather curious what it is."

"Me, too. Curious, but not a busybody. Take care, Mai."

Roisin would have hugged Mai and kissed her cheek, but Moira was a modern businesswoman. They shook hands.

Back in the library, Alexei had waited for Mai's return. He took a penknife from his pocket and slit the tape.

"Nothing nefarious?" Mai asked.

"Not that I can see."

He held the box while Mai slid from it what indeed appeared to be a painting cocooned in bubblewrap. Alexei cut the tape on the wrapping, and Mai pushed it aside to expose the painting.

A water color, perhaps twelve by sixteen, but the matting and framing doubled that. An artist would call it a study or a sketch of a subject to be painted in detail later, but this was far more than that.

Two women, their resemblance to each other obvious, from the color of their hair to the shape of each face, to the same serious but fetching expressions. One had blue eyes, the other brown. A small brass plaque at the bottom of the gilded frame read, "Mother and Daughter by Saoirse O'Saidh."

Mai stared at it, unmoving, not speaking. Alexei's fingers brushed the image that was Mai.

"Perfect," he said. "It's exactly you."

She could only nod, Saoirse O'Saidh having rendered her speechless again. Painting in hand, she rose and left the library.

Alexei found her in the foyer, where she'd removed a Rembrandt of similar size that had hung in Mai's condo and then here. She and Alexei lifted the watercolor onto the empty hanger.

"When can I ask some questions?" Alexei asked.

"Let me re-hang the Rembrandt somewhere. You open a bottle of wine, and I'll explain."

He leaned down and kissed her cheek. "Wine coming up," he said and headed for the kitchen.

Mai was glad he'd left her alone, so he wouldn't see the tears that fell as she looked at her mother's face, now no longer the fading memory of a five-year-old. Mai had a permanent reminder of who she and her mother were and the legacy Katherine Maitland had left her only child.

A spy's legacy, and for that, Mai was grateful.

End of Book One

A Spy's Legacy
November 2021 - June 2024
Staunton, Virginia

ACKNOWLEDGMENTS

Thank you to the usual cast of characters: my Beta Readers extraordinaire, Allison K. Garcia and C. A. O'Neill; my editor, Mary-Ellen Jones; my writing groups; my writer friends who bolster me, and the reader who messaged me and said, "I think it's time we knew more about Mai Fisher's mother."

Thank you to those secondary characters who, once I decided to write about them, i.e., give them the stage, wouldn't leave the spotlight.

ABOUT THE AUTHOR

The author of 30+ published historical espionage works and one mystery, P. A. Duncan is also a former commercial pilot, government aviation safety official, and stodgy bureaucrat, albeit one with a highly overactive imagination.

A graduate of Madison College (now James Madison University) with degrees in history and political science, she lives and writes in the beautiful Shenandoah Valley of Virginia. History and politics often find their way into her writing.

Her short fiction has been featured in numerous literary journals and anthologies and has won or placed in several contests. Her novels consistently reach the top 25 on Amazon bestseller lists, with one rising to #2 twice in one year. She has also edited the works of several award-winning and bestselling authors in a variety of genres.

When not writing, she cheers on the New York Yankees (yes, even after the 2023 season), watches Formula 1 and NASCAR, and spoils her grandchildren.

ALSO BY P. A. DUNCAN

Find all of the author's work at

Short Story Collections

Blood Vengeance, 2012

Spy Flash, 2012

The Better Spy, 2015

Spy Flash II, 2016

Spy Flash III: The Moscow Rules, 2021

Novelettes

A Face in the Crowd, 2017, mini-sequel to *A War of Deception*

Old Love Does Not Rust, 2022

Prologue to Terror, 2022

Prologue to Revenge, 2022

Prologue to Treachery, 2023

Prologue to Rendition, 2023

Novellas

The Yellow Scarf, 2015

My Noble Enemy, 2015

A Change for the Better, 2020

Dateline: Belgrade, 2020

Quintet, 2022

Standalone Novels

A War of Deception, debut novel, 2017

Love/Death, 2021

A Spy's Legacy, 2024

The Devil Passed By, coming 2024

SERIES

A Perfect Hatred

End Times, 2018

Bad Company, 2018

Descending Spiral, 2019

Collateral Damage, 2020

Self-Inflicted Wounds

Welcome to Belgrade, 2020

Dangerous Truths, 2020

And Justice for All, 2020

Meeting the Enemy

Terror, 2022

Revenge, 2022

Treachery, 2023

Rendition, 2023

Box Sets

Quintet, 2022

PROLOGUES, 2024

Secrets, 2024

Writing as Phyllis A. Duncan

Supreme Madness of the Carnival Season, debut mystery novel, 2023

AUTHOR'S SOCIAL MEDIA

Follow me here:

Amazon Author Page: amazon.com/author/phyllisduncan
BookBub: https://www.bookbub.com/profile/p-a-duncan
Facebook Author Page: www.facebook.com/unspywriter
Facebook Reader Group: www.facebook.com/group/RealSpies
Goodreads: http://bit.ly/GRPADuncan
Instagram: www.instagram.com/paduncan1
Substack: https://paduncan.substack.com/
Website/Blog: www.unexpectedpaths.com
X (formerly Twitter): www.twitter.com/unspywriter

NEWSLETTER SIGN-UP

SECRET BRIEFINGS

Bimonthly Issues

Stay up to date on what I'm reading, featured books by other authors, my book events, my preorders and sales, and—this is the best part—*free* excerpts.

Sign up at: https://unexpectedpaths.com/contact-the-author-2

"REAL SPIES, REAL LIVES PODCAST"

"Where we talk about writing, spies, and writing about spies."

Find the "Real Spies, Real Lives Podcast" on your favorite podcast provider: https://linktr.ee/paduncan
Listen to the latest episodes at www.realspiesreallives.com
Join the podcast's Facebook Page:
www.facebook.com/RealSpiesRealLives

DON'T FORGET THE REVIEW!

I'm sure you've heard all the cliches, and I'm a writer so allow me to indulge in a few.

Reviews are a writer's life's blood. We live for them. We weep for joy over the good ones. Bad reviews are inevitable, and we express (inwardly) righteous indignation at them. Without reviews, how would we improve as writers?

Bottom line? All those cliches are reality for us. I will continue to write and publish what I write whether people love my writing or hate it, but putting a few kind words on Amazon or Goodreads or BookBub is all you have to do to make me smile.

P. A. Duncan

DISCUSSION QUESTIONS
A SPY'S LEGACY

1. Did Alexei Bukharin make the right decision in keeping the truth of her mother's fate from Mai Fisher? Was that decision made from love or paternalism?

2. Although keeping secrets is necessary in intelligence work, what about a personal secret? Do such extraordinary lengths have to be taken to keep a personal matter secret?

3. Why do you think Nelson didn't order Harry Thompson's death as he had Zhen's?

4. Beta readers remarked that Alexei was unnecessarily "mean" to Katherine Maitland during their interrogation sessions. Was he, or was he treating her as he would any possible traitor?

5. Did Alexei show Katherine the home movie of Mai as a reward for Katherine's cooperation or from compassion?

TEASER

FOR MY COUNTRY - SECRETS BOOK 2

1957

The Lubyanka
KGB Headquarters
First Directorate Training Unit
Moscow, USSR

Before I, Lieutenant Olga Yevgenia Lubova, knocked on the door, I gave my uniform jacket a tug, set the belt precisely at my narrow waist, and smoothed my skirt. My sensible but chunky shoes had a high polish, as did the brass buckle on my belt. This morning, I made sure to place my collar tabs and epaulets per regulations. The buttons on my jacket gleamed. I had worked on ironing, polishing, cleaning everything most of the night before. The olive-gray color of the uniform was not flattering for me, but it was what it was.

With my regulation hat tucked under my left upper arm, I checked my hair for any loose strands. From judicious use of hairpins, every hair stayed in place. My makeup was minimal, barely a touch of lipstick, and I hoped I radiated professionalism.

I took a deep breath, cut off by the damned regulation girdle, raised my clenched fist, and knocked.

"*Voidite!*" came a woman's brusque, raised voice. Of course, a woman. This was the typing pool. Not the most exciting of jobs in the Training Unit but a place to start fresh out of training myself.

My back stiff and straight, I opened the door, took two steps inside, and closed the door behind me. I came to attention and saluted the woman standing at a desk. The woman returned the salute. She held up a hand to the others in the room and shouted, "*Stoi!*" Stop.

The sound of typewriters faded, and a series of clicks told me the tape decks had been paused.

Before I could announce I had reported for duty, the woman said, "You must be Lieutenant Lubova. I am Captain Mikhailovna." The captain's eyes narrowed at me. "Is that your natural hair? We will have no dyed hair here. That is a decadent perversion of the West."

"Yes, Captain, it is my natural color," I replied, tone neutral. Not the first time I'd been asked. Auburn-haired Russians were beyond rare.

"I see. Your mother had the same color. I always believed she dyed her hair, given her *profession*." A turned-down mouth.

No one laughed, but I saw the smirks, the side glances.

My mother had been an actress, a star of Soviet propaganda films made during the Great Patriotic War, a director of films about the glories of Soviet life post-war. If you watched her war films, and I had in my teenaged years, you would think my mother had killed more Fritzes than the entire Red Army.

From the fire my father had ignited to rid himself of my mother's belongings, I saved one scorched picture: my mother receiving a medal from Stalin himself. All the men in the picture gazed at her with adoration, except my father. He scowled. Fortunately, Stalin was in the part of the picture eaten by the fire. I trimmed my father away from what was left.

When my father had denounced my mother, he called her a *prostitutka*, and the number of her "lovers" arrested at the same time gave that insult credence in an attempt to save themselves. That was the current official conclusion about my mother. Her fame had corrupted her, and she had given her Soviet-owned body to men other than her husband for the money and gifts they could give her. Capitalistic vanity.

"Follow me," Captain Mikhailovna said and marched down the long room of busy typists to an empty desk in a corner far away from anything of importance.

I marched smartly behind her, noting how the others snuck glances at me.

"This is your station," Mikhailovna announced.

A squat, black Cyrillic typewriter sat in the middle of the wooden desk. Beneath it was a thin, green felt blotter, for noise mitigation, I assumed. Beside the typewriter sat a reel to reel tape deck and a pair of heavy headphones.

"You were instructed on the procedures here?" Mikhailovna asked me.

"Yes, Comrade Captain."

"Recite them to me."

"I transcribe what is recorded on the reel, word for word. When I finish the transcription of the reel, I remove it from the player, return it and the typed sheets to you, sign a form that I returned it, receive another reel from you, sign that I received it, and repeat the process."

Mikhailovna waited, an eyebrow raised.

"And forget everything I have heard while transcribing."

"Very good, Lieutenant. You will find one ream of paper in the upper right drawer. When you need more paper, pause the tape, stand at attention at your desk, and I will bring you another ream. At the end of the day, return all unused paper to me along with your final reel, whether it is finished or not. You will note there are no trash bins. Your purpose here is errorless, accurate transcription. I will count your errors. If you do make an error, pause your tape, type over the error with Xs, rewind the tape past your error, and resume. You will receive a ten-minute break morning and afternoon. Long enough for any bathroom business but nothing more. Half of the group go to lunch at noon and return at 1245. The other half at 1300, returning at 1345. You are new. You are in the second group. For lunch, you must use the commissary here. You may not bring in your own food. You may not leave here for food. No phone calls to or from here. No visitors. No fraternizing with our male comrades during work hours. We conclude at 1700, and if you do not finish your last reel, you will resume with that reel the following morning. Any questions?"

"No, Comrade Captain."

"Get started, Comrade Lieutenant."

I set my hat on the upper right corner of the desk, as had every other woman here. I sat in the armless, stiff-backed and cushionless chair and donned the headphones. I pressed "Play" and began to type. Mikhailovna hovered for a moment before she marched back to her desk.

Despite the droning monotony of the recording—an instructor reporting on the progress of his trainees, who were only identified by a three-digit number—I did not get bored. The details fascinated me, and, contrary to what I'd told the captain, I absorbed them. The morning passed quickly, and break time arrived. Each typist stood at attention at her desk and filed out at

Mikhailovna's command to form a long queue. With military precision, the line made its way to the women's toilets and stalled.

After several minutes, I checked my watch.

"Do not worry," came a voice from behind me. "Comrade Captain knows there are but two toilets for all of us. She will excuse a few minutes of tardiness, but each of us has to make sure we tell her there was a line. Otherwise, she deducts how long you were late from your lunch time. Do you smoke?"

I glanced over my shoulder. A diminutive girl with a narrow face and mousy hair. No makeup at all, but she did not need it. She was the typist who sat to my immediate left.

"No. Why?"

"Why, I was going to bum one off you at lunch. I am Masha. Pardon me. Lieutenant Vashnikova, and as we all heard, you are Lieutenant Lubova. You are on the back row because you are new. I am there because of my typographical errors. Keep typing like you are, and you will be right up front, next to the Comrade Captain's desk." Masha winked.

The line inched closer to the toilets.

"How do you know how well I type?" I asked.

"You are close enough I could see you have not backed up to cross out any errors. So, your mother was that famous actress, *da?*"

My jaw clenched. "She was an actress, *da.*"

"I have seen all her films. They were too good to destroy. They simply removed her name from the credits. You look like her."

"Sometimes not a positive aspect," I murmured. "She died in a gulag, where she belonged."

A brief silence, then Masha's voice came from close to my right ear. "No need to be socialistically precise around me, Comrade Lubova. 'Revolutions are always verbose.'"

Stunned, I almost didn't step forward to close the gap in the line. Comrade Lieutenant Maria "Masha" Vashnikova had spoken the latest code phrase of the Red Circle, which meant she knew my status before I arrived.

Now, the question I asked myself was, is she here to assist me in my part of the Red Circle's plan, or is she here to spy on me?

Secrets Book 2
For My Country
Coming in July 2024